Promiscuous

Books by R. Moreen Clarke

Quench My Thirst

Promiscuous

Published by Kensington Publishing Corporation

Promiscuous

R. MOREEN CLARKE

APHRODISIA

KENSINGTON BOOKS

http://www.kensingtonbooks.com

APHRODISIA BOOKS are published by

Kensington Publishing Corp.
850 Third Avenue
New York, NY 10022

All Kensington Titles, Imprints, and Distributed Lines are available at special quantity discounts for bulk purchases for sales promotions, premiums, fundraising, and educational or institutional use.

Special book excerpts or customized printings can also be created to fit specific needs. For details, write or phone the office of the Kensington special sales manager: Kensington Publishing Corp., 850 Third Avenue, New York, NY 10022, attn: Special Sales Department, Phone: 1-800-221-2647.

Aphrodisia and the A logo Reg. U.S. Pat & TM Off.

ISBN-13: 978-0-7582-1681-6
ISBN-10: 0-7582-1681-5

First Trade Paperback Printing: May 2008

10 9 8 7 6 5 4 3 2 1

Printed in the United States of America

1

1990

Pajama parties have long been known as a popular event for young girls; it's where secrets are shared, true friends bond, and those who don't quite fit are revealed. The party at 234 Mulberry Court was no different. Five teenaged girls discussed their secret, and not-so-secret, loves. They discussed who'd done "it," who wanted to do "it," and what "it" might be like when it finally happened. In the midst of their giggling and teasing, the one who didn't quite fit was exposed to the unflattering glare of parental microscopic inspection.

The party was hosted by Constance Jefferson. "CJ," as she was called, lived in a well-maintained estate home in the right neighborhood. Her father was a successful and prominent surgeon. CJ was a pretty, shy, and petite sixteen-year old. She'd invited three of her friends from the cheerleading squad at the private high school they all attended: Petra Engles, sixteen, a snobbish child of privilege who was happy to let everyone know her father was the mayor, Debbie Cardena, a buxom,

gregarious blonde, also sixteen, and Emily Park, polished, reserved, and mature beyond her seventeen years.

Debbie had called CJ earlier in the day to ask if she could
bring along a friend. CJ had eagerly agreed without asking the
identity of the additional guest—as far as she was concerned,
the more the merrier. However, when she opened the door later
that evening to find that Debbie had brought along her best
friend, Andie Moore, CJ wasn't certain how her other guests
would feel. After the two girls entered the foyer, CJ hastily
grabbed Debbie and pulled her down the hallway, whispering
intently.

"Why didn't you just tell me it was Andie? You know Petra
doesn't like her."

"She's really nice, CJ. It's just that nobody takes the time to
get to know her," Debbie replied easily.

Andie, a tall, gangly teenager, with thick, curly brown hair
and hazel eyes, took the opportunity to meander along the hallway and admired the décor of the tastefully appointed home,
and pretended she didn't hear the whispering about her being
there. She didn't care what they said—she was here and that
was all that mattered to her. She could pretty much get dim-
witted Debbie to do whatever she wanted. Convincing her to
call CJ for the invitation had been easy, and she told Debbie not
to tell CJ whom she was bringing along. She knew that if her
name had been mentioned, she wouldn't be there. Polite manners dictated they allow her to stay and she counted on them
relying upon correct manners. Now all she had to do was con-
vince them she belonged as a part of their sphere. Tonight she
intended to win them all over.

In the 1950's, Andie would have been referred to as being
from the wrong side of the tracks. In more modern times, they
politely referred to their poorer neighbors as not a good fit.
Not a good fit for their social clubs, their organizations, their
neighborhoods, and certainly not a good fit to be their chil-

dren's friends. Considering that Andie did not live in an upper-class neighborhood, and her parentage was certainly in question, it was difficult to uncover how she ended up at such a posh high school. The school was discreet enough not to disclose the details.

CJ quickly slipped back into her role of hostess and guided the young women to the family room, where the others were waiting. Conversation halted briefly as they entered the room and then a flurry of whispers could be heard. Determined her party was not going to be disrupted, Connie took charge.

"Hey, everybody, I'm not sure if you all know Andie. This is Andie Moore, one of our classmates, and she's joining us tonight. Everybody say hi," she said in an attempt to break the ice.

Resolute in her determination to win them over, Andie greeted Petra and Emily warmly before choosing the empty space next to Emily on the sofa. CJ began passing around snacks and the five girls easily slipped back into their conversation about school and boys. They watched a few movies before retiring to Connie's oversized bedroom for the night. In the privacy of Connie's bedroom the conversation turned toward sex.

Andie listened to their tales of petting and heavy kissing in silence. She was waiting for her opportunity to impress them with her knowledge and sexual experience.

Debbie admitted she'd let a boy put his hand inside her panties during a date. "He started rubbing me down there and getting all excited. His thing was so big, I could see it through his pants," she explained.

"Well, how did it feel? Did it feel good to have his hand down there?" Petra asked.

Debbie giggled before replying earnestly, "No, it didn't feel so good. I mean, his hands were rough and he was rubbing so hard it was uncomfortable, but he was moaning and groaning like it was so good."

"Did you see his thing?" Petra probed.

"No, but you know he tried to pull it out and show it to me. I turned my head and told him to put that thing away, 'cause I knew what he was going to try next, and I wasn't having none of *that*!" She stated it as though they all knew what "that" was.

"They ain't all that scary once you get used to them," Andie said quietly from her corner of the bed. All eyes turned to look at her.

"You've seen more than one?" Petra asked.

"I've seen a few," she replied, and then continued, "Boys aren't any smarter about sex than girls are. Boys experiment more and are more curious than girls, so that gives them the upper hand."

"We can't go around experimenting like boys do, we could get pregnant," Connie said, repeating the mantra told to her by her parents over and over again.

"Yes, that's true," Emily heartily agreed.

Andie took a deep breath; she had important information to share. They would be so happy once she told them, they would be her friends forever. "You can make boys do things for you and give you stuff without letting them put their dicks inside you. And that's the only way you can get pregnant," she advised.

"Like what?" Debbie asked.

"First, like you said, you let him put his hand inside your panties and he really liked it, right?"

"Yeah, he did."

"But you didn't like it so much."

"No, not really."

"That's 'cause he didn't do it right—"

"Wait," Petra interrupted. "Aren't they supposed to be the experienced ones? So, shouldn't they be doing it right, and how would we know?"

"Girls gotta stop being afraid of their bodies. Boys jerk off all the time. That's how they know what makes them feel good, but girls never explore their bodies. If you knew more about your body—you could control any man and any situation."

"I don't think we should talk about this anymore," Connie said nervously, and looked toward the bedroom door.

"No, Andie's right. We're always told to treasure our bodies and keep our legs closed off from boys, but nobody talks about that other stuff. I think we need to know. I don't want the boy to control me. I want to be in charge," Debbie protested.

"In order to be in charge, you have to know what to expect and how it is supposed to feel, and that way you will know if he's doing it right," Andie explained, and began to wiggle out of her panties.

Shocked, CJ and Emily gasped, "What are you doing?"

Petra giggled nervously and Debbie immediately slipped off her panties.

Emboldened by their rapt attention, good and bad, Andie lifted her nightshirt and exposed her pubic area. As though explaining a science project to a bunch of schoolchildren, she used her fingers to spread the lips of her vulva and expose the tiny pink bulb hidden beneath. "This is the clit, and if you rub it the right way, you can have an orgasm," she instructed while lightly stroking the protruding bulb. Soon she was moaning softly and shaking violently as she climaxed over and over.

The girls sat with mouths agape as they watched Andie masturbating and enjoying it. Debbie, who was quickly getting flushed and excited in a voyeuristic way she never had before, eagerly followed suit, but she had difficulty finding her bulb. "Where is it, damn it? CJ, can you see it?" she asked as she spread her legs wide.

"I don't want to look at you like that!" CJ exclaimed. "You guys better stop, or you're gonna get us all in trouble."

"Chill out, CJ. It looks like fun. I want to try," Petra said, and wiggled out of her panties.

Emily had retreated to the farthest corner of the second bed and watched silently, appalled and intrigued at the same time.

"Help me, Andie. I can't find my button," Debbie cried in frustration.

Andie stopped her own self-pleasing and scrambled across the bed to assist in the lesson. Kneeling between Debbie's knees, she guided Debbie's hand to the exact location and showed her how to rub lightly.

Debbie started moaning and giggling alternately at the sensations she was creating in her own body. Thrilled by the prospect, Petra exclaimed, "Show me! Show me!" Andie happily obliged. Soon all three were spread-eagle on the queen-sized bed masturbating while CJ and Emily looked on.

"I think you should stop now," CJ cautioned. She was feeling very uncomfortable and her body was tingling in very strange places.

Debbie, now overly excited and horny, was eager to try more things. "CJ, Emily, you should try this. You don't know what you're missing. What else can you show us, Andie?"

"Well," Andie replied, "if you're really in control, you can make him eat you, and that's so cool. Usually, boys will want you to suck their dicks. But if you suck his, he has to suck yours too."

"Suck what? We don't have anything for boys to suck on— except our tits, and they're always trying to do that anyway," Petra protested.

"Sure, you do," Andie replied confidently, and with a secret smile. "Make him suck your button."

"What!" Petra exclaimed loud enough to cause CJ to get up nervously and check the door. The hallway was clear. This was getting out of control and she was afraid what Andie would have them try next.

"Oh, suck my button! I want to know what it feels like,"

Debbie exclaimed. "Come on, Andie. You suck mine and I'll suck yours."

"Who's gonna suck mine?" Petra wailed, still playing with her newfound toy, as she looked impishly at CJ and Emily.

Andie eased herself between Debbie's legs and spread her vulva with fingers. She expertly swirled her tongue around the moist pink opening and then flicked the bulb with her tongue.

"Oh, my gosh!" exclaimed Debbie as she enjoyed the feel of Andie's tongue. Andie burrowed deeper and she pulled the tiny sensitive bulb into her mouth and sucked. Debbie's body bucked wildly and her shrill cry of pleasure pierced the stillness of the room.

All the girls froze in place as they waited for the inevitable footfalls of CJ's parents. When no one came, they all breathed a sigh of relief and returned to their former activity.

"You have to keep your mouth shut, Debbie," Andie cautioned, and leaned back on the bed. "Your turn," she said, and lay back on the bed and spread her legs.

Debbie needed no further urging and she buried her face between Andie's legs and sought out the pleasure button. Petra was getting antsy that she was missing out on this extra bit of fun and began to protest.

"What about me? What about me?"

Andie's worldly experience would cause her to make one more bad judgment. "Come on, I'll do you too." While Debbie concentrated on her newfound talent of eating Andie's pussy, Andie showed them how to conduct a proper threesome by having Petra straddle her face so she could suck her button at the same time.

These three young girls in the midst of a taboo, and very erotic, activity was the picture emblazoned on Arlene Jefferson's face as she opened the bedroom door to check on the girls before retiring for the night. Her unearthly scream caused her husband, Carlton, to come running and the girls to scatter around the room.

CJ and Emily began to cry as CJ explained to her shocked mother that she'd tried to stop them, but they wouldn't. Debbie and Petra immediately distanced themselves from Andie, and had the grace to look ashamed.

Andie, who was not ashamed or embarrassed by her body, lacked the humility to realize how bad this situation had just gotten. Her demeanor of nonchalance set her apart from everyone else in the room and identified her as the organizer of the sex fest.

It only took a moment for Arlene to assess the situation and lay blame. Through clenched lips she hissed, "Get that half-breed trailer trash out of my house this instant!"

Humiliation and anger overcame Andie as she realized she was the only one being unceremoniously escorted out of the house. When she was dropped off at her apartment across town twenty minutes later, Dr. Jefferson didn't even wait to see if she got into the building safely as he sped away from the curb. Mrs. Jefferson's withering look was etched in her mind—a look that said she was no better than common street filth. But it was Arlene's parting shot that carried the most sting as Andie passed her on the way out the door to the awaiting car. "You're nothing but a common whore," she hissed, and paused for a moment before adding, "Just like your mother." She then slammed the front door behind her.

CJ, who had followed Andie downstairs, and had been sniffling quietly in the corner, gasped at her mother's cruelty. Arlene whirled around at the sound and her look sent CJ scampering off to her bedroom.

Meanwhile, in spite of the events of the evening, Andie was certain that she'd made some new friends, and it would all turn out okay once the shock wore off. She quickly learned her newfound friends were not her friends at all, for the girls distanced themselves from her. Even the once gullible Debbie no longer had time for her. While the girls never told what truly happened at the party, the whispers of half-breed and trailer trash followed Andie through her remaining year in high school.

It was a humiliation she would never forget or forgive.

2

The café was nearly empty at ten o'clock on a Tuesday morning. It was the slow time that falls between the bustle of morning latte and muffin traffic and the hurried rush of the lunchtime crowd. As she leisurely sipped her caffeine-infused mocha java latte and scoured the local newspaper, Deandra fit into neither of these categories. She stopped there several times a week after her five-mile morning run.

Tall and lean, she was a stunning woman with an olive complexion and greenish-blue eyes. All traces of the awkward teenager she'd once been were gone. Andie Moore had dyed her hair and changed her name in a determined effort to escape her past. Her thick sandy blond hair was pulled up into a ponytail and poked through the back hole of a green baseball cap as she bent over the society section of the paper, studying her subject with the intensity of a high-school senior cramming for her SATs. While she bought the paper regularly, only two sections garnered her attention: the society page and the business section. The society page told her what was happening and where for the local who's who. The business section let her know who were the up-and-coming movers and shakers in town.

This day she made a mental note that it was the third time in six months she'd seen the name of Marshall James. On the second page of the business section was a photograph of him as he received an award for outstanding community contributions. He'd donated a very large sum of money to renovate the local gymnasium of the community center. Although it probably wasn't the best picture of him, Deandra could still clearly see his strong jawline and warm smile, and more important, she immediately recognized the five-thousand-dollar Concord Saratoga diamond watch on his left wrist. The coffers were starting to run a little low and it was time to find another benefactor. Marshall James looked like he would fit the bill perfectly.

A shadow moved across her newspaper and she looked up to see a twenty-something dark Italian cutie standing next to her table. He had smoldering, dark eyes with long, thick lashes. *"Scusami,"* he began, and indicated the chair opposite her as though to join her.

In a glance Deandra took stock of him from head to toe. He was wearing a tight-fitting tank top, lightweight sweatpants, and well-worn joggers. If she were hornier this morning, it might be worth the ride, but at the moment she had much bigger fish to fry. She pointed to the seat opposite her. As soon as he sat down, she collected her newspaper and prepared to leave.

He grimaced as he watched her long, fit frame rise from her seat. Dressed in a green sports bra, white spandex running shorts, and a white thong providing a clear outline of her ass cheeks, Deandra was a toss-up between athletic sportswoman and sex kitten, all in one. She knew she had a body that men lusted after, and used it to her best possible advantage. Her potential suitor looked at her with a perplexed expression and spread his arms in the international gesture of misunderstanding.

Sunlight glinted off a silver key ring in his hand. Her eyes were immediately drawn to the Porsche insignia on his key ring. A quick scan around the parking lot revealed a gray Porsche 911 Carrera, and a change in Deandra's afternoon plans. Perhaps this young man wasn't quite the guppy she envisioned. She discreetly lowered her body back into the chair.

"*Buongiorno,*" she said, and smiled with a new appreciation for his potential as an afternoon playmate.

An hour later they were on their way to her apartment, so he could show his appreciation for her naked body. Paolo was lean and strong. As a long-distance runner, like Deandra, he had the stamina of a racehorse. He'd begun undressing her on the way up the steps to her third-floor apartment. She'd stopped in the stairwell and allowed him to pull her spandex tights down over her hips. His lips blazed a fiery trail across her satiny butt cheeks and his tongue snaked down the crack of her ass.

She grabbed the handrails to steady her weakened knees. As she neared the top steps, she'd bent over and put her ass in his face. Paolo eagerly obliged, and roughly dragged the only barrier between her and his hot, extremely long tongue—her white thong—down to her knees.

He spread her ass cheeks with his hands and slipped his tongue into her moist, wet pussy. Deandra purred in response. Neither seemed concerned that they were in the middle of a public stairwell. Paolo lapped her body juices like a thirsty man in the middle of the Nairobi Desert. When he replaced his tongue with his long, lean dick, Deandra's mind was transported into another millennium. As strong as he was lean, he wrapped his arm under her rib cage and lifted her up off the stairs and carried her onto the top landing. The length of his ten-inch dick was still embedded deep in her pussy when he pressed her face against the closed door of her apartment and continued pounding her with solid, steady thrusts. The thumping of her body against the solid wood door finally brought a curious neighbor into the hallway below.

"What the hell is going on up there?" exclaimed the old man at the bottom of the stairway as he tried to peer into the darkened upper landing.

Deandra reached inside her bra and pulled out her apartment key. She leaned back away from the door, only far enough to slip the key in the lock. When she turned the handle, the door burst open from the weight of their bodies.

Paolo kicked the door closed with his heel and continued his plundering of newly discovered land. Still positioned behind her, he assisted her as she pulled her sports bra over her head. He cupped her large, voluptuous breasts in his hands and squeezed as though testing them for ripeness. He guided Deandra into the kitchen, where he pulled out a chair and sat down, pulling her into his lap.

Deandra screamed as the length of his extra long dick pushed up farther inside her body. He put his hands under her thighs and lifted her closer to his groin and eased the degree of pain she'd felt. It was soon apparent that Paolo was no novice in pleasing women, as he expertly slipped his hand between her open thighs and started stroking her clit.

Deandra jerked uncontrollably as she was overcome with orgasm after orgasm. Pinned on his dick, with his hands securely between her legs, there was no escape from the sensations he created. Wet, milky juices flowed from her body and gushed over Paolo's long, lean fingers as he tweaked her clit. He then smeared the fluid across her breasts and across her open, panting lips.

He finally eased her off his lap and pulled her toward the couch. Deandra was relieved to be on her back for once, and opened her legs wide to welcome him back into her secret depths. Paolo eased between her legs once more and rode Deandra to several more climaxes before finally releasing his cum deep inside his newly charted territory. He stretched to his full height and flexed his muscles and smiled. He gestured toward the bathroom and indicated he wanted to shower before he left.

Deandra nodded her agreement and continued to lie on the couch, regaining her strength. She'd enjoyed her afternoon romp with Paolo; she hoped he'd show his appreciation for her time. When she heard the shower running, she fished his wallet out of his jeans. She found at least fifteen hundred-dollar bills and several 50s. She put the wallet, and the bills, back into his pocket and proceeded to her closet to retrieve a T-shirt.

Paolo emerged from the shower shortly thereafter and strode boldly and naked back into the living room. His hair was wet from the shower and its shiny, silken sheen reflected his use of her shampoo. His body was similarly covered with long, dark, fine hair, although there were thicker patches on his chest and pubic area. His face was handsome and he had dark piercing eyes. Adonis should have been so well put together.

After he dressed, he walked over to Deandra seated on the couch and planted a surprisingly gentle kiss on her lips. *"Grazie, il mio amore,"* he said as he reached for his wallet. He opened it, and seemed mildly surprised to see his money still intact. He pulled all the bills from his wallet and took one of the fifty-dollar bills out of the stack.

Deandra watched in silence. When he took the fifty off the top of that thick wad of bills, her heart sank. Did he think she was that cheap? Why should he pay her at all? Simply because she assumed he would reward her for her time and use of her body.

Paolo chuckled softly at the dismay evident on her face. He chucked her under her chin and pressed the wad of bills into her hand. The fifty-dollar bill he shoved in his front pocket. He said something in Italian, which was totally unintelligible to her, but it sounded so beautiful coming off his lips. Then with a wave and an *"Arrivederci, bella,"* he was gone.

Deandra gleefully counted the money he'd given her. She earned two thousand dollars for her afternoon adventure. Now she could afford to buy a new outfit for the art showing.

Deandra worked hard to remain well-connected, and it was one of those connections that came through with an invitation to a private viewing of a hot, new African-American artist at a local gallery. Her Internet research revealed Marshall James was a patron of African-American art. She was banking on James not missing this event.

Friday evening she dressed in a soft silk chiffon navy dress with a halter neckline and full skirt, cinched around the waist with a wide inset of pleated silk charmeuse. Matching leather navy high-heels complemented her understated look, saying sexy, not sluttish. She arrived at the gallery early to ensure she would have time to survey the premises for the best possible "happenstance" meeting. She flirted with several guests in attendance while keeping a sharp eye on the entrance. She knew it would not pay to pin all her hopes on his showing up and she needed a fallback plan.

When Marshall James stepped into the lobby of the Norton Museum of Art with a woman of obvious style and sophistication at his side, Deandra was only mildly surprised. She could not expect that a catch of his magnitude would be without a date, but disposing of the competition had become a hobby of hers. She quickly assessed the woman's salt-and-pepper hair, which was coiffed to perfection. Simple diamond teardrop earrings bounced softly against her neck. Her flawless makeup brought out the rich tones in her caramel complexion. An elegant black designer dress sheathed her trim and petite figure. She oozed graciousness and class with every movement. Deandra took an immediate dislike to this interloper. However, her resolve to end up with him this evening was not in the least daunted by this development. She would have to choose her moment of introduction very carefully. Immersed in her plans for the evening, she did not hear anyone approach until a voice whispered in her ear.

"Careful, dear, your fangs are showing," he said, and handed her a glass of red wine.

Deandra turned quickly and smiled slyly at the familiar face of Oliver Benson. They had been friends for several years and he was well versed in her predatory nature. She wasn't in the least offended by his comment and laughed deliciously.

"It can't be that obvious. I must be losing my touch," she replied wickedly.

"Obvious only to me, darling. Is he on the menu tonight?" he asked, tipping his wineglass slightly in Marshall's direction.

"Yes, I'm quite ravenous and he does look much better in person than in the photos I've seen of him," she replied as she watched Marshall James from across the room.

Marshall was wearing a three-button black suit, complemented by a gray shirt with crisp white collar and French cuffs. Diamond and onyx cuff links matched the gold, diamond, and onyx ring on his ring finger. He was clean-shaven, with the exception of a neatly trimmed mustache. His attire screamed money and his demeanor projected class.

"He looks positively edible," Deandra purred as she took a sip from her glass. "By the way, not that it matters, but who's the old broad glued to his side?" she queried.

"Ah, that would be Viola. She's looking elegant as usual this evening. Classy lady, and just to let you know, she will be quite a formidable opponent."

"Really," Deandra replied incredulously. She reassessed the woman who had now drifted away from Marshall's side and was engaged in her own conversation with a few of the socialites in attendance. "I can't imagine . . ."she mused.

"Viola James is no joke. Many beautiful women have not survived Viola's inspection or gained her approval," he advised.

"Approval? Viola James?" she pondered aloud as the name tried to register in her brain.

"She's his mother, darling, and she can smell a gold digger a mile away. Be careful," he cautioned, and wandered off.

Deandra's gaze narrowed reflectively as she contemplated the best way to get Marshall away from his mother's clutches and into her bed before the night was over.

Two hours into the evening Deandra had yet to wangle an opportunity to meet Marshall. Each time she managed to get within shouting distance, he was pulled away in another direction. Time was winding down and her feet were beginning to ache. She took a moment to slip into the corridor near the rear entrance and massage her aching feet. She leaned on the wall and slipped off one of her sandals. Balanced on her left foot, she massaged the ball of her right foot with her free hand and held on to her shoe with the other. Unexpectedly, a door opened behind her and bumped her just enough to unbalance her and send her careening face-first into the opposite wall. Flailing helplessly, she tried to prevent her body from crashing into the wall. Suddenly her arm was grabbed from behind and she was snatched from near disaster and landed smack in the arms of Marshall James.

At once angry and relieved, she started to let out a stream of expletives until she realized upon whose solid chest she was resting. Any and all sharp retorts were suddenly swallowed.

"Are you all right?" he asked as he eased her away and allowed her to lean on his arm as she put her shoe back on.

"I'm fine. Thanks to you. I didn't realize I was standing in front of a door until it opened." She smiled and inhaled a deep breath of the most delicious cologne. Tingling sensations started inside her thighs. *This is going to be so good,* she thought.

He extended his hand to her. "I'm Marshall, and you are?" he asked. Her obvious beauty was not lost on him.

"Deandra Morgan, pleased to meet you," she replied easily, and slipped her hand into his. His palm was soft and his handshake firm. Her hand lingered in his a moment more and then she casually looked away. "Are you familiar with the artist?" she asked.

"Actually, not really. I saw the painting sample included in the invitation and my curiosity was piqued, you might say," he replied. The understated dress did not fool him. This woman radiated sex appeal no matter how hard she tried to mask it. He'd seen her watching him from afar most of the evening and wondered when she would make her move.

"Mine, too, peaked, I mean," she replied, and looked directly into his eyes. There was no mistaking the double entendre of her words, or the naked desire in her eyes. A fierce throbbing was starting and she could feel her body growing moist in anticipation.

Marshall took in the appealing package in front of him, from her healthy olive-toned skin to her long and sexy legs, which did not seem to stop. The deep V-neck of the halter top dress displayed just enough cleavage to be enticing and let the viewer know her soft, full breasts were homegrown—not factory made. The excitement of the moment was causing her nipples to strain firm and rigid against the thin chiffon of her dress. Marshall, too, felt the thrill of anticipation in his loins. In his mind's eye he was already deep between her thighs and hard at work.

Reluctantly he reminded himself Viola was here, and it was unlikely he was getting out of here without taking her home first. The two-minute silent conversation took place without either of them saying a word. It was instantly clear to Deandra when his mind drifted back to the present and his mother in the other room.

"I'll be leaving soon," she remarked, although it sounded

more like a suggestion, and then slipped him a gallery card with her cell phone number written on the back. She glided away without a backward glance and mingled effortlessly into the crowd. She had accomplished what she needed for the moment. The meeting had been most important. Now she would wait for him to make the next move.

He smiled as he saw the number on the back and then slipped it inside his jacket pocket. It was time to find Viola and make his exit. There was a change of plans in the evening's agenda.

As Marshall walked his mother to her door, his mind was on Deandra and he planned to give her a call as soon as Viola was safely inside for the night. He opened the front door and made a cursory check of the house from front to back before returning to the foyer, where Viola was hanging her wrap in the hall closet.

Viola had kept a close watch on her son all evening. Her internal antennae were alert for any unsuitable women. She loved her son, but felt he was somewhat naïve when it came to women. When Marshall happened to catch Deandra in the hallway, she had watched the flirtatious behavior that ensued. She knew Marshall was anxious to leave this evening and follow up with that woman.

"Would you like to stay for a cup of tea, dear?" she asked, even though she knew the answer.

"Not tonight, Mom. I have some work to do," he replied as he leaned over and planted a kiss on her cheek.

"I don't like her," she blurted out before she could stop herself. She knew he was on his way back to the gallery. Her innate radar told her that girl was trouble with a capital *T*. A designer dress and shoes were not enough to disguise a gold-digging trollop. She wanted better for her son. She just wished he wanted better for himself.

Marshall straightened up and looked down at his mom and smiled. Viola never missed a trick. He knew she only wanted to protect him, but he wasn't eighteen anymore, and her opinion of his companions mattered less and less as he got older. He wasn't the babe in the woods she feared, and a long-term commitment was not what he had in mind for Deandra tonight.

"Don't worry, Mom. I've been a big boy for a long time now. I'll call you tomorrow." He kissed her again and walked out the front door, closing it gently behind him.

Marshall punched the number on the back of the card into his cell phone as soon as he got back into his car. Deandra answered on the third ring. "Would you care to join me for a late dinner?" he asked.

"I'd love to," she replied, and pumped her fist in the air, mouthing a silent and enthusiastic *yes!* "I'm still at the gallery," she offered.

"Give me fifteen and meet me outside," he replied easily.

Deandra pouted, but immediately thought better of complaining. She wanted to "be seen" with Marshall by the other movers and shakers in the crowd. She didn't want to jump into some mysterious car curbside like a common hooker. "Oh, okay. I'll see you soon," she answered sweetly. She had plenty of time to make a lasting impression on Mr. James. It was best to go along with his game plan for tonight.

True to his word, he pulled up in front of the gallery fifteen minutes later. Deandra took note of the pristine silver CL500 Mercedes-Benz coupe he drove, and smiled inwardly. Excitement rushed through her veins. Marshall James was a big fish, probably the biggest one she'd baited so far. She would have to be very careful to stay on top of her game.

Marshall alighted from the car and came around to open the passenger door for her. He watched as she demurely sat facing outward and then pulled her long legs into the car. He took note that her smoothly shaven legs were devoid of any hosiery. *One less barrier to cross,* he mused. Her toes showed evidence of a recent pedicure and were delicately painted with white French-style tips. He closed the door and returned to the driver's side.

Deandra easily slipped into the luxurious comfort of the expensive car. Sexy jazz tunes floated from the speakers and enveloped her. *This is where I belong,* she convinced herself. She smiled brightly at Marshall and leaned back, crossed her legs and slipped off her shoes. The ball was in his court now; she was curious to see what he would do with it.

He returned her smile, put the car in gear, and eased out into traffic. He was glad he'd called her. It had been a while since he'd spent an evening with a beautiful woman. It was not that opportunities did not present themselves, but he'd been working steadily on a new development and this was the first time he'd gone out socially in a few months. If his mother had not insisted she wanted to be there, he may not have attended the showing this evening.

Deandra turned in her seat so that she faced him while he drove. She studied his profile—confident and determined. She liked his hands—strong with long, lean fingers that held the steering wheel lightly, but still effortlessly maintained control of the road. She surmised he was a man of action, one who would take what he wanted regardless of the consequences. He hadn't spoken a word since she got in the car and long silences made her nervous. Sometimes it meant someone was reevaluating a decision they'd made. She wasn't about to give him time to rethink his decision to call her tonight.

"So, Mr. James, tell me. What is it that you do?" she asked boldly.

He smiled. He was certain she already knew what he did. He'd met her type before. They usually had a full dossier on their mark before they made the initial contact. He may have approached her in the hallway, but like a bitch in heat, she'd been sending out pheromones all evening long.

"A little bit of this and a little bit of that," he replied evasively. He watched as an expression of mild annoyance crossed her face ever so quickly. Before she could respond, he added, "And what is it that you do, Miss Morgan?"

"As little of this and that as I possibly can," she replied candidly. There was no shame in her game. She knew he was on to her, so there was little use pretending to be something she was not.

He laughed aloud. "Somehow I knew that about you."

"So where are we going this evening?" she asked as she leaned back into the soft leather of the seat.

"If you don't mind, I thought perhaps the Lounge at the Ritz would be nice. They usually have a small jazz quartet playing and we can get a light bite to eat," he suggested.

"That's fine with me. I love their spring rolls," she replied. She wanted to let him know this wouldn't be her first visit to the Ritz-Carlton. But she wasn't about to admit that she'd only been there as an event waitress once. She had never actually dined there.

"Then I certainly hope they're on the menu tonight," he said, and smiled warmly at her.

Jeez, she thought, he had the prettiest teeth she'd ever seen on a man, so even and white. It would be a pleasure slipping her tongue between those pearly whites. A thrill of anticipation caused her to give a little shudder of delight.

"Are you cold?" he asked, concerned. The little shudder had not escaped his attention.

"No, I'm fine. Really," she replied happily.

A few moments later they were pulling up in front of the Palm Beach Ritz-Carlton. A valet hastened out to the car and another opened her door to assist her from the vehicle.

Marshall collected his receipt and joined her. He placed his hand on the small of her back to guide her into the lobby of the hotel. He directed her toward the Lobby Lounge, where they were greeted by a hostess and promptly seated. Marshall ordered a martini and the same for her.

"Looks like your spring rolls are on the menu tonight," he remarked after perusing the menu for a few moments.

"That's perfect. I'll have that." She smiled and placed her menu on the table. She folded her hands in front of her on the table and gazed around the lounge.

I belong here, she thought.

Their drinks arrived and he ordered the spring rolls for her and calamari. While they waited for their food to arrive, he had an opportunity to really study Deandra. Yes, he had seen her most of the evening, but now he had the luxury of viewing her with a discerning eye. What he saw was an undeniably beautiful woman with a voluptuous, well-toned body. Her long hair was freshly washed and well kept, as were her nails and toes. She smelled delicious, from an expensive fragrance he couldn't quite recall the name of, although he was sure he smelled it before. Her demeanor intrigued him most. She had an edge about her— an edge that simmered beneath the surface of a highly polished veneer. The edge of someone who's fighting hard to reach a goal that's just beyond their grasp. She hadn't been born with a silver spoon in her mouth, but she did a good job of faking it.

Deandra wondered how the evening was going to end. She'd wanted to be here with the infamous Marshall James, and he was everything she'd imagined and more. He was handsome, refined, and a gentleman. She knew instinctively that he planned to bed her before the night was through, but she wasn't looking for a one-night stand. She wanted to ensure there would be other nights like this, and considered it might pay for her to hold out a little now for a greater reward later on. Despite her own physical desires, she might have to resist the call of the wild.

The waitress arrived with their appetizers, interrupting the solitude of their individual reflections. They spent the next hour musing over the incredible food and enjoying the music played by the jazz quartet.

Marshall was pleasantly surprised to find Deandra quite informed on a number of topics. They chatted about the local and national political climate and a few of the local politicians. She was also up to date on the current national and international golf and tennis tournaments and players. A lively debate ensued over who was the best in women's tennis, past and present. Deandra mentioned she'd won a few local tournaments.

"Do you play?" she asked.

"Not for competition. My schedule usually doesn't permit me to commit as much time as a tournament generally requires. I play golf and tennis for relaxation or the occasional business meeting," he replied.

Deandra was more impressed by Marshall than she expected. He wasn't stuffy like many men of similar stature. He was really laid-back and appeared easygoing. She liked that about him. The fact he was single and unattached was a special bonus. She'd grown a bit weary of married men who didn't want to be seen in public places with her. They were more than willing to spend time with her in out-of-the-way restaurants or hotel rooms, and to lavish her with expensive gifts and money in exchange for her company. Yet, she knew they offered no future or security, because they were already committed to someone else. Tonight, staring across at Marshall, she became abundantly aware she wouldn't be able to trade on her looks forever. Eligible bachelors like him were few and far between. Perhaps it was time to think about a long-term relationship.

While Marshall wasn't thinking long-term commitment, he was considering the possibility of spending more time with Deandra. She was lively and vivacious. He surmised it was time for a little fun. He'd been working steadily for the past several months and just decided a mini vacation might be in order.

"Do you have any plans for tomorrow?" he asked as he finished his drink and watched her face closely for a reaction.

Out of force of habit, she almost wanted to say she had plans for the weekend. She didn't want him to think she was not invited anywhere. Most socialites were always occupied on the weekend. However, logic told her this might be her only opportunity to spend more time with him. The evening was ending and how she answered might determine the outcome tonight. If she said she was unavailable, chances were he would sleep with her tonight and she would quickly fade into a distant memory. Or, if she was available, even if he slept with her tonight, he would have committed to seeing her again tomorrow. All these scenarios danced around in her head delaying her response.

"You must have a very busy schedule. Pardon me for being so presumptive," he said, and signaled for the check. It was a calculated move on his part, because he could clearly see she had no plans for the next day. He knew by indicating the evening was over, it would force a truthful response from her and not allow her time to calculate her next move. She reacted as he expected.

"Nothing so pressing I couldn't put it off to a later date," she replied easily.

He smiled before continuing. "Your company this evening has helped me to realize I am in need of a little break. Care to join me for a quick trip to the Bahamas?"

Unabashed surprise and glee registered on her face. Without hesitation, she replied, "I'd love to."

"Great," he replied, and placed some bills along with the check in the black folder on the table. "Excuse me for just a moment," he continued, and disappeared into the lobby for a few minutes. When he returned, he assisted her from her chair and escorted her out toward the lobby.

As they exited the hotel, Deandra's mind was in a whirl. What should she pack? Should she ask him how many days they would be gone or just stay quiet and not interrupt the mood? Excitement raced through her body and her eyes sparkled in anticipation. She looked across at Marshall standing next to her while they waited for the valet and shivered.

"Are you cold?" he asked once more.

"No, just excited," she said, and smiled up at him.

He took her hand in his and gave it a brief squeeze. He released her hand as soon as his car was brought around and he opened the car door for her. Marshall got into the driver's side and put the car in gear and drove off.

Her mind was so filled with thoughts of what she should take with her to make the best impression on him that she didn't pay attention to where they were going. After fifteen minutes it occurred to her he might need to know where she lived, so he could drop her off.

"Are you taking me home?" she asked.

"Not yet, unless you're ready to go home?" he replied, and continued on his course.

"Oh," she answered, and sat quietly back in her seat. She said nothing for a few more minutes and then noticed they were approaching the local marina. She looked across at him quizzically, but declined to ask any more questions.

He pulled into a parking space at the marina and alighted from the car. She stayed in her seat unsure of why they were here. Suddenly her door was opened and he offered his hand to assist her out of the car. He took her hand and guided her along the walkway toward a huge white boat.

"Good evening, Mr. James," an old man called from the deck of a sleek Sea Ray Sundancer, and climbed down to the dock and began walking toward them.

"Hey there, Sam, everything in order?" he asked.

"Yes, sir, just like you requested."

"Fantastic," Marshall replied, and tossed his car keys to the old man.

Deandra stopped in her tracks as it dawned on her. The trip to the Bahamas was now, not tomorrow. "Marshall, are we leaving now?"

"Yes, I thought it would be a nice surprise," he replied.

"But I didn't pack anything," she wailed as she realized the only makeup she had was a tube of lipstick in her evening bag, and surely this cocktail dress would be out of place on a beach. She didn't even have a decent hairbrush.

"Not to worry," he said, and tilted her chin up with his hand and kissed her briefly on the lips.

His kiss was as unexpected as it was sweet, and she melted instantly. Still in her high heels, she allowed him to guide her along the wooden planks of the dock. She watched each step to prevent one of her two-hundred-dollar Jimmy Choo pumps from slipping through the cracks in the wood.

Marshall assisted her onto the deck of the boat and handed her his suit jacket before he turned to have a few more words with the old man. Deandra stood in the cockpit and took stock of her surroundings. From what she'd seen so far, the boat was immaculate, with a U-shaped comfortable seating area complete with wet bar and sink. She lifted his jacket to her nose and inhaled deeply. It was warm from his body and his cologne lingered in the fine wool threads. She ran her fingers across the expensive material and smiled. This was all too good to be true.

The old man gave a brief wave from the dock before he climbed into Marshall's Mercedes and drove out of the marina. Marshall bounded back onto the deck and joined her in the cockpit. He wasn't quite ready to set sail. With his shirt collar undone and sleeves rolled up, he looked every inch the rich playboy. He reached for her hand and easily pulled her into his arms.

She offered no resistance and slipped her arms comfortably around his waist. Her body tingled in response to the close proximity of his. She explored the solid muscles of his back and shoulders with her hands. His waist was slim and she resisted the urge to run her hands south of his waistline.

He brushed her hair from her neck and kissed the soft skin below her ear. His lips blazed a hot trail from her jaw to her lips before he captured her mouth in a rapturous kiss.

Her knees grew weak as his assault on her senses continued. She eagerly responded as he slipped his tongue deep into the sweet corners of her mouth. Heat rose between her thighs and she ached in anticipation.

Marshall's hand slipped down to caress her ass, but the many layers of chiffon in the skirt of her dress were prohibitive. He gathered layer after layer in his hands without gaining access to skin. He finally gave up, murmuring against her neck.

"This is a lovely dress, but there is just too much material here," he said, and tugged on the chiffon for emphasis.

"Why, Mr. James, it seems you're quite intent on getting under my clothes," she drawled sweetly.

"You noticed?" he replied.

"What kind of girl do you think I am?" she protested weakly as she exhaled in short, quick bursts.

He groaned, accompanied by a deep laugh. "Do you really want to have that conversation right now?" he asked as he finally found his way under the chiffon to the soft skin of her thigh.

Deandra wanted to be offended, but the ache between her thighs could not be ignored. The firmness of his manhood pressing against her belly hinted at a promise of sexual fulfillment. A promise she was eager to collect on.

He stopped his caressing just long enough to escort her to

the cabin below deck. She removed her shoes to descend the steps into the salon below. Marshall locked the cabin door behind them and then walked up behind her and slipped his hands around her waist. He nuzzled her neck only briefly before he untied the silk ribbon around her waist.

Deandra was overwhelmed by the elegance of the salon and still could not believe she was on the boat. She wanted to take it all in, but her physical desire for him was more overpowering. When he slid down the bodice of her dress and his hands cupped her bare breasts, she moaned aloud with pleasure. She felt her dress fall to the floor and she was naked, except for a silken hunter green thong with lace trim.

Marshall scooped her up effortlessly and carried her to the master cabin. He laid her on the bed and took a moment to enjoy the vision before him. Deandra lay reposed on the bed; her long, firm, shapely legs, her large, voluptuous breasts, and her slim, taut waistline created an irresistible package.

She watched him undress and marveled at the body hidden beneath the cloak of a benevolent businessman. There wasn't an ounce of fat on him and it was clear from the taut, rippling six-pack he worked out regularly. His dark skin was smooth as marble, like an African warrior chiseled from the finest stone. He took only a moment to sheath his manhood and then joined her.

He started his exploration at her ankles and licked his way up the supple skin of her legs to the firm skin of her belly. He nuzzled her navel playfully before sliding his tongue along the underside of her breasts. He continued his pursuit to the pink nipple, and gently pulled the large areola into his mouth.

Deandra purred, catlike, in response to his touch. She spread her legs wide, inviting him into her secret depths. She reached out and took hold of his dick as it rubbed against her belly. She wanted to feel him inside her.

Marshall was not in a hurry. He intended to enjoy each delicious morsel of her body. He wasn't sure if he'd have it again. He eased away from her insistent hand and slipped his finger inside her pussy. As he suspected, she was ready and juicy. He rubbed her clit until she bucked slightly from the stimulation. He then inserted a couple of fingers and stroked them in and out, making certain to slide his fingers over her clit each time he eased his fingers out.

She was moaning louder and louder, and whispering passionately and almost unintelligibly. "Fuck me, Marshall, fuck me now," she repeated incessantly while thrusting her hips against his groin.

He decided not to make her wait any longer and he pushed his dick as far inside her hot, wet, and juicy pleasure spot as he could.

Her vaginal walls closed around his dick like a vise grip and he could feel her working her inner muscles to increase his pleasure. It was working since his body temperature was rising steadily as he pounded her with sure and strong strokes. He made love to her for the better part of an hour before she shuddered violently in one final climax and he followed suit shortly thereafter.

Deandra snuggled in his arms and they fell peacefully asleep to the gentle rocking of the marina waters.

Marshall arose early in the morning and started toward Nassau while Deandra slept. She poked her head out from the cabin door just as Marshall was dropping anchor.

"Where are we?" she asked.

"Just a few miles from Nassau," he replied, and smiled as she emerged completely naked from the cabin door. Her body seemed even more flawless in the bright light of day than it had the night before. There wasn't a spare ounce of fat on her body. Her breasts were large and perfectly formed. She had a taut, firm stomach and abdomen. Her hips were slim, with just the right amount of flare to complement her smooth, round ass.

"Then I shouldn't have to worry about any nosey neighbors or Peeping Toms," she said as she stretched leisurely and then approached his chair in the pilothouse.

"Aren't you afraid you'll get burned?" Marshall asked as he ran his hand along her arm.

"I'm hoping for a little burn this morning," she replied coyly, and eased herself between his legs with her back to the wheel.

Marshall placed his hands on her ass cheeks and pulled her close for a kiss. His dick was already hard from the moment she stepped naked out onto the deck and he wanted her to feel his readiness.

Deandra moaned deliciously as his cock bounced eagerly against her rib cage. Marshall slid out of his bathing shorts and slipped on a condom from a small compartment next to the chair.

"Are you always so prepared?" she whispered, and pulled his earlobe into her mouth, and then ran her tongue along the outline of his ear.

"Always," he replied as he lifted her onto his lap and eased his thickened rod inside her waiting pussy. He moaned as the warm wetness closed around his shaft.

Deandra sighed and groaned as the long length of him moved deeper inside her body. She wrapped her arms around his neck for leverage and began to move her pussy up and down along the length of his dick. With his hands on her ass cheeks, and the strength of her thigh muscles she worked them both up to a heated frenzy before Marshall rose from the chair and carried her to one of the sofas on the deck to finish the job.

Spent, they both lay naked on the floor of the deck, soaking up a few rays of sun and resting. They drifted off to sleep. The sound of an engine nearby woke Marshall an hour later.

"Hey, Marsh, you there?" a man called from the approaching boat.

Marshall jumped up as he realized they could be seen any minute now as the other boat got closer. "Wake up, Dee," he said urgently, and shook her arm slightly. He then crawled into the pilothouse and donned his shorts before greeting the visitor.

"Hey, Pete," he called in return, hoping Dee had escaped inside the cabin. The boat continued its approach.

"What you doing out here? I haven't seen you on the water in months," Peter asked.

"I have to escape now and then," Marshall replied as Peter Jensen pulled his cruiser alongside the Sea Ray.

"Mae and Lonnie are in the cabin, why don't you come on over for some coffee and breakfast," Peter offered as his wife poked her head out of the cabin to call a greeting to Marshall.

"Thanks, but—" Marshall replied, but was cut off.

"Sweet Jesus!" Peter cried aloud as Deandra stood up in the middle of the deck and stretched kittenlike with her arms above her head. Her heavy, pendulous breasts swung naturally and erotically as she bent over and stretched the back of her legs by touching her toes. Her fine, round ass was on display, along with every other orifice of her body.

She stood up, smiled, and then waved to the newcomers as she disappeared below deck. Peter and his wife, Mae, stood with mouths agape and then looked questioningly at Marshall.

Marshall was disturbed by her blatant exhibitionism. She had a beautiful body without a doubt, but they were his friends, and a bit of decorum was necessary. He would have to have a serious chat with her. "Not today, thanks anyway," he replied as though they hadn't just seen every inch of his companion.

"Sure, sure. Maybe another time." Peter regained his composure and then restarted his engine and pulled away. "Have a good time," he tossed back over his shoulder with a knowing smile as he headed for the open sea.

Marshall stared out across the ocean and reflected on what

had just occurred. What did he know about this woman aboard his boat, except that she was beautiful, vivacious, and sexually insatiable? *Are you looking for a wife?* a little voice in his head asked. *No. Then what's the problem?* He couldn't change what had already occurred, and this wasn't destined to be a long-term relationship anyway. By the time he finally went below deck, he had decided not to make any comment on her behavior.

He found her draped in a towel and still wet from a shower. She was holding a photograph that had been mounted on the wall next to his dresser. She looked up at him curiously and pointed to the photo.

"Who are these people?" she asked.

The photo had been taken a few years ago on the deck of his boat. It was an older couple, himself, and a young woman. "Why? Do you recognize anyone?" he asked.

Deandra smiled meekly. Yes, she had recognized someone. When she emerged from her shower, she took a look around the bedroom, checking out pictures. Most of them were scenic pictures—the ocean, the sunset—and there was one of him holding a huge fish he must have caught. When she stumbled across this picture, her body froze. She hadn't seen her in fifteen years, but she would bet money that was CJ in that picture with Marshall. CJ, the source of her childhood humiliation, somehow knew Marshall James. It appeared that they knew each other rather well, judging by his arm that was draped over her shoulder and the big grin she was giving him in the picture. "No, not really. Are these your parents?" she said, pointing to the older couple in the picture.

"No, those aren't my parents. That's Tina and Emmett. They are good friends of my mother's and now they're friends of mine, a really nice couple. The other person is Connie. She's a close friend of Tina's."

"Was she your girlfriend at the time?"

"Connie? Oh no. We're just good friends. Connie's not the

kind of girl you just fool around with. Connie's long-term," he said, and smiled.

The glint in his eye when he spoke her name told Deandra that Connie was special, even if she wasn't his girlfriend. "What do you mean she's long-term?"

"Well, if you're going to get involved with someone like Connie, you should be thinking about eventually getting married. Sorry to say it, because it sounds so old-fashioned, but Connie is the kind of girl you take home to your mother."

"Ouch! And I'm not?" she countered.

He laughed and pulled her close, dislodging her towel. He nuzzled his face in her neck and pulled the soft skin of her neck between his lips. "I don't know you that well yet," he replied as his dick hardened again in anticipation of another romp. He cupped her breast with his right hand and brought the pink tip to his lips. He circled the protruding bud with his tongue, before pulling the tit into his mouth and sucking.

Deandra momentarily gave up her interrogation to slip back into bed with Marshall. She welcomed him into her body once again. She marveled at the contrast of his coal black skin melded with her light skin as she watched their reflection in the mirror across from the bed. The muscles in his back and ass cheeks were like steel. His body glistened with a light coat of sweat. His dick filled every inch of her aching pussy as he stroked deeper and deeper inside. She slipped her hand between his groin and her and began to stroke her clit.

Marshall felt her stroking herself. He knew this meant she wasn't coming easily this time. He pulled her hand out and held both of her hands by the wrists above her head. He removed his dick from her pussy and replaced it with his mouth. He sucked aggressively on her clit and tasted the juices of her body.

Deandra bucked wildly under the assault on her clit. She thrashed uncontrollably as orgasm after orgasm rocked her body. Satisfied she'd finally come, he reentered her body and fucked her until he came again.

Marshall arose from the bed to take a quick shower while Deandra remained in bed, her thoughts in a jumble. Marshall shared a definite affection for Connie. She could hear it in the way he talked about her, something deeper than friendship. She wanted to know more about their relationship, but didn't want to make him suspicious by asking too many questions.

She decided it didn't matter at the moment. There was no way CJ was going to stop her from continuing in this relationship with Marshall James. No way in hell.

After she showered again, Marshall took her on a shopping spree in Nassau. She was completely loaded down with clothes, shoes, and accessories by the time they returned to the boat. He enjoyed buying clothes for her, and she was like a child in a candy store everywhere they went. Since it had been so long since he'd spent time with a beautiful woman, he did not mind indulging her.

They returned to the boat, where they made love again, then headed back out to sea and home to Jupiter Island.

3

A thin bead of sweat trickled down the side of her forehead as she basked in the plastic lounge chair on the white sandy beach. Her dark brown hair was loosely pushed up under an orange straw-woven hat. A modest orange bikini covered her small but perky breasts and contrasted perfectly with the cinnamon tones of her skin. The Florida heat added its own highlight to this perfect picture by creating a glowing sheen to her skin in the form of tiny beads of sweat. Connie Jefferson was oblivious to the enticing package she made that day on Juno Beach, but someone watching her from a distance was not.

Listening to her internal clock, she opened her eyes and reached into her beach bag for her watch. It was three o'clock. Another Sunday afternoon spent alone. She sighed and tossed the watch back in the bag. There was no real need to race home; she could stay at least another hour. Turning over on her stomach, she rested her face on her forearms and closed her eyes, allowing the sun to do its job on her well-formed back, shoulders, and shapely legs.

Thoughts of Marshall drifted unchecked across her mind.

She wondered what he was doing and with whom he was doing it. Pangs of unexpected jealousy and dislike arose sharply toward the unknown woman he was probably making love to at this moment. Two years had passed since their afternoon on the lake and he'd never mentioned it. What had she expected? Not as much as a phone call, a note, a card, or something to acknowledge the fact that they had shared an intensely intimate and passionate afternoon together. How about "I'm sorry about the misunderstanding"? There had been no misunderstanding. He'd given her exactly what she craved at that moment. Maybe he could have said, "I'm sorry for slipping between your thighs and leaving you wanting more, for creating a void no man could fill." Agitated by her thoughts, Connie turned her face to the other side and brushed away an errant tear. She acknowledged the mixed feelings he evoked in her. She hated Marshall James. Hated him for being everything she ever wanted and knew she would never have, and she loved him for giving her one unforgettable moment in time.

Two years ago in the summer of 2003, Connie took a weekend trip to the Isle of St. John in North Florida with a group of friends. The retreat was hosted by a former employer and close friend. Connie was originally supposed to attend the party with her beau, who unfortunately broke up with her a few weeks before the trip. Her friend Tina assured her the cabin would be filled with several other single guests and it would do her good to be around people and not home sulking. Reluctantly Connie agreed to go alone. She'd always looked forward to any opportunity to stay at the cabin and decided to make the best of her time out at the lake.

The trip was actually a success, because Connie did forget all about her heartbreak that hot, long weekend, but she replaced it with a memory that would stay with her forever, when fate tossed her a curveball in the form of a well-meaning, gorgeous, compassionate, and sexy Marshall James.

It was the first time she'd been out to the cabin at the same time as Marsh. They'd met on earlier occasions at the Millers', but never really spent any appreciable amount of time in each other's company. Marshall was also a close friend of the hosts, and often acted in the capacity of second host, making sure all the guests were taken care of and had everything they needed. At six feet two inches tall, with a dark bittersweet chocolate complexion and well-formed muscular body, Marsh was rarely without female companionship. He was a successful real estate developer, and his financial stability rounded out the already appetizing package. Women fawned over him and competed for his attention on a regular basis.

He'd arrived at the cabin with a stunning dark-haired beauty. She was tall and slim with voluptuous enhanced breasts and a smooth mocha complexion. While the women snickered and whispered behind her back, referring to her as a Black Barbie doll, the men suddenly developed a newfound respect for Marshall. They were hoping to live vicariously through a few stories with him. But Marshall was a gentleman above all else, and kiss-and-tell boasting was not his style.

It was the gentleman and host in him that noticed how out of sorts Connie was, early on that weekend. Although they had not spoken more than a few words at previous meetings, he went out of his way to lift her spirits. He'd offered to take her canoeing. She agreed, because it was an opportunity to get away from the throng of guests milling around the cabin. They were out on the water about twenty minutes when she told him of her recent breakup. She felt comfortable talking with him and gave him her thoughts on why the relationship failed, and expressed her disappointment at being unsuccessful with men. He assured her it was not her fault; she simply hadn't met the right man yet. She was staring reflectively out at the water, mulling over his statement, when they were hit with a sudden fierce rain shower.

As often happens in the "Sunshine State" of Florida, there had been no warning signs. One minute the sky was clear, and the next they were hit with a deluge.

By the time they reached the shore, they were both drenched. After assisting her from the canoe, Marsh grabbed her hand and they ran toward the cabin. As they reached the steps, he realized that if they rushed inside, they would track water all through the cabin.

He pulled her around to the shed behind the cabin, certain he could find towels inside. When they reached the shed, they both darted inside out of the pelting rain. Marsh searched until he found the pile of spare towels. He handed one to her and draped the second over his shoulders. They looked at each other and burst out laughing at their predicament.

Connie dried her hair and face with the towel he'd given her. Her eyes were filled with mirth, and twinkled up at him in the dim light of the shed. He thought she looked absolutely inviting. As his gaze traveled down her body, he noticed her wet cotton shirt was plastered against her firm round breasts. He felt a familiar stirring in his groin, and with the sole intention of trying to be a gentleman, he removed the larger towel from his shoulders and wrapped it around her shoulders.

He knew she was unaware her breasts and erect nipples were clearly visible to him through the thin cotton blouse she wore. Holding on to the ends of the towel, he pulled it snuggly around her shoulders and up under her chin.

She reached up to take the ends of the towel in her hand, and her hands touched his. His intention changed as the sensation of her warm hands on his lit a fire in the pit of his stomach. With the ends of the towel still in his grasp, he pulled her closer to him. She looked up to see him staring at her intently. It was clear what was on his mind. Alone in the shed, she knew it would be impossible to resist him.

Embarrassed by the naked desire she saw in his eyes, she

tried to lighten the mood. "Hey" was all she was able to get out before he leaned down and kissed her. His lips were warm, soft and yet demanding at the same time. Tingling sensations raced through her body. Somehow she secretly knew it would be like this with Marsh. She willingly gave in to the desires raging inside and opened her mouth under the gentle pressure of his. The passion of their kiss deepened.

Connie began to feel weak in the knees as the tingling sensations traveled lower and settled in the depth of her feminine core. She offered no resistance as he walked her backward to a cot in the far corner of the shed. He lay down on the cot and pulled her down next to him. Overcome by her own physical desires, she was powerless to resist him. She nestled in the crook of his arm, and returned his kisses with equal ardor. His hand, which had been caressing her midriff, was moving up under the rising mound of her breast. Arching her back, she longed for the feel of his hands on her. She was not disappointed. His warm hand cupped her breast and he began massaging the sensitive bud of her nipple with his thumb. She could feel the moistness starting between her legs as the full length of his erect manhood was etched along her thigh.

They rode along with the waves of unbridled passion engulfing them. Marsh deftly began to unbutton her blouse. At the same time she reached over to unbuckle his jeans. An urgent need for physical connection spurred their actions. He eased her out of her blouse and unsnapped the front-hook bra she was wearing. Her breasts sprang free. He paused for a moment to behold the physical beauty of this woman in his arms, and then dipped his head to latch onto her nipple with his mouth.

She moaned aloud in pleasure as he teased the rigid peaks with his tongue. The sensations cascading through her body were driving her crazy with desire for him. Reaching inside his unzipped pants, she slipped her hand inside his briefs and touched the hard, yet velvety smooth, skin of his organ. A sharp intake of breath from Marsh let her know the pleasure he derived from her touch.

His attention turned back to her mouth. Her lips were trembling with anticipation as he began kissing her deeply again. His free hand now slipped inside the elastic waistband of her shorts. He found the pleasure spot he was seeking and began massaging her lightly. Waves of ecstasy cascaded through her body at his touch as he brought her to a fierce climax.

He released her and stood up to remove his jeans. Staring down at her, he hesitated for a brief moment, having second thoughts about what he was going to do next. The hesitation disappeared as she reached up for him. He climbed back on the cot and slid between her open and welcoming legs. She arched her back and raised her hips to accept him as he drove deep into the warm moist comfort of her body. Her fingers gripped the sinewy muscles of his biceps as the ensuing sensations overwhelmed them both. Their bodies met in a fierce union of passion and desire. Minutes later they lay spent in each other's arms.

Reality and clarity returned more quickly for Marshall than for Connie. Concerned he'd allowed his passion to overrule his head and taken advantage of her in a vulnerable state, he asked, "Are you okay?"

Against the warmth of his chest, she murmured, "Yes."

Instead of easing his concern, it was suddenly elevated. Connie was nestled in his arms like she belonged there. He, too, felt at peace having her there. But he knew she was still vulnerable from her last relationship. He also remembered he had not come to the cabin alone that weekend. He'd brought along a date, who was probably wondering where he was.

"Connie," he started. She looked up at him and saw the concern in his eyes. She misinterpreted the look on his face as regret. Reality came crashing back. What had she done? In those wanton, lustful moments she had wanted to feel loved and desired. She'd lost her head and just made love to someone else's man. It was something she never thought she would do. How could she face the woman now, knowing what she'd done?

"Oh, I'm . . . Oh boy . . . ," she said, suddenly feeling very naked, emotionally and physically. She sat up and reached for her bra and blouse. She snapped the hooks on the bra, but her trembling fingers had difficulty closing the buttons on the wet blouse. Marsh watched in silence as a tear trickled down her cheek. He zipped his pants and knelt in front of her and closed his hands over her trembling ones. She stopped attempting to button the blouse and allowed him to do it for her. Her tears continued to fall silently, wetting his hands. He leaned over and kissed her trembling lips.

"This was not your fault," he said. "I shouldn't have taken advantage of you, of your feelings. I'm sorry. I'd never hurt you for anything in the world, Connie. Believe me, I wouldn't," he finished earnestly, and pulled her into his arms.

"I know you wouldn't, Marsh," she said, and wiped the tears off her cheeks. Steeling herself, she continued, "Neither one of us was thinking beyond the moment. I can't pretend to be sorry for what we shared, but what about your girlfriend?"

"She's not my girlfriend. I've only been seeing her for a couple of weeks. I mean, I know it was still kind of disrespectful. Damn," he said. "I'm not saying I'm sorry it happened either. I think you're a little vulnerable right now and I should have taken this into consideration before coming on to you, but you were so . . ." He'd known Connie as an acquaintance and he always admired her, but right now he was feeling more than a little confused by the turn of events. His mind was battling with his heart to understand how these feelings snuck up on him. There were many things buzzing around his head he felt he had no right to voice. Instead, he stood up and turned back to look out the door. "I think it stopped raining. I'll go back to the cabin first. You can follow me in a few minutes. I don't want us to walk in there together, feeling or looking guilty."

Connie thought she understood what he was trying to say so ineloquently. Much to her disappointment, it was all about sex. A hot, lustful moment of unbridled passion and she gave in to it without a second thought. A quickie. It would be foolish for her to even think there was, would, or could be more between her and Marshall James. "Okay," she agreed, determined to be as nonchalant about the whole incident as she thought he was. She watched him leave the shed. A few minutes later she felt composed enough to head back to the cabin. She spent the rest of the weekend avoiding direct contact with him and his insignificant other.

After the interlude of the weekend Connie was sure Marsh would call. Just to say hello or something. Three months of anxiously checking her voicemail finally convinced her he was not going to call. Six months of silence convinced her he had forgotten all about her and their moment. His feelings about their time together finally became crystal clear to Connie; it had meant nothing to him. Over time they'd run into each other socially and the tension disappeared as a comfortable friendship grew between them. Yet their intimate encounter was never discussed.

The sky darkened overhead and a chill wind blew across her spine. The beach had emptied, except for a few hardy souls. It was time to go. Connie arose and began gathering up her beach chair, towel, and bags. She pulled a T-shirt from her bag and slipped it over her head. As she put on her sandals, a book slipped from the top of her bag. Hefting the bag back onto her shoulder and setting down the beach chair, she reached for the book.

"Allow me," a gentleman said from behind her. He stepped in quickly and retrieved the book. He brushed off the sand it collected and handed it to her. A warm smile crossed his face and he extended his hand to introduce himself. "Hi, my name is Victor. Can I help you to your car?"

Connie took in his clean-shaven face and head. His skin was the color of toasted macadamia nuts and his smile was warm and friendly. Six feet tall, slight of build with a baby smooth, hairless chest, he was an attractive man. Maybe the fates were smiling on her after all. She handed him the plastic lounge chair and replied, "Thanks, my name is Connie."

Victor called Connie several times the following week. They agreed to meet for dinner on Friday. Connie hadn't been out on a date in a few months and was eagerly anticipating his arrival. She found him charismatic and a good conversationalist. He seemed well-informed on many topics.

For the evening she'd chosen a simple peach floral sundress with matching peach sandals and purse. After speaking with Victor throughout the week, she felt comfortable enough to allow him to pick her up at her home. Connie lived in a small two-bedroom villa not far from the beach. Her grandmother had passed two years earlier and left the villa to her. It needed a little work, but Connie was quite handy and creative. She'd turned it into a little haven filled with plants and a collage of pictures.

Victor arrived punctually at seven-thirty in a small sports car. He was attired as though he'd stepped off the cover of *GQ*—Florida style in a muted striped shirt, linen shorts, and a pullover sweater draped loosely across his shoulders.

When Connie answered the door and invited him inside, he presented her with a tiny gift-wrapped box. Genuinely surprised, she asked, "What's this?"

"Just a small gesture to say I'm glad we met," he replied.

She sat down on the couch and opened the box. Inside was a miniature bouquet of three tiny roses with a silver-plated bow around the stem. The crystal in the rose blossoms reflected a prism of colors from the light in the room. Connie was speechless. She'd never received such an exquisite and unique gift on a first date.

"Victor, you shouldn't have. This is gorgeous," she exclaimed with delight.

They dined at a local seafood restaurant. Victor would prove to be a perfect gentleman as he opened the car door for her and pulled her chair out for her in the restaurant. He asked what food she liked and made suggestions from the menu of what he thought she would enjoy. Connie was pleased by the lengths Victor went to ensure she had a good time. He was personable and even funny at times. He asked polite questions about Connie, but didn't pry too deeply.

Connie, on the other hand, didn't feel she'd learned very much about Victor. He'd mentioned siblings in passing and that his parents lived in the Northeast. He'd moved to Florida only a few years ago and said he hadn't made a lot of friends during that time. He stated he was a bit of a loner.

After they took a drive out to the beach and strolled along the boardwalk by the ocean, Connie was surprised when Victor took her hand as they walked. She looked down at their hands clasped together and smiled.

"What's so funny?" Victor asked, and raised her hand to his lips and kissed the back of it.

"Oh, nothing really," she replied. "I was just surprised, that's all."

"Surprised that I would hold your hand? You're a very beautiful woman, Connie. Any man would be a fool not to want to touch you," he replied, and stopped walking for a moment to face her.

She blushed and turned away toward the railing. As she looked out at the rippling ocean waves, she said, "That's a really nice thing to say, Victor."

"It's the truth, plain and simple, Connie. I've only had the opportunity to know you for a week and already I can see how special you are." He leaned on the rail next to her.

Connie faced him. She studied his face and thought about this evening. He'd been wonderful to her all evening. It had to be fate that brought him to the beach last week.

Victor watched the play of emotions on Connie's face. Her dark brown eyes sparkled in the moonlight. Impulsively he leaned forward and kissed her gently on the lips.

Connie's eyes registered surprise at first. Then she relaxed into the simple kiss for a moment before breaking away.

Victor eased up behind her and placed his hands on either side of hers. He leaned into her ear and whispered, "You're special, Connie."

Connie relaxed against his solid chest and sighed. She felt good. For the first time in a long time, she felt comfortable with someone.

Victor cupped her chin with his palm and turned her mouth upward. He kissed her again, this time with a little more coaxing. His tongue flicked her lips lightly, until she opened her mouth slightly. He slipped his tongue into the warmth of her mouth and he heard her moan with pleasure.

Connie's body started tingling when his mouth touched her more intimately. She felt his hand on her abdomen as he turned her in his arms. When his tongue slipped inside her mouth, a hunger surfaced inside her being. She tasted the essence of him and enjoyed the increasing passion of his kiss. She wrapped her arms around his waist as he pulled her close against the length of his body. His arousal did not escape her. Her body ached in response to the feel of his manhood against her thigh.

Suddenly she broke off the kiss and looked away. What was she thinking? She'd only known this man a week and she was wantonly engaging with him in a public place.

"Connie?" he queried. "Did I do something wrong? I apologize for coming on to you like that." Victor quickly tried to regroup.

Connie looked up at him. He looked so sincere, like a soulful puppy who'd trampled on your white carpet with muddy feet. She realized she was being a bit overly prudish. After all, there was no one around for miles, and Victor had done nothing she hadn't encouraged him to do.

"No, Victor. You didn't do anything wrong at all. It's just me being a bit silly." She smiled in an apologetic manner.

"Hey, do you want to walk on the beach?" Victor asked, brightly trying to recapture the mood.

"Sure, I'd love to," she agreed, and started toward the steps to the beach. At the bottom step she stopped to remove her sandals.

Victor took a moment to remove his loafers before capturing her hand and racing her toward the rolling waves.

They stopped just short of the wave as it lapped ashore. Their toes dug into the sand and the water washed over their feet.

Connie danced along the water and couldn't remember having felt so carefree in a very long time. They walked along the beach, hand in hand, and waded in and out of the water for almost a mile.

Victor finally sat down on the sand next to a formation of rocks and well back from the waterline. He pulled Connie down to the beach floor with him. She settled down between his legs and rested her back against his chest. With her head resting on his shoulder, she gazed at the overwhelming expanse of ocean in front of them. The sea air was intoxicating and the sound of the waves rolling ashore was erotically enticing in its own way.

"Connie, do you know how much I want to make love to you right now?" Victor whispered against the soft skin of her neck.

"Yes, Victor, I think I do," she whispered back as her body cried out for fulfillment she hadn't experienced in a long time. She scooted back farther between his thighs until she could feel his hardened dick against her ass.

"Are you sure?" he asked as he slipped his hand inside the bodice of her sundress and cupped her bare breast.

A small cry of pleasure escaped her lips as his hand touched her breast. He kissed her lightly on her shoulders as he methodically pushed down one strap of her dress and then the other, exposing her breasts. Cradled between his legs, Connie allowed Victor to pleasure her slowly and sensually. When the cool night air blew across her breasts, she shivered only slightly before he cupped both breasts in his hands and tweaked her rigid nipples playfully and expertly.

The heat in her body was building at a rapid pace and her pussy was throbbing in anticipation. She started to move out of the circle of his arm, but he held her tightly. "Not yet," he whispered, and circled his tongue around her ear and sucked on her earlobe. He slipped one hand down the inside of her dress and massaged her taut abdomen.

Connie whimpered pleasurably under his skillful assault on her senses. His other hand slipped under the skirt of her dress and sought the moist warmth between her thighs.

She cried aloud as he pushed aside her silken panties and touched her aching clit. Her body jerked as he rubbed the protruding sensitive bulb, but his hand on her abdomen kept her firmly in place. Trapped between his legs, her body jerked violently as he worked her clit until she climaxed uncontrollably. When he felt her cum flush over his hand, he released his grip on her abdomen.

Connie moaned aloud as he lay her back down in the sand. He took only a moment to slip out of his trousers and into position between her legs. He donned a condom and quickly eased into her aching pussy.

She arched her back and raised her ass up off the sand to assist his entry into the moist, hot depths of her body. All she could think of was how thick and hard his dick was as she shuddered and accepted the satisfying length of him.

Victor stroked long and slowly while he enjoyed the feel of her tight pussy grabbing and sucking his dick back inside her secret depths. Her eager willingness only heightened his excitement. He cupped one breast in his hand and sucked the small buttonlike brown tit. Her breasts weren't large, but the teat fit perfectly in his mouth. He sucked intently and swirled his tongue around the rigid tip. When he felt her body tense and a rush of hot fluid encased his dick, he knew she'd come again. He groaned aloud as his excitement reached a feverish peak and released his cum deep inside her pussy.

He rolled off her and lay back on the sandy beach. He laughed aloud and then turned to look at her, where she lay next to him. "I never go this far on a first date," he confessed.

Connie returned his smile. "Neither do I." She suddenly realized her dress was filled with sand, as well as her hair. "Oh, my goodness! How are we going to get to the car without being seen?"

"Don't worry. I think the restaurant is closed now anyway. No one will even notice us," he assured her, and began to shake the sand out of his clothes.

She shook as much sand as she could from her dress and smoothed it back down where it had wrinkles from being bunched up in the sand. They both looked quite rumpled and it would be obvious to anyone what they had been doing.

"That's what they make dry cleaners for. Our clothes will be fine. Come on," he said, and they started back down the beach to the boardwalk.

They didn't talk much on the ride back to Connie's home. As Victor walked her to the door, he paused for a moment on the sidewalk.

"Any regrets?" he asked seriously.

"None," she said, and smiled sincerely. She'd had a wonderful evening. She hadn't anticipated they would go as far as they did, but at the moment she didn't regret it.

"I had an amazing night with you, Connie. May I call you tomorrow? I'd love to see you again," he asked.

"I'd love to see you again, Victor," she replied, and hoped he was as sincere as he sounded. He was almost too good to be true.

He kissed her lightly on the lips and then waited for her to put her key in the door. "I'll talk to you tomorrow," he said, and walked toward his car.

"Good night, Victor. Thanks for a wonderful evening," she called toward his retreating back. She stepped into the foyer and leaned back against the door. A small laugh slipped through her lips and she giggled happily as she headed toward her bedroom for a shower.

4

Marshall and Deandra spent a lot of time together during the first month. Most of that time was spent in intimate little restaurants or expensive hotels. While she was being luxuriously wined and dined, Deandra had yet to visit Marshall's home and was beginning to wonder why. When the local Children's Home Society hosted a fund-raising dinner dance, Deandra knew Marshall was sure to attend. It was getting perilously close to the date of the event and he had not mentioned it to her at all. The weekend before the dance, they were having dinner and she popped the question.

"Marshall, are you planning to attend the CHS fund-raiser on Saturday?" she asked.

He had suspected sooner or later she would want to accompany him to a very public event. However, his mother was on the board of CHS and he usually escorted her to these events. He weighed his answer carefully.

"I will be attending, as I usually do with my mother. She is on the board and I like to make sure she gets there and back home safely," he said, and paused to gauge her reaction. She was staring down at the table. He continued, "If you like, I can pick you up after I take her home and we can spend the rest of the weekend together."

Deandra immediately felt his rejection of her, real or imagined. She wasn't good enough to be seen as his date. Her anger filtered out through the slit in her lips as she asked, "Do you expect me to wait at home like a good little girl until you are done parading your mother around and have time for me?"

"Dee, we've spent a lot of time together since we met and I think that's a bit unfair," he countered.

Chastened, but undeterred, she persisted. "I want to go to the dance."

"Sweetheart, I'm not stopping you from going. I just won't be able to escort you there," he said, and then added, "Not this time anyway."

She immediately jumped on the ray of hope he tossed her way. "Then we will attend functions together in the near future?" she asked.

He acquiesced and replied, "Sure we can. If she wasn't on the board, and I didn't take her every year, I'd be happy to take you. But my mother is a very demanding woman and I'd prefer not to upset her right now."

She considered the results of pressing this issue and remembered the warning that Viola would be a formidable foe. She needed Marshall more squarely in her corner before she took on Viola. Contrition filled her voice as she backed down on the issue of the dance.

"I wouldn't upset her, but I understand. I don't want to cause problems before I even get a chance to meet her. I do want her to like me."

Much like Deandra, Marshall recognized when the pendulum had swung his way and immediately seized the opportunity. He pulled Deandra into his arms and gave her a warm hug.

"Honey, she will like you as much as I do." He whispered

assurances he knew were untrue, but he didn't want to give up Dee yet. His mother was not going to be happy when she realized he was still seeing her. He was going to put that revelation off as long as he could.

In the meantime he could spend the rest of the night convincing her how much he enjoyed her company. Instead of taking Deandra to her apartment after dinner, Marshall decided to take her to his home. When they pulled into the courtyard of his estate, Deandra turned in her seat and looked at him curiously.

"I gather this is your home?" she asked.

He pulled into one of the four garages before answering. "Yes, I thought it was time I brought you to my place."

Deandra checked out the other cars in the garage. In addition to the sport Mercedes he usually drove, there was a Range Rover, a large Mercedes 500 sedan, and an older model four-door sedan. The moderately priced car seemed a bit out of place next to the other expensive vehicles.

"Whose car is that?" she asked.

"It's mine," he replied as he alighted from the car and came to her side to open the door for her.

"Is that your first car or something? Is there sentimental value attached to it?" she asked as she stepped out of the car on the concrete floor of the garage.

"No, it's not that old. There are just days that I'd rather be incognito or don't necessarily want to flaunt my success in the face of some of my friends."

"You've earned your success. Why be embarrassed about it? Heck, like they say, 'If you've got it, flaunt it,' " Deandra replied, and scoffed at the idea of hiding her affluence once she had attained it.

"It's not always that simple," he countered, and decided to drop the discussion. It was clear that Deandra did not have a sensitive bone in her body when it came to relating to others.

He had many friends he'd made along the way who were not as successful as he was, but they were still his friends. They accepted him for who he was, a regular guy who happened to make a lot of money. Sometimes he only wanted to be that regular guy, and that's how he felt when he drove that car.

They entered the house from the garage and walked down a short hallway to the foyer. There were large marble tiles of varying sizes across the foyer and into the dining and formal living room. Deandra wandered into the living room and admired the rich interior. She ran her hand along the frame of an Italian leather sectional. The house smelled new, with a subtle hint of an amazing potpourri that was not flowery, but aromatically pleasing. Her eyes were drawn to a large purple vase on the sofa table near the entrance to the dining room. She approached the vase, and upon closer inspection, she could tell it was actually a vase in the shape of the petals of a flower. Her eyes sparkled as she looked at him and lightly touched the edges of the vase.

"What flower is this?"

Marshall smiled as he answered. "That's a tulip. You have very good taste. That is a Daum piece from France. It's one of my mother's favorites."

"How much would something like this cost?" she inquired.

He pulled her away from the vase and nuzzled his face in her neck. "I didn't bring you here to study the artwork."

"But I want to know," she moaned as her body began warming up for the next activity.

"If I tell you, will you stop asking questions?" he cajoled.

"We'll make a deal," she responded breathlessly. "For every question you answer, I will remove an article of clothing. Is that fair?"

He smiled devilishly at her. He could easily get into this game. "I hope you don't have more questions than clothing. But that sounds fair. That vase costs about twenty-five hundred dollars."

"Really!" she replied. She liked it even more now. She untied the chain-link belt around her waist and tossed in onto the sofa. Next she pointed to a framed portrait of an older gentleman on the wall over the mantel. "Who is this?"

"That's my father, Edward James. He passed away two years ago," he replied as he walked up behind her and unzipped her dress. "After he died my mother didn't want to live here anymore, so I moved back here to care for the estate."

She turned coyly toward him before slowly sliding the sleeves down her arms and across her fingers. "Your father was a very handsome man, I'm sorry I'll never meet him." She gave the dress one final downward push and it fell to the floor at her feet in a small heap. Gingerly she stepped out of the dress and smiled. Clothed only in a satiny black slip, she continued her tour of the room.

Marshall appreciated her sexy form. Her long legs were perfectly accented by the high heels she still wore and the sexy slip. His dick was already erect and eager to slip between her silken thighs. Slip into the comfort of a body he had come to know so well. He watched as she sat on the sofa and crossed her legs slowly. The satin slip rose to the tops of her thighs. With her right leg crossed over her left, one of the Jimmy Choo high heels he'd bought her earlier in the week dangled enticingly off the tip of her toes.

"How long have you lived here?" she asked, and kicked off one shoe.

"About five years," he replied as he approached the wet bar and began to prepare a drink for himself.

Deandra stood up and kicked off her remaining shoe before posing another question. "Have you always lived here alone?"

"Yes. Can I offer you a drink?" he asked as he poured a healthy shot of vodka into a glass.

She stood in the entrance to the living room and smiled. Slowly she raised the satin slip, revealing her delectable body underneath, inch by inch, until she was able to pull it over her head. She removed the clip from the back of her head and shook her long, thick hair until it fell loose and cloudlike around her shoulders. She was naked except for a minuscule thong as she stood under the arch between the foyer and the living room. She did a slow pirouette for his viewing pleasure. Her ample breasts swayed like ripe cantaloupe above her taut and narrow waist. She coyly pointed to the stairs leading to the second floor. "May I?" she asked deliciously.

He nodded his assent and voraciously watched her as she sauntered up the stairs. Her ass cheeks were smooth and perfect oval pillows at the top of her endless shapely legs. Her olive skin had a perfect tan from head to toe. The thin wispy line of a black lace thong disappeared invitingly between her ass cheeks. His fully engorged dick ached with anticipation as he downed the last of his drink and removed his jacket. He tossed it on the couch and then followed her exit. Marshall jogged up the steps and stopped in his tracks when he realized she was seated at the top of the landing on the first step.

Deandra was poised on the top step with a wicked come-hither grin on her face. Her legs were spread invitingly as she fingered her clit. She mewed aloud as her body shook gently from the stimuli.

"You are so bad, so damn bad," Marshall whispered huskily as he quickly slipped out of his remaining clothes.

"Do you have something for me, Marshall? Give it to me, give me all of it," she groaned, and raised her buttocks off the step to give him easier access to her body. His dick was so hard, it literally hurt. He wasted no time in filling her request—his dick was soon embedded deep inside her hot, juicy love canal. He pulled her thighs to his groin and stroked as deep inside her pussy as humanly possible. His heightened level of excitement and need for release was reflected in his aggressive assault on her pussy. He pounded her fast and furiously until beads of sweat glistened on his skin and his breathing became deep and relaxed.

Deandra's screams were long and constant in response to the pleasure and pain generated by his rough and dominant love-making. Her body was rocked by orgasm after orgasm under his masterful hands.

Marshall extricated his still rigid manhood from between her thighs and gently pulled her to her feet.

"You didn't come," she protested weakly as he helped her to stand on her still tingling and not quite steady legs.

"I'm not finished with you yet," he replied, and guided her in the direction of the master suite.

"Oh!" she giggled and followed his directions through a double-door arch into his bedroom. A king-sized bed was the focal point of the room, and Marshall took only a minute to re-move the comforter before lifting Deandra onto the center of the bed.

As her body sunk into the soft comfort of the expensive mattress, she watched as Marshall donned a condom before he returned to the bed. She realized that was why he had not given in and climaxed earlier. He wasn't protected—protected from her. A dark mood settled over her and she turned on her side away from him.

Marshall climbed into bed behind her and spooned lovingly up against her back and ass. He wrapped his arm around her waist and pulled her close against his chest. He immediately recognized the stiffness of her body. "What's the matter, sweet-heart?" he asked, and began to nibble on her ear. She did not re-spond. He rubbed his hand along her abdomen and asked again, "Dee, what's wrong? Did I do something?"

She turned on her back and looked at him accusingly. "Why did you just put on a condom?"

Shocked, Marshall sat up before he responded. "I always wear a condom, don't I? Why is that an issue?"

Tears unexpectedly sprung to her eyes. She was hurt and she couldn't even begin to put her finger on why. She didn't want children, so he was protecting both of them. Rationally she knew this, but somehow it hit her as rejection—rejection of her.

"What are you afraid of?" she demanded. "Are you afraid I'll get pregnant and you'll be stuck with me?"

"Dee, what are you talking about? Aren't you on the pill?"

"Yes," she replied quietly.

"So you're not ready for children yet either?"

"No."

"Then why are we arguing about something neither one of us wants to happen right now?" he asked softly.

Deandra realized the rationale of what he was saying. She knew she'd reacted to her own insecurity and nothing he'd done. She smiled weakly. "I'm sorry, Marshall. I don't know what got into me."

He relaxed and lay back down on the bed. He pulled her into the crook of his arms and kissed the salty tears from her cheeks. "I've never seen you cry before," he whispered. "You're very sexy when you cry," he continued, and slid his palm down her abdomen and into her crevice between her thighs.

Deandra smiled demurely, still embarrassed and confused by her outburst. She pointed to his soft dick lying undisturbed and uninterested in a thick patch of curly pubic hair. "I'm sorry I spoiled the mood," she said.

"You didn't. I just think my dick went to sleep. Do you think there's anything you can do about that?"

Deandra was once again in an arena where she felt confident. She placed her hand around his softened manhood and squeezed gently. His dick responded positively to her stimulation and grew hard and firm. She straddled him easily and he slid deep inside her warmth. Deandra placed her hands on Marshall's chest and allowed her breasts to brush his lips.

Marshall sucked gently on her tits until her rocking became more aggressive. In response to her frenzied grinding on his dick, he grabbed her ass cheeks with his hands and raised his hips with each downward thrust of her body. They returned to the comfort of past lovemaking, and all thoughts of earlier distractions disappeared as they worked feverishly to please each other. Marshall's gentle sucking became more intense as he palmed her breasts and sucked passionately, running his tongue around the rigid peach nipple. He alternately bit and sucked the delicious fruit.

Deandra fucked him with an urgency she'd never experienced. She fucked hard to make him forget about her outburst. She fucked him hard so she could forget about her display of weakness. She wanted him to remember how good she could make him feel, so he wouldn't want her to leave. Deandra threw her hair back and moaned aloud like an angry lioness. An orgasmic wave crested at the top of her head and rushed through her body before gushing from her pussy. She gasped aloud as tears of unchecked emotion, raw and vulnerable, rained down her cheeks.

Marshall seized the opportunity to take control once again and rolled her underneath him and drove his voracious rod deep inside, before spilling his seed inside his protective sheath.

He took a moment to dispose of the condom in the bathroom before returning to bed. Once in bed he pulled Deandra close to his side before drifting off to sleep. Exhausted physically and mentally, Deandra followed suit. Soon she began dreaming.

Andie's sleep was disturbed by loud voices, and she pulled the pillow over her ears to block out the noise. Her mother was crying and her father was angry again.

"Will you stop with the fucking tears? You've been carrying on like this for days. Get ahold of yourself, for crying out loud!"

"What more do you want from me?" Julia Moore pleaded.

"I want you to knock it off. I can't take much more of this," her father said.

"I'm trying, you just don't understand. He, he . . ." She began crying again.

Her father could barely contain his anger as he interrupted her. "He's dead! He's fucking dead. He ruined my life and yours. Now you can finally stop moping around here, hoping he'll come and rescue you. He's gone!" he yelled.

Her mother wailed even louder at this outburst, and the sound of a chair crashing to the floor startled Andie. She pulled the pillow tighter against her ears, she knew it wasn't over yet.

"I've been here for the last seventeen years. I stuck by you even after you embarrassed us in front of this whole fucking town! You made me look like a fool and I still stayed with you anyway!"

"Why? Why did you stay?" she screamed, and took a deep, ragged breath through her tears. "Did you stay to torment me? To make me pay for a mistake I couldn't help?"

Her father's voice suddenly broke, and she could hear him struggle to get past the lump in his throat as he confessed, "I stayed because I loved you Julia! But you wouldn't let me love you. I forgave you and you still only wanted him!"

"That's not true, it's not true," she wailed. "I do love you."

"Just not as much as you loved him. I'm tired of being second best. I can't do this anymore," he said. A door slammed in the distance and the only sound that remained was that of her mother sobbing uncontrollably.

Deandra turned restlessly in her sleep and felt tears on her cheeks. She rubbed the moisture from her cheeks and sat up on the side of her bed. Why did her parents arguing haunt her so much? She never saw her father again after that last fight. When she'd confronted her mother about the subject of the argument, her mother just waved her off and refused to discuss it. She knew Dan Moore was not her biological father, but her mother would never give her any information about her birth father.

She insisted that Dan raised her as his own daughter, and it was all she needed to know.

Deandra got out of the bed quietly. She found a robe in the bedroom closet and tied it around her. Without disturbing Marshall, she left the room and wandered back downstairs to the living room. She stood in the doorway and gazed around the room. It was a beautiful room in a gorgeous home. It was a home and a lifestyle that were within her grasp, but outside her reach. As much as she wanted the fairy tale with Marshall, she was afraid of getting her hopes up. She wandered to the French doors leading to the balcony outside the dining area. As she pushed open the door and stepped into the night air, a chill enveloped her body, and she pulled the robe closer.

The sky above was filled with tiny sparkling diamonds. The dream she'd awoken from spoke to her insecurities. She'd loved Dan Moore as much as any girl loves her father. He tried to keep her at arm's length. He'd provided for her as any father would, but whenever she got too close, he'd almost imperceptibly pull away. When she was seventeen, he'd left them and never returned. Deandra believed she was somehow to blame. In spite of her mother's assurances to the contrary, she knew his leaving had something to do with her. She stared out across the expanse of property and wondered how long this dream of being with Marshall would last. When was she going to screw up so badly that it would drive him away too? Deandra knew, given her inescapable past, it was inevitable this dream would one day end. She just needed to hang on as long as she could.

The following Saturday, Viola called Marshall to advise she just wasn't feeling up to attending. She suffered from debilitating migraines on occasion and today she'd been unable to find any relief. Attending tonight's function was out of the question. She asked him to extend her apologies to the board. Although it was a last-minute invitation, Marshall decided to call Deandra and see if she still wanted to go.

Although she was enormously excited by the prospect of going to the fund-raiser as his date, she was clever enough to offer her sympathies for his mother's health before she graciously accepted his invitation. He said he would pick her up at seven that evening.

5

Deandra was excited by the prospect of attending the high-society dinner with Marshall. It was being held at the mansion of one of the local benefactors. Deandra had made a silent promise to take advantage of this opportunity and show Marshall how well she fit in with the upper crust. She was tastefully attired for the evening in a David Meister gold-and-blue abstract brocade dress. The dress was sleeveless with a boat neckline, ruched bodice, and slim skirt. A tiny gold clutch bag and matching high-heeled sandals rounded out her look of understated elegance.

Marshall arrived promptly at seven, as promised. When he saw her emerge from the building, he emitted a low whistle of appreciation under his breath. She was a stunning woman. He assisted her into his car and then got in on the driver's side.

"You look exquisitely beautiful tonight, Dee," he said as he put the car in gear and pulled away from the curb.

"Thank you for taking me with you. I've always been interested in the Children's Home Society and the work that they do with the children of our community."

"You don't have to be financially well-off to participate, Dee. There are many different ways that people of all economic levels can contribute time and energy. It's not always about money," he replied.

"I suppose that's true," she mused. She wanted the recognition of being a part of a socially recognized, affluent group. She really wasn't thinking about spending time with those children.

"It's about the kids. That's why it's important to me. I've even mulled over the idea of adopting one or two children at an appropriate time," he added with an easy smile.

Puzzled by the idea, she turned in her seat to look at him. "You would actually take on someone else's responsibility and raise their kids?" she questioned.

"Someone has to do it. We can't save all the kids that are trapped in the system. Sometimes the parents aren't fit, but it could be a case of where the parents are dead and there is no one else to step in. If we don't get these kids out of the system early, we may lose them."

She thought about her father, the man who raised her. She knew he wasn't her biological father, but he'd still done the best he could to be a father to her. Still, something was missing in their relationship and she'd often wondered if it would have been different, possibly better, with her real father. She was not likely to ever know.

"I don't think I could adopt. I don't think I would be able to bond with another woman's child. I'm not in any hurry to have children anyway. Are you?" she asked.

"No, I've still got a lot I want to accomplish before I slow down and have children," he replied as he turned into the driveway of Estelle Bancroft's stately home. The tickets for the dinner started at forty thousand dollars for benefactors. This usually included a total of ten tickets for dinner. He'd given away the other eight tickets to his employees and expected at least half of them would show up for the event.

Deandra was on her best behavior all evening. She was pleasant and conversational with the other attendees, but not overly chatting. The evening was nearly over when they bumped into an older couple, whom Marshall knew very well. Marshall greeted them warmly and then made introductions.

"Tina and Emmett, I would like you to meet a friend of mine. This is Deandra Morgan," he said as the group exchanged handshakes. He went on to explain, "Tina and Emmett are like family to me. They knew my parents before I was born."

"Where's Viola? She's never missed one of these dinners before," Tina asked.

"She's a bit under the weather. Unfortunately, she turned up with a migraine this morning, and you know those can knock her off her feet for a few days," Marshall replied.

"Yes, I remember well. I'll give her a call later in the week to check up on her," she replied as she gave Marshall a kiss on the cheek before she and Emmett made their departure for the evening.

After they left, Marshall turned to Deandra and asked, "Are you ready to go, sweetheart? I've seen everyone I need to see tonight."

"Yes, I'm ready," she replied, and slipped her arm through his.

It had been a wonderful evening. She was particularly pleased when he'd introduced her as his friend. Although he hadn't said "girlfriend," the designation of "friend" was better than none at all.

"Where would you like to go?" he asked as the valet brought his car to the front entrance.

"It's probably going to sound silly, but I'd like to go to the boat. We haven't been out on the water since our first date," she replied.

"Sure, we can do that. However, we won't be able to go anywhere, because I have a business appointment tomorrow."

"On a Sunday? That's okay. I just like being on the water, even if it's only for a little while."

"Then that's where we will go," he agreed.

A short time later they pulled into the marina parking lot. It was quiet and peaceful just as Deandra had hoped it would be. He assisted her onto the boat and she made her way to the pilot's chair. She leaned on the wheel and stared wistfully toward the open sea. The vastness of the sea represented escape. Freedom from her past, an escape from all the lies she'd told and deeds she'd done that she couldn't outrun. Deeds that would one day catch up with her if she didn't get away from here.

"Have you ever thought of taking off and never coming back?" she asked.

As he stood next to her, he could sense her desperation to get away. He pondered this before he answered.

"Sure, I have, many more times than I can remember. But I have responsibilities I can't escape," he said.

"Like your mother?" she asked, and tried not to let any bitterness creep into her voice.

"She's one of them, yes. I also have a responsibility to the business my father built. I must preserve his legacy for future generations. So, my dear, as desirable as it may seem to run away, we can never go far enough away or stay long enough to outlast our responsibilities or demons," he replied, and pulled her from the chair into his arms.

She relaxed into the comfort of his arms. Their bodies swayed gently with the rocking of the boat. He held her for a few moments, and then silently led her down to the main cabin and master suite.

Viola attended her monthly ladies' group meeting the following week. It did not take long for the conversation to get around to the CHS fund-raiser.

"We missed seeing you on Saturday, Vi," Tina said as she took a shortbread cookie from her plate and bit into it.

"I'm so sorry I missed it. You know I never do," Viola replied.

"I swear that son of yours gets more handsome every time I see him," added one of the guests at the other end of the table.

"Why, thank you, he does take after his father," Viola replied as she luxuriated in the compliment.

"Who was that young lady he was with?" asked another guest.

Viola, who raised her teacup to her mouth to take a sip, paused with the cup in midair. "I didn't realize he'd taken anyone," she said quietly.

"Yes, he did. She was a rather tall, fair-skinned young woman with sort of dirty blond hair. She was very pretty, though," the helpful guest added.

Viola's cup clanked unceremoniously back onto its saucer. She couldn't believe he would dare to parade that strumpet around her friends.

"I didn't mean to upset you, Viola. It was just that none of us had seen her before and—"

"Actually, I have seen her before, Viola. I must tell you, since it's been brought up. I was rather surprised to see her with Marshall a second time. I mean, after the first incident," another guest added, to Viola's distress.

"Incident?" Viola asked quietly. She was seething inside and was afraid to hear what the incident was all about.

"Well, Peter and I were out boating near Nassau a few weeks ago, maybe more, and we saw Marshall's boat. So Peter pulled up alongside to say hello and invite him to join us for breakfast," Mae described. "Now we all know there's no way a boat the size of our old one is quiet, so they had to hear us coming. Lo and behold, we're chatting with Marshall and this girl stands up in the middle of the back deck, naked as a jaybird.

She had the audacity to bend over and stretch her naked ass—excuse me, buttocks—in my husband's face and then wave at us before she sashayed down to the cabin." She paused as she noticed the expression on Viola's face.

Viola felt near to fainting. This mortification was beyond words. The walls in the room were suddenly closing in on her.

"I will say this, Vi. Marshall did look quite embarrassed by the whole thing. That's why I was so surprised to see that young lady again. I will say, she did look much better in her clothes—"

"Excuse me," Viola interjected, and rose abruptly from the table. She'd heard more than she wanted to hear this afternoon.

Tina excused herself and rushed after Viola. She caught her in the parking lot of the restaurant. She grabbed Viola's shaking hand as she tried to fit her key in the lock.

"I'll drive, Vi. You're too upset," Tina suggested.

"I'll kill him, Tina. I swear I will kill him for embarrassing me this way. His father must be rustling in his grave," she said, and reluctantly handed the keys to Tina. She walked around to the passenger side to get in. She slammed the door and sat fuming inside while Tina started the car.

"He's a grown man, Vi. You can't tell him what to do anymore," Tina said, and tried to appeal to her rationale.

"Don't try to reason with me, Tina. I'm not in the mood. He has a reputation to maintain. I knew that girl was a slut the moment I laid eyes on her in the art gallery. That boy, man, whatever, needs to stop thinking with his dick," Viola spat.

"Vi!" Tina exclaimed, shocked by the language her friend used. It was not like Viola to be so vulgar.

"I'm sorry," Viola said, and remained silent the rest of the way home.

Tina decided she would not want to be Marshall when his mother got hold of him later on today. Grown man or not, it was not going to be pleasant or quiet in the James household.

* * *

Once she got home, Viola decided she'd better calm down before she talked to Marshall. She poured a short glass of vodka and drank it in one quick gulp. Her agitation had her pacing around her living room for an hour before she finally picked up the phone to call her son. He answered on the first ring.

"Marshall, I need to speak with you. Can you come over this evening?" she asked through clenched teeth.

"I wish I could, Mom, but I have a business meeting tonight. I'm trying to solidify the Anse Cochon development deal. Is something wrong?"

Viola hesitated to get into it with him over the phone, but she didn't think she could stay quiet much longer. She decided to attack the problem head-on.

"Who did you take to the fund-raiser the other night?" she asked. Maybe her sources were wrong and there was another blond whore lurking around her son.

Marshall knew this conversation was inevitable. He'd wondered how long it would take for word to get back to her.

"I took Deandra. We had a very nice time, as a matter of fact," he replied with ease.

"Do you have any idea how embarrassed I was today to find out in front of all my friends?"

"Mom, why would you be embarrassed? Deandra looked perfectly beautiful on Saturday."

Viola was growing angrier by the minute. How dare he defend his decision to take that woman to an event of such social significance.

"She's trash and I don't know why you refuse to see it. Don't think I didn't hear about that other little striptease too. She was parading around naked on your boat in front of other people!"

That had happened so long ago, he'd almost forgotten about it. Leave it to those old hags at the ladies' club to bring that one up. He could understand why his mother was upset, but Deandra hadn't done anything seriously wrong for him to stop seeing her.

"I apologize, Mother. If anything I have done has upset you, it was certainly not my intent. However, I happen to like spending time with Deandra and don't intend to stop seeing her," he said with quiet firmness.

"Do you know anything about this woman, other than how good she is in bed?" she hissed.

"Mother, we will not continue this discussion in that vein. It is beneath you and me," Marshall cautioned.

"No, Marshall. The only thing beneath you is that gold-digging whore and it'll be over my dead body that she gets away with this!" she said angrily, and slammed the phone back into its cradle.

She was so furious, she was literally shaking as she poured another shot of vodka. She downed it and then hurled the glass toward the fireplace. It shattered on impact. She sat down dejectedly on the settee. The argument had taken a lot out of her. She'd never argued with her son before. Although suspect at times, his choice of women had never shamed their good family name. Somehow this woman was different, and Viola would bet good money Marshall hadn't even bothered to check into her background. Maybe a different tactic was needed to get rid of this one. She retrieved her address book from the desk drawer and began looking for a phone number she hadn't needed in a very long time.

6

Three weeks later Marshall took Deandra to the theater for the opening night of *Les Misérables*. It was a grand affair and he'd even taken her shopping for a new evening gown for the occasion. Everyone who was anybody in Palm Beach County seemed to have packed the theater. Whether that was to see the show or to be seen was the question. The opening night was an invitation-only affair. Men in tuxedos and women in ball gowns enjoyed silent competition for best dressed.

Deandra was in awe as they entered the lobby. Marshall looked extremely handsome in his tuxedo. He'd bought her the most beautiful gown she'd ever seen, a Carmen Marc Valvo designer garment. It was a stunning midnight blue tiered gown of satin and lace, with a strapless sweetheart neckline. The gown and accessories cost more than five thousand dollars. Marshall had paid for it without batting an eye. He wanted to be certain that when the tales filtered back to his mother this time, there would be no question regarding the suitability of his date's attire.

During intermission Deandra headed for the ladies' room. She had finished her toilet and was intent on fixing the bodice of her dress in the stall at the far end of the restroom when she heard several people enter. Her hand was on the latch and she was about to exit the stall when she heard them discussing her. She paused to listen.

"Did you see that girl with Marshall James? She's very attractive, but I've never seen her before," the first woman said.

"She is pretty, but she looks vaguely familiar to me. I wish I could remember where I know her from," the second woman chimed in.

"You know, now that you mention it, she does look a little like a girl we went to high school with. Man, what was her name?" the first woman said.

"What girl? Oh, wait a minute. I think I know who you're talking about," said the second woman excitedly.

Terrified these women might actually remember her, Deandra leaned against the tile wall and held her breath.

"Andie! Andrea Moore!" shouted the first woman.

"You're right. That is who she reminds me of, but that can't be her. Andrea Moore—my word, what a fucking whore she was. That girl screwed everything but a lightbulb," added woman number two.

"That can't be her, though. I mean, come on, seriously— with Marshall James? He wouldn't even step over filth like Andie on the street. This girl is someone else. Viola James would have a full dossier on any woman her son dates," said number one.

"People can change. You know what they say about turning a cow's ear into a satin sleeve, or something like that," said number three, who had been silent previously.

"No, Debbie, it's 'you can't turn a sow's ear into a silk purse.' Gosh, will you stop with the misquotes. You know you always did like Andie and I could never figure out why," said woman number one.

"Well, don't worry if that is our old trashy Andie, she'll get caught sucking off an usher for a free seat, just like in high school, and that will be the end of her and Marshall," added woman number one, and they all broke out in laughter.

Deandra sat down on the toilet seat as tears streamed silently down her face. It was like being thrust back into high school and the bad memories associated with those years. She remembered how nobody understood her, or wanted her around. The only friend she had back then was Debbie. It was the same Debbie who had participated in her silent humiliation tonight. They had been friends until the slumber party, and Debbie had stopped being her friend because of CJ.

The color had drained from her face and her hands were shaking. They didn't know for sure who she was, but the thought of Viola digging into her past frightened her. She wasn't Andie Moore anymore. She was Deandra Morgan now, and she wanted to forget all the things Andie had done to survive, and to take care of herself and her mother. Her body was her commodity and she used it to her advantage. She wasn't doing that anymore. She was Marshall James's girlfriend and they needed to respect her position.

She pushed out of the stall and dabbed at her face with a damp towel. After she reapplied her makeup, she felt ready to face the public again. With her head held high, she exited the restroom in search of Marshall. A waiter with a tray of champagne stopped to offer her a glass. She gratefully took one and downed it quickly to bolster her courage.

It took three sweeps through the crowd, and two more glasses of champagne, before she finally saw Marshall in conversation with another couple at the foot of the stairs leading to the opera boxes. She linked her arm through his and smiled brightly at the couple.

Marshall paused in his conversation to introduce her and then continued his earlier discussion. He took note of the unusual flush to Deandra's cheeks.

It didn't take long for Deandra to begin fidgeting as the bubbly she'd hastily consumed on an empty stomach saturated her blood. The conversation taking place was boring her and she wanted to go back to the show.

"When can we go back inside and sit down?" she asked Marshall, and rudely interrupted the gentleman who was speaking.

Marshall looked at her curiously before he replied, "In a minute, Dee. I'm sorry, Ed. What did you say?"

Deandra noticed a bar in the corner, where appetizers were being served. She moved away from Marshall, who was still deep in the middle of his business conversation, and headed toward the food station.

Halfway there, she began to feel a little unsteady on her feet. She slowed her steps to make sure she didn't fall. Her exaggerated gait did not go unnoticed. She reached the bar and gleefully plopped down on one of the bar stools. She giggled and gushed at the woman next to her.

"I wasn't sure I was going to make it." She laughed a little loudly as she hung on to the counter edge.

The woman smiled demurely in response and looked around the room to see if someone was on his way to take hold of this obviously inebriated young woman.

Deandra reached across the woman next to her and pulled a tray of crackers and cheese within her reach. She proceeded to pop one after the other in her mouth as though she hadn't eaten in months.

The woman next to her politely eased off her stool and melded into the crowd, lest anyone think she was associated with this uncouth individual.

A few moments later Marshall appeared at Deandra's side. He'd been watching her since she left his side and was appalled by her behavior. However, he'd been in the middle of securing an important contact and hadn't been able to follow her immediately.

"Deandra, what's the matter with you?" he asked as quietly as he could, trying not to draw more attention than she already had.

Her eyes sparkled and her cheeks were deeply flushed. When she spoke, her words were slightly slurred; it was evident that she was drunk.

"Nothing happened. Why? What's the matter with you?" she asked as he took her arm to pull her gently from her position on the stool. "Where are we going?"

"I think it's best that we leave, Dee. You obviously need to get some real food in your stomach to soak up some of the champagne. How many glasses did you have anyway?" he whispered.

Deandra did her best to stand tall and walk out of the theater with as much dignity as her current disposition would allow.

Marshall was embarrassed, as well as puzzled, by her behavior. She'd been fine up until intermission, when she'd gone to the restroom. He wondered what had transpired between then and when she rejoined him to cause her to get drunk.

Deandra fell asleep in the car on the way back to Marshall's house, and instead of them having dinner together, he ended up putting her to bed. Marshall changed out of his tuxedo and went to the kitchen in search of food.

Deandra's sleep was again disturbed by demons from her past.

It was late in the afternoon when the landlord knocked on the apartment door and demanded the rent. He said they were two months behind and he was tired of waiting. Andie tried to rouse her mother from her drunken stupor, but the older woman only swatted at her to go away.

The landlord watched with disgust the exchange between the younger woman and her mother. Things had gotten really bad once the husband left. The mother kept up with the rent for a short while, and then her drinking took over and she stopped working. He felt sorry for them at first, but it had been too much. He needed his money and they had to go.

"Tomorrow," he yelled from the hallway. "Have my money tomorrow or I lock you out!"

Andie sat down on the floor with her head in her hands and cried. They had no place to go. It was bad enough there was barely any food for them to eat. Tomorrow they would be out on the street.

"Andie," a young man called from the doorway.

She looked up to see her neighbor "Chuy" from across the hall peering inside. "What do you want?" she asked, annoyed. She brusquely wiped the tears from her cheeks.

"I heard old man Gardner say you had to leave. I don't want you to leave, Andie," he said, and stepped inside the apartment and closed the door behind him.

"We don't have a choice anymore. We don't have the money for the rent. It's not Gardner's fault. He could have put us out a long time ago," she said.

"But I have an idea of how we can get some money. If you are willing to try," he offered.

"I'll do anything, Chuy," she said, suddenly interested in his idea.

"Anything?" he asked.

"Yes, anything, damn it. What's your idea?"

Two hours later Andie was standing outside Chuy's uncle's house a few blocks away. She was frightened and nervous. Chuy waited on the corner. He pointed toward the house and gestured for her to go inside. She stayed rooted to her spot on the sidewalk.

Chuy watched her for a few minutes and then ran up to her. "What are you waiting for?" he asked urgently.

"I don't know him, Chuy," she replied nervously.

"Look, Andie, you need money. He will give you money. It

ain't like you're a virgin or something. Go ahead and hurry up before he changes his mind."

Chuy returned to his position at the corner and Andie walked up to the front door and knocked. A burly, dark-skinned Hispanic man opened the door. He eyed Andie up and down before he gestured for her to enter the house. He checked out her slim figure and round ass as she preceded him into the living room. He liked what he saw.

"I ain't got all day, get them clothes off," he instructed in a gruff tone.

Andie tried to look anywhere in the room, but at the gross, fat man that was about to put his hands on her body. She peeled off her top and jeans while he sat on the couch with his pants down around his ankles and watched her every movement. He ran his hand up and down his rigid penis in anticipation of ramming deep inside her tight, little pussy.

"Come over here, honey. How much money you want?" he asked. A lit cigarette dangled from the corner of his lip and his head was encased in a blue haze.

Andie walked up to the couch and stood in front of him. Except for her small breasts, she could have been mistaken for a boy. Her slim hips did not yet have the flare of woman-hood.

"How old are you?" he suddenly demanded, and continued to masturbate.

"I'm seventeen and I want five hundred dollars," she replied with more bravado than she felt.

"Well, you ain't gettin' that much outta me. I'll give you two hundred for letting me fuck you and another fifty if you suck my dick," he advised.

Andie looked down at his tiny, little penis. It couldn't have been more than four inches erect. She swallowed hard and got down on her knees in front of him. She took his tiny dick in her mouth and nearly gagged. It tasted salty and smelled musty. She steeled her nerves to continue. She sucked his dick for a few minutes while he moaned and groaned and tried to push her face into his hairy groin.

She finally pulled away and climbed into his lap and tried to insert his wet slippery dick into her pussy. He wasn't sustaining an erection long enough for her to sit on it.

Annoyed, he finally pushed her off and made her get on her hands and knees on the couch. He managed a weak rear entry and stroked for only a minute or two before he groaned so loud, she thought he was having a heart attack. After he came, he threw the two hundred fifty dollars on the table and walked out of the room.

Andie dressed quickly, grabbed the money, and ran from the house. Chuy was still waiting at the corner. Together they raced all the way back to Andie's apartment.

Seated at the table in the kitchen, Andie pulled out the money and laid it on the table. She was disgusted with what she'd done, but relieved to have some money to give the landlord.

"He only gave me two-fifty. It's not enough to pay the rent," she said sadly.

"I know. He's a cheap, dirty bastard. But while you were busy sucking his tiny, little dick, I was in his bedroom hitting his stash," he said, and pulled out a wad of bills.

Andie jumped out of her seat, grabbed Chuy, and hugged him with all her might. "You're the best, Chuy!" she exclaimed. After they counted all their money, they had enough to pay the rent and buy some groceries.

They were at the grocery store later that afternoon when they passed the condoms. Chuy looked at Andie curiously.

"Did he use a condom, Andie?" he asked.

"No," she said.

"Andie, you can't be stupid like that. Don't let nobody fuck you without a condom," he advised passionately. "You don't know what people got that they might give you. If they want to fuck you, they will put it on, believe me."

"Okay, Chuy. I promise." She smiled and gave her new best friend an impromptu kiss.

"You know, I love you, Andie. Right?" he confessed.

"Yes, Chuy, I love you too. You were my first love, remember," she teased, and grabbed a pack of a dozen condoms and put them in the shopping cart.

It was the beginning of a partnership that lasted a long time. Chuy would find a man willing to pay for sex and Andie would oblige. If there was extra money to be found, Chuy would steal it while Andie entertained their mark. When Andie wasn't fucking for money, she and Chuy practiced on each other. They spent a considerable amount of time poring over sex books. They mastered the best positions and perfected their own personal techniques. Their alliance helped Andie pay the rent and take care of her mother for two years. After Chuy graduated from high school and went off to college, Andie was left on her own to find money to support them.

Deandra rolled over in the bed. Her head was throbbing from the champagne. She vaguely remembered the evening, and her recollections weren't good. Those women had gotten to her and she'd had too much to drink. She put on her bathrobe and wandered downstairs in search of Marshall. She found him in his office reviewing a file of papers.

"Hi, Marsh," she said quietly.

He looked up at her and took in her tousled hair and smeared makeup. He laid his reading glasses down on the desk and closed the file.

"Do you want something to eat?" he asked, and walked past her toward the kitchen.

"Yes, if you don't mind," she replied, and turned to follow him.

"I can make you an omelet, but that's all we have in the house right now," he offered, and took a carton of eggs from the refrigerator.

Deandra settled on a bar stool at the counter. "That's fine," she agreed.

Marshall began the preparation for the omelet and waited to see if Deandra would bring up her behavior this evening. When she didn't, he felt compelled to ask about it.

"What happened tonight, Dee?" he asked as he whisked the eggs in a bowl.

"I'm sorry, Marshall. I had too much champagne on an empty stomach," she explained. She knew this conversation was unavoidable and she had no excuse for her behavior that she could share with him.

"You were fine before intermission. Did something happen that made you drink?" he prodded. He was afraid his mother may have been right about her, and her unwillingness to explain was not sitting well with him.

"I was so overwhelmed by the crowd and all those people— important people—I got nervous and I just took one drink to calm my nerves."

"One drink, Dee?"

"Well, no. It was more than one. I just don't remember the others so clearly. I'm sorry, Marshall. I swear it won't happen again," she implored him to understand.

He didn't, and he'd hoped she'd take this opportunity to open up to him. He could tell there were things that haunted her, but she didn't trust him enough to share them. It bothered him. It was one thing to have skeletons, but her secrets were now impacting him and his reputation. It was the one area in which he agreed with his mother. His reputation and standing in the community could not be jeopardized by his association with Deandra. Up until tonight he hadn't taken that advice seriously enough. He hated the fact that his mother could be right, and decided to give Deandra another chance.

He set the omelet on a plate before her and watched as she devoured it ravenously. Deandra smiled impishly at him between bites. She was beautiful, but flawed. He could see that now. He hoped he would not regret his decision to keep her around a little longer.

7

Victor seemed to be pulling out all the stops in his effort to woo Connie. He sent flowers for no special occasion. Little note cards would arrive in the mail unexpectedly. Connie was thrilled by the attention. It was refreshing to find a gentleman so attentive and concerned for her well–being. Ever since their first date Victor called her every evening to make sure she'd arrived home safely, and they would chat on the phone for hours.

She found Victor to be quite an accomplished lover and she did not lack for sexual gratification. He'd been spending more and more nights at her home. She'd been pleasantly surprised on more than one occasion by his sexual spontaneity and creativity. She tried not to dwell on the fact that Victor had begun to ask questions about her, her family, her job, and at one point he'd even asked about any investments she might have. When Connie hesitated in answering, he immediately backed away from the subject. He explained that he was a financial investment counselor, and let her know that if she ever needed any financial advice, he'd be happy to assist. Or if she was more comfortable, he could refer her to someone. He only had her best interest in mind.

The law firm she worked for was having a celebratory dinner this coming weekend and she planned to attend. Victor had expressed an eagerness to meet the people she worked with and they were looking forward to the event.

They arrived at the restaurant early and waited at the bar for the rest of the firm to arrive. Victor ordered drinks for them. He was attentive to her needs as usual.

Within twenty minutes most of the office staff had arrived and joined them at the bar. They were shown to a private room for dinner. Victor ended up seated between Connie and a young woman from the clerical staff. She was about twenty and was wearing all the bloom of youth in a slim, figure-hugging, short spandex dress.

Connie had always considered Victor a good conversationalist, but she was surprised to see him flourish under the attention of the women in her office.

He offered to get drinks for the young woman. He advised her on the menu choices and he was ultracharming to any other woman within listening distance. The more attention he seemed to get, the more he wanted. By evening's end Victor's effervescent charm had begun to sorely wear on Connie's nerves.

A few of her coworkers made comments to her about how lucky she was to have such a charismatic boyfriend. "A keeper," they called him. Connie noted that as charming and handsome as Victor was, he hadn't been as attentive to her needs once the other women were around.

The evening dragged on for Connie and she was more than ready to leave at the end of the dinner. She'd seen another side of Victor this evening and it wasn't one she cared for. His charm bordered on flirtatious, and in her opinion it was disrespectful. As they were getting ready to depart, she noticed the young woman slipping Victor a piece of paper. He slipped the paper so casually into his pants pocket, Connie almost wasn't certain she'd witnessed the exchange.

In the car on the ride home, Connie was noticeably quiet. Victor was still feeling the bloom of his evening. He reached over and patted her affectionately on the leg.

"Are you okay, honey?" he asked.

"Yes, I'm fine," she replied. Her disappointment with him was evident in her quiet tone.

"Talk to me, Connie. You seem a little distant. Didn't you have a good time?"

She turned her face and looked out the window. She didn't want to get into this with him and she didn't want to appear petty. It would be better if she could have some time to think about the evening with a clear head; she was too annoyed at the moment.

"No, I didn't have as good a time as I'd hoped," she replied.

"Was it something I did? It must have been, because I can tell you're upset with me. What did I do?"

"Did you even notice I was there, Victor? You hardly said two words to me all evening," she answered.

"Oh, babe. I'm sorry. I was just trying to make a good impression on your friends. That's all it was."

"It seemed like more than that, Victor. You were flirting with those women," she argued.

"No, honey. Now, really, do you think I would be so disrespectful as to do that right in front of your face?" he cajoled. He patted her leg again to get her attention. "You are my girl, Connie. I am not going home with anybody but you. Don't let that other stuff bother you. It's part of the business, baby. We have to network. That's all I was doing, networking."

She wasn't going to be swayed so easily, but she declined to argue the point any further. When he pulled up in front of her home, she opened the door without waiting for him to shut off the car.

Victor jumped out and cut her off before she could get to the front door. He blocked her path and looked at her seriously.

"Connie, I'm sorry. I didn't mean to upset you. I just thought I was being friendly. I promise I will never disrespect you again. Don't go away mad, baby. Let me make it up to you," he pleaded.

She wanted to stay mad at him, but he did look sincere in his apology. Maybe she was making a mountain out of a molehill.

"All right, are you coming in?" she asked, and continued up the walk to the front door.

Connie headed for her bedroom and began to undress for bed. She could hear Victor in the kitchen and assumed he was getting something to drink. When he entered the bedroom with two glasses of champagne and a large mixing bowl, she was surprised and curious.

"What do you have there, Victor?" she asked, and tried to peer inside the bowl.

He placed the bowl on top of the dresser and brought her a glass of champagne. He offered a toast and she sipped her champagne slowly while he undressed.

She admired his thin, wiry body. He had muscles in his arms and his pectorals were decent, but no one would call Victor stud material. That is, until they saw the impressive size of his dick. When aroused, it was quite sizeable in girth, as well as length.

Connie had learned to handle it quite well over the past few months. As he approached the bed, she reached out and captured it with her hand and tugged him gently toward her.

He pulled her up off the bed and guided her toward the bathroom. Once inside the bathroom, he turned on the shower and began to undress her. He pulled her tank top off and assisted her out of her shorts. Both naked, they entered the shower, where Victor stood behind her and applied shampoo to her hair as the spray of the shower rained over them. He lovingly and slowly washed her hair and then applied a conditioner.

Connie basked in the attention. She tried to ignore the prodding of his stiff dick against her butt cheeks every time he got close.

When Victor finished with her hair, he lathered a sponge with shower gel and gently washed her all over, from her breasts to the secret areas between her thighs and ass cheeks. Nothing was off-limits to the gentle, sensual exploration of his fingers.

She took her turn washing him next. She followed the same path he'd taken along her body as she lathered and massaged his butt, then turned his body toward her and lovingly washed the length of his long, steel-hard dick. She ran her soapy hands up and down his thickened rod. Her sweetness ached and throbbed, so she pressed the rod against her crotch and rubbed it against her clit. She cried aloud from the tingling sensation it created.

Victor turned off the spray and left the shower stall. He draped a towel around her as she exited the shower and wrapped another around his waist. Connie took a moment to lightly towel some of the water from her hair before she followed him back into the bedroom. The mysterious bowl was now at her bedside and she could see it was filled with whipped cream.

"Victor, the sheets?" she queried, and wondered if this was a good idea.

"The sheets are washable," he replied, and pulled off her towel. "If you would get in the bed, please."

She climbed on the bed and watched with fascination as Victor spooned dollops of whipped cream on each breast. She squirmed with delight as he methodically sucked the cream off each breast with his mouth, then licked each nipple clean. When he placed a large dollop on her navel, she waited patiently for him to remove it. She was eager for her turn.

Victor spooned several dollops of cream on her crotch, before dipping his dick in the bowl. When he removed it, it was completely and invitingly covered with melting whipped cream.

Connie eagerly straddled his face with her pussy and began lapping up every delectable inch of cream from his dick. She hungrily licked up and down his voraciously pulsing dick while he applied the same dedication to eating her cream-laden pussy. When his rod was clean, she took her exploration to his balls and swirled her tongue around the sensitive sac, holding the hairy, little jewels in her mouth and gently sucking them clean.

With a fever pitch of sexual excitement reached, he quickly donned a condom before he turned Connie on her back and eased his dick between her thighs into the dark depths of her feminine heat.

She bucked wildly and more aggressively than ever before as she subconsciously tried to remind him that sex with her was as good as with any other woman, and he didn't need to shop around. A half hour later both lay spent and sated in her bed. All evidence of their whipped-cream adventure had disappeared. Connie enjoyed making love to Victor, but she knew there were a lot of things she didn't know about him. Those doubts gave her an uneasy feeling as she drifted off to sleep.

8

The month of April celebrated the city of Riviera Beach's annual "Jazz on the Beach" music festival. It was a star-studded event that drew thousands from across the country to the relatively small town of Riviera Beach, Florida. "Riv Beach," as it was affectionately called, was a town rife with drugs and gang violence. Current razing of undesirable and condemned properties, along with reconstruction efforts, was under way in anticipation of bringing more upscale clientele into the area. A relative stone's throw away from exclusive Palm Beach, Riviera Beach and its close proximity to Singer Island was ideal for investors.

Marshall had been busy with a new development and hadn't spent much time with Deandra in recent weeks. He thought a trip to the festival might be a nice treat and help to get them back on track.

Similarly, Connie and Victor were experiencing a bit of tension in their relationship. Connie had always wanted to attend the event and this year the list of music talent would be unmatched: Michael McDonald was headlining that evening, along with Angie Stone, and a host of other talented performers. She looked forward to a great show.

The concert started at two in the afternoon and ran until midnight. Connie and Victor strolled through rows and rows of vendor booths. She loved browsing through the different display tents at the festival in hopes of finding eclectic works of art.

She noticed Victor had difficulty keeping his wandering eyes from roaming all over the place. He openly stared at nearly every woman who crossed his path. His blatant disrespect was wearing on her nerves. She was determined to have a good time in spite of him. When Victor wandered off to get a beer and a soda, Connie took the opportunity to chat with a local vendor who was selling unique purses handmade from colorful silk scarves.

Marshall and Deandra had just finished a funnel cake. Deandra excused herself to freshen up in the restroom. Marshall surveyed the crowd and sauntered over to a nearby booth to check out the wares. A young woman at the back table was sharing a laugh with the owner of the booth. Something about the customer seemed familiar, and when she turned to exit the booth, her eyes connected with his.

Connie smiled broadly when she recognized Marshall. In a few short strides he was close enough for her welcoming, friendly embrace. His surprise at seeing her was equal in measure to her enthusiastic hug.

"Connie, how are you? I haven't seen you in a while," he said, and took an admiring, long look at her. Her jeans were fashionably figure-hugging, and her V-necked blouse displayed a pleasing view of her breasts.

"I'm fine," she replied, and basked in his smile. He was still as handsome as she had remembered, if not more so.

"Are you here alone?" he asked, since he did not see anyone who appeared to be with her.

"No, actually, I do have a date," she replied, and looked around to see if Victor was in the vicinity. She could see him in the distance as he made his way through the crowd.

Victor saw the man approach Connie from his vantage point at the snack station. He watched the warmth of their exchange and even now it appeared Connie was bubbling over with excitement in the presence of the stranger. He collected their drinks and headed back across the beach.

Deandra also witnessed the reunion and her reaction wasn't quite as nonchalant. At first glance she wasn't sure that was CJ laughing and giggling with her man, but as she quickly moved closer to the pair, she recognized her old schoolmate. In her haste to get back to Marshall's side, she ran smack into Victor, who almost spilled his beer.

"Hey, slow down there. What's the rush?" he said as he tried to avoid spilling beer on his clothes.

Deandra paused for only a moment to look at him with annoyance. She had more important things to worry about as she rushed on her way. How in the world had CJ managed to find Marshall amongst thousands of people? They didn't see her coming as she walked up behind Marshall and confidently and possessively slipped her arm through his.

"Hey, sweetheart, I hope I didn't keep you waiting too long," she said as she clung tightly to his arm.

"Dee, I'd like you to meet a very dear friend of mine. This is Connie Jefferson," Marshall said as he introduced the two.

Connie extended her hand in greeting and Deandra reluctantly released her hold on Marshall to accept the handshake. Connie and Marshall both noticed Deandra's hesitation. Connie raised a curious eyebrow in Marshall's direction as she wondered what that was about.

Victor walked up to the group and handed Connie the soda he'd purchased for her. He assessed the group assembled there as Connie made introductions. When he made eye contact with

Deandra, she looked away evasively. As he shook hands with Marshall, he noticed the sparkle in Connie's eyes as she gazed up at Marshall. He wondered how long they'd known each other.

"So how did you two meet originally?" Victor asked.

"Connie's mother and mine are old friends, so I've known Connie since she was a young girl. We never saw a lot of each other as kids, but I knew who she was and vice versa," Marshall explained.

"Did you go to the same school?" Deandra asked. She was certain she would have remembered Marshall if he'd been in high school with them.

"No, I spent many of my formative years in boarding schools. As I got older, I attended a preparatory school, as opposed to a regular high school. Connie and I didn't meet again until we were adults and found ourselves traveling in the same circles."

"Oh," Deandra replied. She wanted to get him as far away from Connie as possible. She'd had enough of their reminiscing about old times. She tugged on Marshall's arm. "Honey, I think the band is starting to warm up. Can we go grab a spot?"

"Sure. It was nice meeting you, Victor. Connie, it was nice to see you again. Please give my regards to your mom," Marshall said as he and Deandra started off toward the bandstand.

"Yes, absolutely, and it was nice to see you again. Deandra, nice meeting you," Connie replied as Deandra cast a parting wave in her direction.

"She's kind of rude. Don't you think?" Victor said as he took a sip of his beer and watched the two walk away.

"Maybe she's just not a people person," Connie suggested. She hadn't particularly cared for her either, but didn't want to bad-mouth someone she really didn't know.

"I think she's rude. She darn near knocked me over getting back over here to interrupt your conversation with her boyfriend," he said, and smiled seductively at her. "I bet she was intimidated by your beauty and thought you were trying to steal her man."

"You're crazy, Victor. There's no way that woman was worried about me," Connie replied, and giggled happily at the compliment.

"You just don't know how beautiful you are, sweetie," Victor replied as he grabbed her hand affectionately. "Come on. Let's get good seats before all the decent spots are gone."

9

Marshall enlisted Deandra's help as hostess for a small dinner party he wanted to throw to celebrate the huge development deal he'd recently secured. She was thrilled by the prospect and looked forward with eager anticipation to the party.

The night of the party arrived and everything was going very well. Deandra had purchased a new dress for the evening. She'd selected something that she felt was elegant as well as sophisticated. Attired in a short-sleeved shimmering silk chemise, with a rounded neckline with ties, she'd added a detachable crystal rhinestone brooch and looked every bit the part of the graceful hostess. She'd complemented the dress with strappy evening sandals in silver metallic Spanish leather, with a rhinestone ornament at the arch.

The dinner party was a completely catered affair, and only required Deandra to greet the guests and make sure everything was flowing smoothly. The bulk of the responsibility fell to the event organizer Marshall always used. Deandra had enjoyed being consulted on the menu and theme choice for the evening.

Deandra was beginning to revel in her role, when Viola

showed up. Although she knew she'd been invited, she'd never actually met Viola face-to-face. She was a bit intimidated by the prospect.

Viola arrived, escorted by a very handsome older gentleman. This evening she wore a black taffeta shirtdress. Her winged-collar silk dress had a slightly gathered bodice falling into a full-waist skirt. A satin tie had been added to give the dress a romantic look. She was a stunningly beautiful older woman, with a figure to match. Viola commanded a room with ease the moment she entered it.

Marshall greeted his mother with a kiss on her cheek and then guided her across the room to meet Deandra. Deandra watched Viola's eyes as they approached and steeled herself not to wither under the caustic stare. Deandra was surprised when Viola extended her hand warmly in greeting.

"Deandra, it is a pleasure to finally meet you. I have been hearing so much about you," Viola said, and smiled brightly as she clasped Deandra's hand in hers lightly.

Caught off guard, Deandra gushed in response, "Why, thank you, Mrs. James. I have been looking forward to meeting you as well."

Viola's smile never faded, but her eyes narrowed suspiciously. "Have you, my dear?" she asked. She studied the attire of her son's lover—from Deandra's French-painted toenails to the garish silver sandals—and found it wanting. Viola was singularly unimpressed. "Nice frock, dear," she said, and turned her attention to Marshall.

Deandra did not miss the fact that she had just been assessed and dismissed. The "nice frock" comment hit its intended target. Deandra had spent a lot of time selecting this outfit and had nearly depleted her small stash with the five-hundred-dollar dress and two-hundred dollar shoes. She hadn't wanted to ask Marshall for the money, since he'd been so generous already. She wanted to exert a little financial independence, hopeful she would recoup it later on. Viola's comment was cordial enough, so her son wouldn't get upset, but noncommittal enough so Deandra would get her subtle message. Deandra recognized that her prospective mother-in-law had suddenly morphed into a Joan Crawford villain, and she was just as dark and calculating. Every warning she'd received about Viola James was apparently true. She would have to watch her step.

"Marshall, are Tina and Emmett here?" Viola asked as she glanced around the room through the assembled guests.

"No, unfortunately, they had a prior commitment," he responded.

"Well, if you don't mind, I'm going to chat with a few old friends," she said, and started across the room without a backward glance.

"She doesn't like me," Deandra stated flatly.

"She doesn't know you yet, Dee," Marshall countered, and then continued, "Can I get you something to drink?" He was hoping to distract her attention.

"Yes, as a matter of fact, you can." She smiled defiantly and looped her arm through his.

"That's my girl." He laughed and escorted her to the bar.

Viola spent a considerable portion of the evening watching the interplay between her son and his unsuitable new girlfriend. It would be over her dead body that this two-bit whore secured a permanent position in Marshall's life. Viola had always accepted that he could date and bed whomever he chose, but she'd heard stories of this Deandra person and behaviors that were totally outrageous. Marshall usually displayed much better judgment and he was more discreet. She almost wondered if his parading this trash around their friends was a result of her own outburst. It would not be above Marshall to champion this woman, simply because Viola did not like her. She decided she might have to intervene and stop this ridiculous charade.

Deandra was acutely aware of being under Viola's microscope all evening. She was weary from second-guessing everything she said and did. She'd never been so uncomfortable in her own skin. An escape to the bathroom in one of the guest bedrooms brought her face-to-face with her nemesis.

Deandra had bent over a footstool next to the bed to adjust the strap on her shoe when Viola emerged from the bathroom. Both were momentarily surprised to find someone else in the room and stopped what they were doing.

Deandra, on edge and weary from a long evening, made a serious misstep with a woman she should have been trying to impress. She allowed her emotions to get the best of her. In her agitated state she confronted Viola.

"Well, spit it out. I can see you've been itching to say something all night," Deandra said.

Viola looked a bit taken aback at first, but then a sly smile slowly started at the corners of her lips. The smile never reached her eyes as she replied, "I noticed you seemed to be getting a little comfortable acting as hostess this evening."

Deandra removed her foot from the stool and straightened up to her full height. She towered over Viola as she pushed her dress back down over her knee. Refusing to be intimidated, she looked Viola straight in the eye and replied, "And your point is?"

"Don't get used to the lifestyle, my dear. You may be good at"—she looked Deandra up and down so her intent would be clear before she continued—"what you do, but you're only a temporary distraction."

Angered by the implication that she wasn't fit to be Marshall's wife, she snidely countered, "Don't be so sure of that, grandma, Marshall loves me."

"Ha!" Viola scoffed, and ignored the age insult. "You, my dear, need to stop dreaming. You will never bear my grandchildren."

"Who said I want children?"

"And that, my dear, is exactly my point. You don't know my son as well as you may think you do," Viola stated, and then opened her purse and began rummaging around inside, looking for something. She found what she was looking for and continued, "When I was a young girl, my father gave me a dime to take along on my first date. His instructions were that I was to keep that dime between my knees at all times. I understood clearly what he expected of me." She paused and curled her lips into a wicked sneer before stating, "I imagine if your father had given you that symbolic dime on your very first date, you probably lost it on the way to the car. And when that dime dropped, that's when you lost the potential of ever becoming a member of my family." She tucked her purse under her arm and watched the simmering rage in Deandra's eyes. Undaunted, Viola smiled and held out her hand, palm up. Nestled in the palm of her hand was a shiny new dime. Slowly she turned her hand over and the dime fell to the floor with a tiny *clinking* sound and rolled away. She looked at Deandra and whispered vehemently, "Never!" then walked out of the room.

Deandra stood transfixed in her spot as anger and hurt suffused her body. Her breathing was labored as tears filled her eyes and rolled soundlessly down her cheeks. She was instantly transported back to her childhood, where she had never quite fit in with the affluent crowd. They either ignored her totally or whispered behind her back. She saw the same distaste in Viola's eyes as she had seen in Arlene Jefferson's so many years ago. She hadn't been this humiliated in a very, very long time. This was far worse than the eavesdropping incident in the restroom. She decided then and there, Viola would pay for this moment. She wasn't sure how, but she would pay.

Viola was already engaged in a conversation with a few guests by the time Deandra repaired the damage to her makeup caused by the tears she'd shed and returned to the living room. Viola caught Deandra's eye as she reentered the room, grimaced, and then turned her back on her.

Deandra looked for Marshall and saw him in the library across the hall. He smiled and nodded in her direction. She returned his smile weakly, but the pain in her soul was clouding the thoughts in her head. She wandered aimlessly amongst the guests. Through the haze her eyes fell upon the delicate purple flower. *It's so beautiful,* she thought as she made her way toward it. She touched the fragile crystal petals and began to feel better. The coolness of the smooth crystal soothed her nerves. *"It's my mother's favorite,"* she heard Marshall say in her mind. Suddenly her mood darkened and she looked around the room for Viola.

Meanwhile, across the room Viola watched her adversary's movements intently. She could tell Deandra was up to no good. When Deandra paused next to the Daum crystal vase, which had been a gift from her late husband, a cold chill passed through her body. She was too far away to prevent the travesty unfolding before her eyes.

Deandra looked cautiously around the room to see if anyone was watching her. When her eyes met Viola's across the room, a wry smile crossed Deandra's face and quickly disappeared. Within seconds she turned the heel of her shoe and pretended to lose her balance. In a wild effort to catch herself, she swept her hand along the tabletop and deliberately bumped the Daum vase, sending it crashing to the floor. She emitted a loud gasp as all eyes turned in her direction. Clasping her hands over her mouth in feigned horror, she looked up to see Marshall striding across the room in her direction.

"Oh, my God, honey! I'm so sorry!" she exclaimed.

As Marshall rushed to her side, he didn't have to survey the damage to know the vase was lost. "Are you all right? Are you hurt?" he asked.

"I'm fine, but I'm so sorry!" she exclaimed, and managed to look totally distressed as she stated, "I know how important that vase was to your mother. It was an accident, I swear."

Until she'd added that last part about his mother, he'd believed it was an accident. Now he wasn't so sure. He looked at her closely before he responded. "I never thought otherwise," he said. He glanced around the room to see if his mother had witnessed the accident.

Viola was still standing near the window and had not moved. Her face looked pale underneath her makeup as she met her son's inquisitive glance with a cold stare. She was heartbroken, but refused to show that Deandra's actions had affected her in any way. Stoically she turned her back on the room and returned to her previous conversation. She would deal with that bitch later.

As the attendants cleared away the mess, Deandra melded into the crowd. She'd gotten back at Viola, but her gut instinct told her this battle had just begun.

10

Viola scheduled a last-minute appointment at Tina's spa the following Thursday afternoon. She had an engagement that evening, and even though she'd just had her nails done a few days earlier, she wanted a fresh look for the event. As she drove her Jaguar XK convertible coupe up to the front entrance, an eager valet immediately rushed to the car to greet her and assist her to the curb. She smiled in response to the attention and thanked him politely as he opened the door to the establishment for her.

Viola entered the bustling salon and gave her name to the receptionist. Almost immediately a technician escorted her to a private booth for her manicure. Tina's business catered to high-profile clientele and the layout included private booths for all services. If a customer had wicked-looking toes, corns, or calluses on her feet, or even unsightly hair growth, the only one who had to know was her private technician. Tipping was not allowed and Tina's technicians were compensated well for their work. Therefore, a client never had to worry about one of them spreading unpleasant tales. The techs took an oath of confidentiality, and if they wanted to continue working for Tina, they kept their opinions to themselves.

Viola was almost done with her manicure when Tina stopped in to say hello. She wasn't alone; there was an attractive young woman who waited patiently behind for an introduction.

"Vi, do you remember this young lady," Tina said, and pulled the young woman into the booth. "This is Constance Jefferson. Connie, this is Viola James."

Connie stepped forward and extended her hand, then immediately retracted it as she realized Viola's nails were still wet. "It's a pleasure to meet you, Mrs. James."

Viola's quick glance took in Connie's mauve business suit, cream silk scoop-necked blouse, and classic high-heeled chocolate pumps. She accessorized with a simple pearl necklace and pearl drop earrings. "Well you do look familiar, my dear," Viola replied, and cast a questioning look at Tina. "Jefferson you said?"

Tina interjected quickly, "Connie, this is Marshall's mother."

"Oh," Connie replied, and smiled easily at Viola.

"You know my son?" Viola's curiosity was now piqued. Marshall had never mentioned this young woman. A young woman who, on first inspection, was clearly more suitable than that trollop he'd been dragging around town.

"Yes, ma'am. I've known Marsh for a few years now. He's a great guy," she gushed, and then hastily corrected her statement. "I mean he's always been a perfect gentleman."

Viola laughed delicately. This was a delightful young woman and she wanted to know much more about her. "Please sit down, Constance, and chat with me for a while. These minutes pass so slowly when I have to wait for my nails to dry. What do you do?"

"I'm an attorney. I'm doing some pro bono work down at the courthouse right now, but I take on paying clients now and again."

"Pro bono work, my child? That can hardly keep you in those Jones New York suits and Charles Jourdan shoes," Viola queried.

"She's Arlene Jefferson's daughter," Tina said as she walked back into the booth.

This news propelled Viola to the edge of her seat. Almost unable to contain her excitement, she exclaimed, "You're Arlene and Carlton's little girl! My goodness, I haven't seen you since you were in pigtails. You've grown into such a beautiful young woman. Your father was a brilliant surgeon. It was so sad when he passed. Where's your mother now?"

"My mother moved to the Keys a few years ago. She said it was time to get away from the hustle and bustle of Palm Beach County. She spends a lot of her time painting. It was something she always wanted to do, but never had the time."

Viola's eyes sparkled as she glanced at Tina. Now she understood why she'd introduced her to Connie. As mothers they were of like minds. Connie was a perfect match for Marshall. However, a woman as attractive and financially sound as this one surely had to be involved with someone. Viola wouldn't be so gauche as to ask her now, but she'd get that information out of Tina later on. She glanced at her watch and realized she'd better get going if she was to have sufficient time to prepare for the evening's festivities. She rose from her seat and extended her hand to Connie.

"It was wonderful to see you again, Constance. Please give my regards to your mother the next time you speak with her." She gave Connie's hand a gentle squeeze.

"I will, Mrs. James. It was nice chatting with you."

Viola exited the booth and Connie turned to Tina. "What was all that about? Why did you want me to meet Marshall's mother?"

Tina looked away evasively as she answered, "She was a good friend of your mother's a long time ago. I just thought it would be nice for her to see how you've grown up."

Connie laughed. She didn't believe Tina for a minute. However, she never doubted whatever Tina was up to—she had her best interests at heart. It was time for her to leave as well, so she stood and embraced her friend warmly.

"I have to run. I'm meeting Victor for dinner," she said, and tucked her purse under her arm. "I'll talk to you soon. I love you," she called as she exited the booth.

Tina stared after her and sighed. She hoped the introduction to Viola would be enough to get the ball rolling. She didn't like this Victor person Connie had been seeing and she knew Viola didn't like Deandra at all. Maybe it was time this situation got a little help moving along.

In an attempt to smooth things over with his mother and Deandra, Marshall invited his mother to the house for dinner. He asked Deandra to take charge of the preparations and he would cook the dinner.

Viola arrived promptly at five in the evening. Marshall greeted her at the door and ushered her into the living room. Deandra served appetizers she'd helped Marshall prepare, and the conversation with cocktails was light and nonthreatening.

In fact, Marshall thought his mother was being unusually nice to Deandra. It was out of character, given her previous vocal displeasure. He wondered only briefly what was up her formidable sleeve.

He wasn't alone in his suspicions of Viola's sudden cordiality toward Deandra. She hadn't gotten this far in life without knowing when to put her guard up. Deandra waited patiently for the other shoe to drop. She just wondered what it would be this time.

Marshall enjoyed cooking and prepared a London broil steak, along with seasoned red potatoes and asparagus tips. Deandra's contribution to the meal was fresh flowers, along with an elegant table setting.

Viola complimented her son on his cooking expertise as they finished the meal. She'd grown tired of being cordial to Deandra. She hadn't been able to stop thinking about Constance Jefferson and what a wonderful daughter-in-law she would be. First she had to find out what Marshall thought of Connie. Although she was certain she really didn't care. The fact that he'd kept this woman around as long as he had was proof he wasn't thinking clearly. It was time for her to start taking some steps to end the relationship. She hated this woman, and Deandra's proprietary attitude was grating on her nerves.

"May I have a cup of coffee? I need to be awake for the drive home after such a delicious meal," Viola asked, and looked directly at Deandra.

Eager to do something to please her nemesis, Deandra quickly offered to make the coffee. "Would you like caffeinated or decaf?" she asked politely as she rose from her seat.

Viola bit back the nasty retort that immediately sprung to her mind, and replied sweetly, "Caffeinated, please."

Deandra retreated to the kitchen, and Viola leaned back in her chair and closed her eyes briefly. Marshall cleaned up the remaining dishes on the table and took them to the kitchen. Viola could hear the muted conversation, and when Deandra laughed delightedly, it annoyed her immensely. She didn't understand why he kept seeing this trollop, except for the obvious reasons. It was time for him to start thinking seriously about settling down with an appropriate partner. When Marshall returned to the dining room, she smiled sweetly at him. She leaned forward in her seat and folded her arms in front of her.

"Darling, I met the most delightful young woman at Tina's salon. She seemed to know you, but I hadn't seen her in years," she relayed.

"And who might that be?" he asked as he leaned back in his chair.

"Her name is Constance. Do you know her?" she asked demurely.

"Constance? Oh, Connie. Yes, I know her. She's a real

sweetheart," he replied, and laughed easily as an image of Connie floated across his mind.

Deandra returned from the kitchen and placed a tray on the table with three cups of freshly brewed coffee. She placed a cup in front of Viola and then put the crystal creamer and sugar dish within her reach.

"Thank you, dear," Viola said, and then smiled sweetly at Deandra before continuing her conversation with Marsh. "So, have you ever dated Constance or thought about asking her out?"

Deandra stumbled as she started to sit down and almost missed the seat of the chair. She was appalled by Viola's rude behavior. She glared directly at Marsh, waiting for his response.

"Mom, that's not only inappropriate, but you're being rather insensitive to Deandra," he replied.

Viola waved a manicured hand in the air, theatrically tossing off any hint of impropriety. "Oh, pish-posh," she declared. "I was merely asking a question. I understand she's an attorney and she does pro bono work down at the courthouse. I knew her parents many years ago, wonderful people. They would be so proud of her. She's grown up into a delightful young woman. Her mother and I—"

"Mom!" he interrupted. He could tell she was winding up for a nasty, little scene and hoped to cut her off.

Viola was not to be deterred. Out of the corner of her eye, she could see Deandra's clenched fists on the table and a red flush of anger appearing in her cheeks. Viola was never one to step away from her opponent until she struck the deathblow. "Well, I don't know why you're getting so huffy. You said yourself she was a sweetheart," she continued, and paused to take a sip from her coffee cup. She glanced at Deandra surreptitiously and noticed her thin lips were pulled tight against her teeth. Viola smiled impishly.

Deandra had just about all she could take of Viola's disregard for her role as Marshall's girlfriend, and the old bag was treading very heavily on her last available nerve. She was stuck between her insane desire to knock her out of the chair onto her pompous ass, and her fear of upsetting Marshall.

Viola wasn't quite done yet. "It's a wonder no one has snatched her up yet. Have you noticed she's got those good, strong childbearing hips?"

Deandra stood up and threw her napkin down on the table. It was that damn CJ again. Viola was going to hand Marshall over to CJ on a silver platter—whether she wanted him or not. Not this time, Deandra decided. She wasn't going to roll over and play dead so Viola could slip Connie into her place. She had to fight back. She glared down at her. "Look, you old bitch. I've taken more than enough of your disrespect," she spat.

In an attempt to avoid the catfight that was about to take place, Marshall tried to calm Deandra down. "Deandra," he called to gain her attention.

She ignored him and cocked her fist menacingly. Viola stared back at her, daring her to make a move. She'd take the blow willingly if it would get rid of this interloping piece of trash.

"Deandra!" Marshall said with more firmness.

Deandra realized she'd let Viola get the best of her and had almost slapped her. That would have been the death knell in her relationship with Marshall, and exactly what Viola wanted. She abruptly turned on her heel and stormed out of the room.

Exasperated, Marshall turned his attention back to his mother, who was calmly sipping her coffee as though nothing had happened. "Was that really necessary, Mom?"

"I've made no secret of my feelings for that woman. I wish I could understand why you are wasting precious time with a woman you have no intention of marrying. She's not wife material. Did you notice the temper on her? Is that the woman you want raising your children?" she asked.

"Mother, children with Dee isn't even an issue right now," he replied.

"Right now? It shouldn't be an issue ever with that one. You're not getting any younger, Marshall, and you need to start thinking about settling down. I'd like some grandchildren before I die," she stated emphatically, and got up from her seat and headed toward the foyer. She collected her purse from the hall table and turned back toward the dining room. "And, son, I don't want any grandchildren with flaxen hair and blue eyes. I want some pretty little mocha ones," she added, and exited through the front door.

Marshall sighed deeply and passed his hands across his face. *"Arghh,"* he growled as he rose from the table and went in search of Deandra. He found her standing on the deck in the back of the house staring out toward the lake. He moved up close behind her and encircled her rigid body with his arms. "Hey, sweetheart, I'm sorry about that scene with Mom," he said.

She turned and pushed him violently away. "Don't you dare 'sweetheart' me! Apparently, I'm not the only sweetheart you have," she shouted, and pointed her finger at him.

"You're letting her get to you. You know she wants to get under your skin," he cautioned.

"And you let her! What kind of man doesn't protect the woman he loves from such a malicious attack?" she demanded.

"Honey, she didn't attack you. She was goading you, and you fell for it."

"Call it what you will. You always take her side."

"She's my mother!" he replied.

"She's an evil old bitch," she countered viciously.

"Okay. I need you to tone that down a notch. Yes, I agree she has not always been nice to you, and I'm sorry about that. But she's still my mother and you will respect her."

Deandra seethed inwardly. She would get back at Viola in

her own way, but right now a bigger issue had come to light. "Where is this relationship going?"

Marshall shook his head. He was not in the mood to deal with this discussion. "What?"

"Apparently, your mother doesn't think I'm good enough to marry you. I want to know your position on this. Are you going to marry me?" she asked.

"Deandra, we're getting a little off track here. I understand you're upset, but that doesn't call for a reassessment of our whole relationship," he replied.

"Are you going to marry me?" she repeated.

"I'm not planning to marry anyone right now. We're having fun. I enjoy your company and I think you enjoy mine. I'm not ready to think beyond that right now," he answered.

"Is that your diplomatic way of saying no?" she demanded. She was furious—she was good enough to sleep with, and to show off whenever he felt like it. But she was beginning to realize he had no intention of putting a ring on her finger.

"I didn't say that," he said, exasperated. He hated arguing and he had his mother to thank for this confrontation.

"Somehow that's what I heard," she replied with quiet anger. She brushed past him and snatched her purse from the hall table. The front door slammed and a short time later he heard her tires squeal as she peeled out of the driveway and raced off down the street.

11

Tina and Emmett's annual midsummer soiree was in full swing by the time Marshall entered the foyer of their estate home behind Deandra. He surveyed the crowd from the living-room entrance. He wasn't feeling very sociable tonight. Lately parties were not his favorite pastime. Even though he was well aware of the not-to-be-missed networking opportunities these parties presented, it was really his desire not to disappoint his friends that brought him there.

He'd had a small tiff with Deandra on the way to the party, which only served to further dampen his mood. After the last blowup with his mother, she'd become more demanding—and it wasn't sitting well with him. Deandra was accustomed to using her looks to get what she wanted, and unfortunately, the general male population was more than eager to fulfill her outlandish requests. He, too, had initially been very generous with her, and only now was being faced with the results. She'd adopted an annoying air of entitlement, and he'd grown weary of it.

He took note of the usual partygoers and hangers-on. Melding with the muted jazz tones filtering through the room, the hum of many different conversations indicated a successful party was in progress. He did the usual meet-and-greet routine as he worked his way farther into the room. Suddenly his eyes fell upon the woman he had been subconsciously seeking. Almost simultaneously he felt a nearly imperceptible lightening of his mood. A slight upward turn at the corner of his mouth was the only indication of the change. The slight touch of a hand on his arm brought him sharply back to the moment as he warmly greeted an approaching couple and introduced them to Deandra.

Connie desperately wanted to go home, but Victor was deep in conversation with a small group near the fireplace. Victor loved to hear himself talk, and parties always gave him a prime opportunity for that. She stared at Victor across the room. He was still an attractive man, she surmised. Unfortunately, he knew how attractive women found him and used that to his advantage. He turned out to be an outrageous flirt. If there were women around, Victor was sure to be holding someone else's attention. Connie had grown weary of Victor and the games he constantly tried to play with her mind. He assured her she was the only woman for him, and no matter whom he talked to, he was always going home with her. So there was no need for her to worry. Initially Connie had been annoyed by his behavior, jealous even. She found as time went by, she became less worried about what he was doing or even who he was doing it with. She was just tired of Victor, period.

This evening she was dressed seductively in a black silk jersey dress, which hugged her waist and flared slightly at the hips. The dress swung casually above her knees and exposed shapely legs accented by a pair of sling-back black high heels. Alighting from her stool at the bar, she wandered toward the buffet.

"Good evening, Connie," a warm male voice spoke quietly

behind her as she leaned across the buffet table to reach for an hors d'oeuvre. "You look stunning tonight," he finished as he admired the deeply cut V in the back of her dress, which exposed a fair amount of enticing brown skin. Her unintentional posture gave him an alluring view of her shapely rump.

Straightening up quickly without retrieving her appetizer, she turned to greet him. Marshall was standing directly behind her and his secret smile left no misunderstanding as to where his attention was focused. She felt a warm flush creep into her cheeks. Why did the room always seem to get warmer whenever he was nearby?

He was wearing a black silk crewneck, with a tan linen sport coat and matching slacks. The breadth of his well-formed shoulders and muscular arms were muted, but not indiscernible under the loose-fitting linen jacket.

"Hi, Marsh," Connie said, and smiled back at him. "I'm just a little tired and ready to go home. But, as usual, Victor is not," she finished, and looked down at the still-empty plate in her hands.

"Yeah, I saw him. They were getting into a sports battle over who has the best team this year. Sometimes I can flow with that and other times, like now when my team has had a terrible year with no chance for making it into the playoffs, I just don't feel like dealing with it. Here, try the coconut shrimp. I think Tina made them herself," he said, putting one on the small dessert plate she was holding.

"Thanks," she replied, watching as Marshall spooned a little marmalade sauce on her plate for the shrimp. "Where's Deandra?" Connie asked.

"She's out in the back sitting near the pool with Tina and a few others," he replied. Originally from the Caribbean, Tina and Emmett loved to entertain, and did it quite often. Emmett was an investment banker and Tina ran her own very successful spa/salon. Although they were both in their early fifties, they attracted a wide spectrum of friends. Parties were second nature to the couple and everyone looked forward to the next gathering. The food was always guaranteed to be delicious and the conversation stimulating.

Connie glanced out to the deck area in the back and saw Deandra stretched out on one of the chaise lounges, holding a martini in one hand and a cigarette in the other. "I thought Deandra quit smoking?" she queried.

"From your lips to God's ears. I tried to get her to quit several times, but she can't stick it out more than a day or two. She's tried the patch and the nicotine gum, but she keeps giving in to the cravings," Marshall replied.

Shaking her head, Connie walked over to the trash to deposit her empty paper plate. "Well, I guess she'll stop when she's ready," she said.

"Can I get you another drink, a glass of wine maybe?" Marshall asked.

"No, that's okay," Connie replied, wiping her hands on a small napkin.

"Are you sure? I'm headed to the bar anyway." Connie shook her head in response. "How about a soda or a bottle of water?" he pressed. She looked at him and laughed—it was the first time she'd laughed all evening.

"At loose ends, Marsh?" she asked, and tossed the napkin into the trash bin.

"I guess so. I'm ready to hit the road, but it looks like I'm stuck in the same situation as you. Deandra isn't ready to leave yet," he replied, although he hadn't even bothered to speak with her in the last hour.

"Okay, I'll take a Sprite. But I'll go with you," she said, and turned toward the bar. Marshall placed his hand on the small of her back as he guided her through the crowd to the bar. The warmth of his hand on the bare skin of her back gave her an oddly comfortable feeling.

* * *

Deandra watched the interchange between Marshall and Connie from her seat on the patio. Her eyes narrowed as she watched him casually place his hand on the small of Connie's back as they moved away. What the hell was going on? she wondered. Marshall was going to have some questions to answer when they got home. Tossing back her drink, she lit another cigarette and resumed her conversation with Tina.

Victor finally agreed to leave the party around two in the morning. All the other guests had departed, and Emmett was too polite to put them out. Connie had long since dozed off in a chair in the corner of the living room, and Tina had gone to bed. Victor shook her shoulder lightly to wake her up. Sleepily she kissed Emmett good night and followed Victor out to the car. He was quiet on the ride home. When they arrived at her home, he assisted her from the car. Once inside, she immediately proceeded to her bathroom. She washed her makeup off and changed into a nightshirt. Connie had just fallen asleep again when Victor climbed into bed. She awakened to the feel of his hard cock pushing against her flesh. Aware of what was happening, but not really wishing to participate, she pretended to sleep. Victor was undeterred. Spooning up behind her, he raised her nightshirt and attempted to enter her. Unsuccessful, he roughly rolled her over onto her back and pushed her legs open with his knee. Opening her eyes slightly, she could see his rigid, sheathed organ as he mounted her. Still sleepy, she watched the events as though they were happening to someone else. But her body was dry and unyielding. As he forced himself inside her, she was brought back to reality when she let out a sharp pain-related breath. Deep inside her, Victor began biting on her neck and shoulders. He pumped and ground himself into her body, working his way to a frenzied climax without regard for her comfort, or pleasure. Connie lay prone underneath the weight of his body, staring at the ceiling above her in the darkness. He lay on top of her a few moments longer, then got up to flush away the condom. Connie turned on her side, facing away from him, as he climbed back in the bed and promptly went to sleep. Her body ached from his assault. Sex with Victor had become a chore, and an unpleasant chore at that. Her body no longer responded to his touch and he, in turn, no longer even attempted foreplay. He got his, and nothing else seemed to matter. She gingerly touched her private areas and found them tender and sore. Pulling her nightshirt back down over her hips, she tried to go to sleep.

Marshall was sitting on the screened balcony of his bedroom reading the Sunday papers, when Deandra appeared in the doorway. He felt her presence, but said nothing and continued to focus on his newspaper.

He was still annoyed at her for her unbridled attack on him last night. They had barely gotten into the car at Emmett's when she lashed into him about spending too much time talking to Connie at the party. He didn't think he had spent more than ten minutes with Connie and felt blindsided by her venomous attack. He explained that it was a party, and since she was otherwise occupied, he had mingled with several of the guests, not just Connie. She, of course, never acknowledged seeing him with anyone else. She continued her tirade for a good twenty minutes, until she realized he was taking her to her apartment and not his home. "Why did you bring me here?" she asked accusingly.

"As pissed off as you appear to be, I didn't think you wanted to spend the rest of the night with me," he replied quietly.

"What are you trying to say?" she asked angrily.

"Look, I'm tired and you're tired. Let's just call it a night," he said.

She sat there, sulking for a few moments, and then said, "I'm sorry, I don't want to go home alone. I want to be with you tonight."

He looked at her in the glow of the moonlight. Her long hair was flowing across her shoulders and her rounded bosom was rising and falling with every breath as it crested above the deep V-necked sweater she wore. He could feel himself becoming excited at the prospect of making love to her tonight. Sometimes she annoyed the hell out of him, but she was still a very beautiful woman, and she was *his* woman. "All right," he said, and made the first available U-turn and took her home with him.

Due to the lateness of the hour, they had retired immediately to the bedroom. It only took Marshall a few moments to realize the makeup sex he had been anticipating was not going to happen. Once in bed Deandra turned her back on him and shrugged off his advances. She muttered something under her breath, but the only thing he could discern was the name Connie. Thoroughly pissed at this turn of events, he turned on his side away from her. It crossed his mind to make her get dressed and then send her home in a cab, but he knew that would have created more aggravation, and he'd had more than enough already.

He had awakened in the morning and gotten up without waking her. After he had made a pot of coffee and collected the newspaper, he had gone out to the balcony for some fresh air. That had been over an hour earlier. Now she stood in the doorway, sleepily rubbing her eyes as though nothing had happened.

"Good morning, Marshall." She yawned.

"Humph," he grunted in reply.

"I'm sorry about last night. I must have had too much to drink. I didn't mean to fall asleep so quickly."

"No big deal," he replied. He wasn't buying her act of contrition. She hadn't fallen asleep, and he knew it. It was her way of punishing him. If she didn't want to have sex with him, she could have gone to her own home. But in her twisted mind, it made more of an impact to go to his home and then brush him off. She wanted to make her point and she had. He suspected she was only acting contrite now, because there was something else she wanted.

"Let me know when you're ready and I'll drop you off. I have to go to see Viola today," he said.

"I was hoping we could have breakfast together and maybe go over to the Downtown at the Gardens," she said sweetly.

"I'm sorry. Not today. Mom has some work she needs done around the house and I've been putting off getting over there too long," he said flatly.

She didn't want to push him too far, and realizing from his tone she may have overplayed her hand, Deandra, pouting, turned from the doorway and went back into the bedroom. A few minutes later, Marshall heard the shower running. He hadn't planned on visiting his mother today, but he knew the two of them did not get along, and Deandra would not want to deal with her today. He went back to reading his paper while he waited.

12

Connie and Tina met for lunch later in the week. It was their regular once-a-month luncheon that was scheduled for the third Thursday of every month. It gave them an opportunity to relax and spend time together. Tina was like a second mother to Connie and it was important to both of them to maintain the relationship. Connie arrived first at the restaurant and secured a booth while she waited for Tina to arrive.

Tina came bustling into the restaurant a few minutes later, laden down with shopping bags. She easily spotted Connie in the corner booth and made her way toward her, carefully trying not to assault other customers on her way through the tight aisle with her bundles. After she reached the booth, she shoved her bags along the seat to the wall, leaving barely enough room to sit down.

"Well," Connie commented, and smiled, "it looks like you've been busy this morning."

"Emmett and I are heading up to the cabin in a few weeks and there are some items I needed to replenish. It was a slow morning at the shop, so I decided it was as good a time as any to get my shopping done. Besides, there are great sales going on this week," Tina replied, and picked up her menu from the table.

"I think I'm going to have the grilled mahi mahi with the fruit salsa and veggies this time," Connie said, and closed her menu.

"Me too," Tina agreed, and put the menu aside and reached into the closest shopping bag and pulled out a small jewelry box. "These are for you," she said.

"Tina, you shouldn't have. What's the occasion?" Connie asked as she accepted the small black box from her friend.

"I saw them and I thought of you. That's it. I hope you like them," Tina replied as she eagerly waited to see Connie's reaction.

She opened the small velvet box and saw a pair of gold pierced earrings, shaped like the crescent moon with a little star on the inside of the top edge. Embedded in each star was a small diamond. Connie caught her breath at the sight of the generous gift.

"Tina, you shouldn't have," she said as she stared at the earrings in her hand.

"I'm glad you like them," Tina replied, and signaled the waitress to come and take their orders.

Connie slipped the small box inside her purse and slipped out of the booth. She walked to the other side and enveloped Tina in a warm hug and kissed her cheek.

"Thank you," she whispered. "You've made my day."

The waitress arrived and they placed their lunch orders. After the waitress brought their soft drinks to the table, Tina broached a subject, which had been on her mind since the night of the party.

"I've been a bit worried about you lately," Tina said.

"Me? Why? I'm fine," Connie replied.

"Well, pardon my saying so, but you don't look fine. You

look unhappy. You never could hide your feelings very well. What's going on with you and Victor?" Tina asked.

"Not much. Really," Connie answered evasively, not wanting to burden Tina with her woes.

"Connie, you and Victor hardly said two words to each other at the party last weekend. Did you think I wouldn't notice?"

"You don't miss much," Connie said, and smiled at her friend. She took a sip from her glass and twisted it around in her hands. She took a deep breath and said, "I don't think Victor and I will be together much longer."

Unfazed by the admission, Tina asked, "And how long have you been feeling this way?"

"You don't even seem surprised," Connie replied.

"I'm not. I never thought Victor was right for you anyway. But you seemed quite happy for a while there. So I stayed out of it. What happened?" Tina asked, leaning back against the back cushion of the booth.

"We've been together for a long time now and at first it was exciting. Victor couldn't do enough for me. He called all the time, bought me presents. He was very considerate. We had a good time together. Well, honestly, we had a good time when we were alone. Whenever we are in a crowd or a group, he's an outrageous flirt. That really bugs the heck out of me," Connie replied, and sighed deeply.

"Have you confronted him about his flirting?" Tina asked. She wondered why Connie would put up with that kind of behavior.

"Yes, he says it's harmless fun and I shouldn't worry so much. He told me he isn't going to leave me." She laughed. "Funny thing is, sometimes I wish he would. As time went by, he began to leave more and more things at my house and stayed over often. Things were okay for a few weeks. He paid for groceries and offered money for utilities. Then about a month ago, he suddenly didn't want to leave the house. He claimed he didn't have any money and seemed angry all the time. He said business was slow and people didn't have money to invest. Finding clients was getting difficult. I don't need his money, but I'm not going to have him living off me either. He's there almost every night now. I've tried to be supportive. You know, sticking it out through good and bad times, all that BS. He isn't the man I thought I knew. It's been very tense lately," Connie said as she finished her tale of woe.

"Well, it sounds to me like you've done more than your share to make it work," Tina said. "When are you going to tell him it's over?"

"I don't know," Connie said, and shrugged her shoulders.

"Do you want to stay with Victor?" Tina asked, hoping the answer would be no.

"I just don't want to feel like I dumped him while he was going through a bad spell," Connie replied.

"Do you still love him?" Tina asked, silently praying for a negative response. She really didn't like Victor.

"The sad part is that I'm not sure I ever really did. Victor came along while I was going through a very rough and very lonely period. He took my mind off other things and he was so attentive, I just got caught up in the idea of being with someone." Connie sighed, looking down at the lemon sliver swimming in the ice tea in her glass.

"Okay, let's do this. I already told you, Emmett and I are going to the cabin for a week. Why don't you and Victor come along with us? It will give you a chance to get away from everything. It's very romantic and you can relax. See if you two can reconnect," Tina suggested.

"Are you sure you want to be bothered with us while you're on vacation?" Connie asked.

"You won't bother us at all. It may give you the time you need to make up your mind. At least I hope it will. Victor can hang out with Emmett for a bit. Does he fish? Well, even if he doesn't, the change of scenery may do both of you some good," Tina said seriously.

"I'll talk to Victor tonight. When are you two leaving?"

"Week after next, so get back to me. I want to make sure I pick up enough food. And, Connie, don't say no," Tina implored.

"Okay, I'll try not to. I've always loved it out by the lake," Connie said as their lunch arrived and they began to focus on the delicious meal.

Convincing Victor to go hadn't been easy. He complained he really didn't like Emmett, and he thought Tina was a phony. Connie bit her tongue as she listened to him degrade her friends. She said fine, he could stay home if he wanted, but she was going up to the lake. Victor did not like the idea of her going off without him and reluctantly agreed to go with her. Connie had already cleared her schedule, determined that she was going one way or another.

A week and a half later, Tina and Emmett were at the local wholesale food warehouse stocking up on supplies for their trip. Tina wandered off to get some fresh vegetables and Emmett made his way to the meat section. Tina came back carrying a container of red, green, and yellow peppers and noticed in the meantime Emmett really loaded up on meat.

"Hey there, how much meat do we need for four people?" she asked, counting at least four packs of steak, a large salmon, catfish, and several pounds of chicken.

"Four? Honey, I thought you said Connie and Victor were coming?" Emmett replied.

"Yes, you, me, Connie, and Vic. That's four," she replied.

"What about Marsh and Deandra?" he asked.

"Marsh and Deandra?" she repeated incredulously.

"I told you. I invited Marsh when we first talked about going last month. Remember?" he asked. "We're going fishing."

"Oh, that's right. But that was just Marsh. How did Deandra get invited?" Tina replied.

"Tina," Emmett said slowly. He knew she did not like Deandra. "It wouldn't be fair to Marsh to be the fifth wheel, so I told him about Connie and Victor and suggested he bring Deandra."

"You're right, Emmett. It wouldn't have been fair. I'm glad they're coming," she said, and turned away. She didn't want to spoil the upcoming weekend for her husband. She knew how much he enjoyed fishing with Marsh, but she could do without having to entertain Deandra. At least Connie would be there to keep her company.

Victor insisted on driving his own car and Deandra didn't like to feel crowded, so they ended up in a caravan of three cars headed to the Ocala National Forest. After parking near the marina, Marsh and Victor helped Emmett load the boat for the ride out to the Isle of St. John, where the cabin was located. Emmett expertly docked the boat at the pier, and Marsh tied the boat's anchoring rope to the mooring posts. This was the first visit for Victor and Deandra, and Victor climbed out of the boat onto the pier and appreciatively looked up from the pier at the cabin, which was surrounded by trees and shrubs. It lay nestled about four hundred feet back from the water's edge and was framed by the dense woods behind it. It was a huge log cabin with a long expansive front porch. On one side of the porch was a swing that hung from the roof beams above. A double post railing framed both sides of the front porch. Victor noticed there were solar panels on the roof, the only exterior concession to the twentieth century on this rustic-looking cabin.

"Vic," Marsh called to him from the boat to get his attention. Deandra was standing there with her hand extended, waiting for Victor to assist her out of the boat. Vic turned to her and smiled as he offered her his hand and pulled her out of the boat. He then extended his hand to Tina and Connie, in turn. Tina led the way up to the cabin, while Deandra and Victor followed close behind. Both were eager to get a glimpse of the cabin they committed to spending a week in. Connie stayed behind at the pier to assist Marsh and Emmett with the coolers of rations for the week. She was embarrassed that Victor had not offered to assist. Marsh refused to let her carry any of the heavier items and gave her the lighter bags to carry. "Don't worry. It's going to take us several trips to get everything anyway. I'm sure Vic will come back and help," he said to her as if reading her mind. She blushed, admonishing herself silently for being so transparent, and started up to the cabin with her bags of groceries. Marsh and Emmett continued unloading everything onto the pier.

Connie walked into the cabin to find Victor relaxing on the sofa. Deandra was staring out the front bay window at the view across the lake. Tina was pulling protective sheets off the furniture and opening blinds to allow in the sunlight. Connie proceeded to the kitchen with her groceries and turned on the water faucet. Tina always told her to let the water run for at least ten minutes to clear the pipes, especially if they hadn't been here in a few months. It prevented them from getting spiders or bugs in their first glass of water. She placed her bags on the counter and headed back out to see if she could assist with the unloading. As she passed Victor on the sofa, she said, "Victor, there's a lot more to bring in. Can you give us a hand?"

"Oh," Victor replied, startled, "sure. I don't know what I was thinking," he said loudly. He stood up, stretched, and then followed Connie out the door. Clearly, his comment had been for the benefit of Deandra and Tina, because his act didn't fool Connie.

Marsh and Emmett had completed the unloading by the time Connie and Victor reached the pier. Victor grabbed their suitcases and took them back up to the cabin. Connie watched as Marsh hefted the larger of the two coolers. His biceps were bulging as he easily managed the weight of the filled cooler. She felt an irresistible urge to reach out and touch his arm, run her hand along the sinewy muscle, but refrained from doing so. Flashbacks passed through her mind, and shaking her head, she dislodged the memory. She picked up a few more bags and followed Marsh back.

Emmett brought up the rear, carrying a smaller cooler. Connie darted ahead of Marsh just as they reached the cabin to open the door. She continued to hold the door open for Emmett to pass through as well. After several more trips to the pier, they managed to get everything inside the cabin. The cabin had three levels; there was a deep sunken living area, which contained two sofas, two chairs, and coffee and end tables in the living-room section, and a large dining table and chairs on the opposite dining-room side. On the right side of the room was a stairway leading up to a landing that encircled a third of the living room; two guest bedrooms branched off each end of the bridge. Down a short staircase to the left of the room was the entrance to the kitchen. Through the kitchen and up a back stairwell was a loft, which had been turned into a master suite. Out of habit Connie had Victor place their luggage in the room she normally stayed in. She was starting to unpack her suitcase when Deandra appeared in the doorway. "I'm sorry," Deandra said. "I thought Marshall said this was our room." She stepped into the room and looked around, taking stock of it. Connie stopped unpacking and looked up at Deandra, who was slowly making her way around the room.

"No, I always stay in this room when I'm here. Your room is at the other end of the landing," she replied.

"Oh, that must be my mistake. Nice view you have from

here," she said coyly, looking out at the lake in the distance. She looked down into the backyard and said, "Oh my, they have a hot tub out here too. I sure hope they plan on opening that up while we're here. I have a new swimsuit I've been dying to wear. This is an amazing cabin. I didn't realize the Millers' were so loaded." She giggled as she turned back from her position at the window to look at Connie. "How long have you known them?"

"About ten years. Tina was my boss when I was in college. I worked at her shop," Connie replied. She was going to be here with Deandra for six days, she had to try to get along with her for Tina's sake.

"Oh yeah, I think I heard about that. Well, I've taken up enough of your time. I think I'll go check out my room. Ta," she said lightly, and departed.

Connie rolled her eyes and smiled to herself. Talk about phonies; just wait until Deandra saw the view from her own room, or rather lack of view. Connie left Victor's bag untouched; she reasoned he could unpack it himself when he was ready. As she went out to the landing, she could hear Deandra complaining to Marshall in their room. Quietly she went back downstairs in search of Tina.

The group decided that a barbecue would be the easiest dinner to prepare that evening. Tina and Connie got busy in the kitchen seasoning steaks and chicken breasts for grilling. Tina put Deandra to work making a tossed salad. The guys were responsible for setting up the picnic table and chairs and getting the grill fired up.

They had a pleasant first night at the cabin. After dinner they had played cards until late. Tired from the trip and unpacking, Tina decided to retire early. Emmett followed behind her. Victor wanted to go to the clubhouse to see if there was anything happening there. The island clubhouse was a ten-minute drive from the cabin. Connie declined to go with him, since she had come here for a little peace and quiet. Deandra considered joining him, but when Marsh begged off, she changed her mind. She did not like the idea of him being alone with Connie. There were two cars in the garage and the keys were always hanging on a hook in the kitchen. Connie showed Victor where the keys were and gave him directions for getting into town. Once he had driven off, she returned to her bedroom. She reapplied her bug-protection spray and grabbed a sweat jacket and a blanket. Not wanting to pass through the backyard and alert anyone about where she was going, she exited through the front door and walked down to the dock. Carefully she laid her blanket down on the wooden planks and sat on the edge of the dock, allowing her legs to swing freely. It was a crystal clear night and the moonlight reflected in the ripples on the lake. She saw the lights from the town, and when she listened closely, she heard the faint music coming from the clubhouse.

She wasn't sure how long she had been sitting there when she heard footfalls behind her.

"This is one of my favorite spots out here," Marsh remarked as he walked up behind her.

"Hey, Marsh," Connie greeted him. "Where's Deandra?"

"She finally decided to turn in. I think that's what she thought you had done, when you didn't come back after Victor left," he said as he sat down on the blanket next to her.

"When was the last time you were out here?" she asked.

"About six months ago. Emmett and I came out here to fish. It was just the two of us. We had a good time, caught a lot of bass that weekend. I wouldn't be surprised if Tina doesn't still have some of it in the freezer out back." He smiled at the memory. "What about you? When was the last time you were here?"

"Almost a year ago," she replied. "I actually stayed out here by myself for a few days. That was a real treat. It was just before I met Victor."

"It's probably not my business, but you seemed a little tense earlier. Are things okay with you and Victor?"

"You're right. It is none of your business," she said, and smiled gently at him, softening the sting of the words before continuing. "I think this is the last hurrah for Victor and me. We're not good together. What about you and Deandra? She's very beautiful."

"Yes, she is, but things aren't always what they seem. Sometimes we see what we want to see and it takes a while for us to accept that some people can't change. It's not in their nature," he answered.

"I know what you mean," she said. She wondered if he was talking about Deandra or Victor. Perhaps they'd both been misled. This conversation was taking them into dangerous territory and she wasn't sure she was quite ready to get into a personal conversation with Marsh. She stood up. "Anyway, I think it's time for me to go back inside. Are you coming?"

"No, not yet. You go on ahead. I'll see you in the morning," he said, and turned back to the lake. "Good night," he called over his shoulder as she headed back up the dock.

"Good night, Marsh," she said softly. As she approached the cabin, she saw an orange glow from a cigarette on the porch. Deandra was the only one who smoked and Connie surmised she was waiting for Marsh to return. Not wanting to risk any kind of confrontation, she detoured through the woods and entered the cabin through the back door. She was pretty sure the dock wasn't visible through the trees in the darkness, and hoped for Marsh's sake Deandra hadn't seen them. She made her way through the cabin and up to her bedroom, where she entered and closed the door quietly behind her.

Marshall stayed on the dock about fifteen minutes longer. Then he collected the blanket Connie had left behind and walked back to the cabin. Deandra was still waiting on the porch for him. "I thought you had gone to sleep," he said when he saw her sitting in the swing.

The chill wind blowing from her direction preceded the icicles hanging from every deliberately enunciated word as she responded, "Did you now?"

"You seemed tired, that's all," he answered as he climbed the steps to the porch. "I'm going inside. Are you coming?" he asked.

"Where's Connie?" she asked. Rising from the shadows, she moved into the light of the front porch and he could see the barely contained anger in her eyes. He wasn't certain how she knew he'd been with Connie and wasn't about to volunteer any information.

"Connie?" he queried as he stopped at the front door, and opened it for her to enter ahead of him.

"I saw the two of you out there by the water. At first I thought you were alone, so I started to go down there and join you. But the closer I got, I could see you both sitting there. Quite a cozy picture, I must say. So I came back here to wait for you. Then I saw her sneaking around the back of the house, like I wouldn't see her," she said venomously. She walked over and pushed the door closed and stood there with her arms crossed. "Don't you even think of making a fool of me, Marshall. I won't tolerate it, I swear I won't."

"You know, Deandra, you've gotten into a nasty habit of threatening me lately. It's not a good idea. Connie has been my friend for a very long time and we were just talking. You can believe that or not. I honestly don't give a damn," he replied. He entered the front door and left her standing on the porch.

Victor finally stumbled into bed with Connie at three o'clock in the morning. His pawing at her while she slept awakened her. She turned over in the bed and was faced with his liquor-laden, hot breathing. Groaning in distaste, she pushed his hands from her body and moved away from him in the bed. Not deterred, Victor grabbed her around the waist and pulled her up close to his body. She felt his nakedness against her.

"Victor, please stop. You're drunk," she pleaded, and she

tried to push him away. He reeked of women's cologne. She didn't want to think of what he had been doing at the clubhouse and she was pretty sure the clubhouse wasn't open this late. Where had he been before he decided to come home? He clasped her tighter around the waist and tried to push his hands inside her panties. She grabbed his hands firmly. "No, Victor, not tonight. Not like this," she pleaded, fighting to keep him off her. In his inebriated state Victor tired of the battle. He shoved her away from him, nearly causing her to fall out of the bed. She grasped the nightstand to stop her forward progress.

"Frigid bitch!" he muttered under his breath, and turned on his side, away from her. In a matter of moments he was snoring. Tears stung her eyes as she lay there with her arms wrapped around her. What had happened to the Victor she first met? The one who was so tender and caring? Had it all been an act? It certainly seemed so now. She no longer knew the man beside her, and she no longer wanted to try to help him. He was on a self-destructive path and she couldn't let him take her down with him.

13

After breakfast the following morning, Tina suggested a few sets of tennis at the clubhouse. Everyone was game, except Victor who complained of a bad knee, but went along to watch. They retrieved several rackets and ball cans from the front storage closet and piled into two cars to go there. Emmett and Marsh got the first available court, and Victor and the women watched as Marsh easily beat Emmett in three straight sets— even though it appeared he had been trying very hard to take it easy on Emmett. On the next available court Tina, Connie, and Deandra were able to find a fourth female for a round of doubles. They teamed up, with Tina and Connie against Deandra and the other woman. The guys, now relaxing on the sidelines, leisurely watched them play.

From the very beginning it was clear Deandra was out to show up Connie as an inferior opponent. Connie, who was of the mind-set that they were all out for an afternoon of fun, soon found herself being jerked all over the court by Deandra's zinging backhands and powerful forehand strokes. Deandra was an exceptional tennis player, but Connie was no slouch either. Connie stepped up her play to meet Deandra's challenge, powering her serves past Deandra for aces. This only served to bring out the aggressor in Deandra. Connie was playing the back off the net when Deandra sliced a backhand drop shot that fell just over the net. Anticipating the shot, Connie made a quick sprint and scooped it back over the net, and down the line past Deandra's partner for a point, deuce. Next Connie stepped back to accept the serve from Deandra. A powerful fastball came zinging over the net, deep in the corner of the service box. Connie jumped for the shot and managed to hit a powerful forehand return crosscourt and caught Deandra going the other way. Advantage: Connie and Tina. Next Deandra sent an easier serve over the net to Tina. Tina returned the shot and it fell just outside the base line. Deuce again. Connie stepped back once again to receive the serve. She returned the serve crosscourt to Deandra, who was prepared this time and sent it flying back. A fierce crosscourt rally ensued for at least five passes. Victor had risen from his seat and moved closer to the fence enclosing the court. Marsh and Emmett remained seated. Deandra hit another expert drop shot, hoping to catch Tina off guard. Tina couldn't move quick enough to reach the shot, but Connie crossed in front of her and lobbed it back. The lob cleared the net, but was going to drop midcourt and not deep. That set Deandra up for a great smash shot. Tina dropped back to attempt to return the smash, but Deandra deliberately twisted her body as she made contact with the ball and sent the shot zinging straight at Connie, standing at the net. The ball was intended to hit her square in the chest, but Connie managed to turn her shoulder just in time. The ball smashed into her shoulder, and stinging pain shot down her arm, advantage Deandra. Connie dropped her racket and reached for her shoulder with her other hand. Victor yelled from the fence that next time she'd protect herself and Tina ran up to see if she was okay. Marsh jumped up from his seat and started toward the court, then thought better of it. He let Emmett run past him as he and Tina checked to see if Connie was okay. Best to let Tina and Emmett handle this, he thought. He would speak with Deandra later. He knew that had been a deliberate shot intended to hurt Connie. There was no mistaking the satisfied gleam in Deandra's eye as the ball hit its target. Connie insisted she was fine to continue the game, but Tina called a halt. Deandra apologized—she hadn't intended to hit Connie, she explained. Her aim was off on that shot. No one believed her.

Victor hadn't yet played a set and asked Marsh if he was ready to take him on. Marsh, pissed at Victor's nonchalant attitude toward Connie, agreed. He took out all his pent-up aggression on the court as he soundly beat Victor, 6–1, 6–2, 6–0. When they were all done with tennis, Tina and Emmett were ready to head back to the cabin. Deandra wanted to stay and catch some sun at the beachfront. Connie was eager to get back to the cabin. Marsh wanted to head back to the cabin as well. Victor volunteered to stay with Deandra and said he would drive her back. Deandra wasn't pleased with this turn of events, but realized that Marsh would have plenty to say when they got back, and she was going to put off hearing it as long as she could. Besides, hanging out with Connie's man might have some advantages.

Victor and Deandra put her racket in the car and headed toward the beachfront, while the rest piled in the second car for the trip back to the cabin. Victor found them lounge chairs on the beach and retrieved towels for Deandra and him. After sitting down, Deandra pulled her tank top over her head, revealing a deep-cut blue sports bra underneath. She pulled the top off and wiggled out of her shorts. She wore blue panties under her shorts. She turned to see Victor looking at her with an amused smile on his face.

"Is that a bathing suit or your underwear?" he asked.

Deandra winked at him and said, "I won't tell, if you won't tell. I am no less dressed than those women out there in bikinis. This won't make for great tan lines, but I just have to soak up some rays."

"You're my kind of girl," Victor said slyly. He unabashedly stared at her breasts and the long smooth length of her legs from her thighs down. "I don't think Marsh appreciates you the way he should," he continued.

"I don't think so either." She sighed. "But what's a girl to do?" she said, looking right at Victor. She arched her back and pushed her breasts up, and as she pulled the straps of her bra down over her shoulders, her large, round breasts strained against the ridge of her bra. "I hate tan lines," she said coyly. She slipped out of the straps and let the bra dangle, half on her breasts and half off. She leaned back and closed her eyes, but not before she saw Victor licking the moisture from the top of his lips. Deandra was getting the reaction she hoped for. Marsh barely acted like he noticed her anymore, but she liked to be admired and desired—and that's what she saw in Victor's eyes.

Victor sat there staring at her. He was thinking all kinds of things he shouldn't have been, considering her boyfriend was back at the cabin waiting for her. He could tell she was in need of a real man, not a softy like Marshall. She needed someone to rock her world and take that smug look off her face. A man who could show her she didn't have as much control as she thought she did.

"Victor?" she asked, and brought him back to the present. "How are things with you and Connie?"

"Connie's not half the woman you are, and I hate to say that, but it's true. You were amazing out there on the tennis court, but she wimped out. I've told her before about protecting herself on the court. It was bound to happen one day. Maybe now, she'll listen to me," he said in a matter-of-fact tone.

"But how's your relationship? I mean, are things okay?" she queried. She needed to find out if Connie was really a threat.

"Yeah, sure they are. But, hey, I'm not planning to marry her. That isn't part of our deal. So, if you're so inclined, let me know," he replied. Deandra knew exactly what he meant. She hadn't come here to screw around with Victor, but he was a very good-looking man. There was something aggressively appealing about him that drew her to him.

"You're a bad boy, Victor. That's what I like about you," she said softly, and closed her eyes again. Victor leaned back on his lounge chair and pictured himself screwing her brains out. A satisfied smile came over his face.

Upon arrival at the cabin Tina and Emmett began the preparations for dinner. They were planning on grilling a large piece of red snapper and some fresh vegetables. They assured Connie and Marsh their help was not needed. Connie headed straight for her room. A short time later she heard a knock on her door. She opened it to find Marsh standing there with an ice pack wrapped in a towel. She smiled at the thoughtfulness of his gesture.

"You didn't have to do this, Marsh. I'm fine really," she explained.

He touched the purple bruise forming on her shoulder and she winced. "You don't have to be brave for me," he said as he placed the ice pack lightly against the bruised area.

"I'm not really. It was stupid of me not to see it coming. I was just glad I turned away in time. My shoulder can take it a lot better than the other part of me." She smiled up at him and took the ice pack from him, holding it in place on her shoulder.

"I'm really sorry. I think she did that deliberately, and I will speak to her about it. She has this crazy-jealousy thing about you and she let it get out of hand," he said.

"No, Marsh, don't. If you defend me to her, it will only make matters worse. Let's just get through the rest of the week.

I don't want to make trouble for Tina and Emmett. They've been wonderful having us all out here. The least we can do is try to get along. Please," she implored. He looked into her eyes and wanted to take her in his arms and assure her that everything was going to be fine, but he couldn't. Instead, he leaned over and kissed her on her forehead.

"Okay. If that's the way you want it, I'll try. But I can't promise to remain silent if something else happens," he said as he stood up to leave. "Why don't you get some rest and I'll see you later."

"Thanks, Marsh," she said quietly as he left. She watched him as he walked away. She longed for him to wrap her in those strong brown arms and hold her close against his chest so she could feel his heart beating against hers. She remembered what it was like and she knew she wanted to experience it again. Sighing deeply, she got up from the bed and turned on the shower in the bathroom. A cold shower was just what the doctor ordered. It would be good for her shoulder and maybe it would stop the fever raging through her body.

Victor and Deandra stayed at the beach for about two hours before departing for the cabin. As he assisted Deandra into the car, Victor allowed his gaze to trail the length of her body as she swung her long tan legs into the car. On the drive back to the cabin, he decided to test the waters a little with Deandra. He reached over with his free right hand and put it on her leg, just above her knee to see how she would react. She didn't react, only looked out her window. He left his hand there a few moments longer, then squeezed her leg and inched his hand up her thigh. He heard a sharp intake of breath as his fingers lightly touched the smooth, soft skin of her inner thigh. Still driving, and realizing she was enjoying his touch, he slipped his fingers inside the elastic of her panties. Deandra closed her eyes and slid lower in the seat. She opened her legs slightly to allow Victor the access he craved. As his fingers touched her curly soft pubic hairs, he felt his erection straining against his briefs. Probing farther, he touched the wet mound of her vulva and knew she was as excited as he was. He lightly rubbed the tiny protrusion until she cried out loud in climactic joy. They were just reaching the end of the driveway to the cabin. He stopped the car and grabbed her hand and placed it on his engorged member. "We'll take care of this another time," he said as he rubbed her hand along the length of it. Still weak in the knees from his touch, Deandra smiled up at him. The unabashed desire in her eyes told Victor all he needed to know. He could have her anytime he wanted. He put the car back in gear and drove up to the cabin.

They dined in the cabin that evening. The conversation around the dining table centered on vacation locales and who had been where. Which were the recommended islands in the Caribbean to visit? Connie expressed a desire to see the Mexican Mayan ruins, and Marsh agreed it was something he was interested in doing as well. Victor scoffed at the idea and said he would rather spend his vacation week at Hedonism in Jamaica. That was his idea of a good time. Deandra laughed and agreed with him. Connie intercepted a secret smile, which passed between Deandra and Victor, and wondered what had transpired while they were gone. Deandra turned her gaze to Connie and fixed her with a Cheshire-cat grin. The quizzical look on Connie's face prompted Deandra to look back at Vic and roll her tongue around her lips. At this blatantly sexual gesture from Deandra, Connie looked at Vic to gauge his reaction. He looked at her and then looked away without reacting. Vic thought that Deandra was going a little over the top with that one. Fooling around with her was one thing, but letting everyone know was something else. He may have been a flirt, but he felt he was a discreet one. This woman was out of control. Though the conversation had continued around them, Connie was not the only one to see Deandra's intimate gesture. Marsh appeared deep in conversation with Emmett, but he had not missed the exchange. The simmering began deep in the pit of his stomach. Her brazen behavior embarrassed him. She was disrespecting Connie and him right to their faces and enjoying it. He wished he'd never brought her here. In retrospect he was wishing he'd never allowed her to seduce him the first time they met. Her behavior then was a precursor to her behavior now, and he had been too blinded by physical attraction to see it. The sex had been exciting for the first several months. Slowly he'd begun to realize there was very little depth to her personality. Lately he was seriously considering how to extricate her from his life with as little complication as possible. After this week he was finished with her. Deandra was not the type of woman he wanted for the long haul, and he'd made the mistake of keeping her around longer than his other casual flings.

Connie got up from her chair and began clearing the dishes from the table. Her right arm was still very sore and she cradled the plates in her left arm. Marsh arose from his seat to take the plates from her. He carried them into the kitchen, while Connie followed behind after collecting some of the glasses. Tina had risen to assist, but Connie assured her that she and Marsh could handle it, since Tina and Emmett had prepared the meal. Tina sat back down. She wanted Marsh and Connie to have some private time, so she engaged Deandra in conversation to distract her attention from the kitchen. Marsh's solicitous behavior did not slip past Victor either. He did not like it. Connie was his woman, and Marsh always being Johnny-on-the-spot to assist her was beginning to grate on his nerves.

The sound of dishes being washed came from the kitchen, along with a few giggles from Connie. She and Marsh had been in the kitchen for about thirty minutes when Victor came through the door. He said everyone was going to sit out in the back by the Jacuzzi for a while. Connie said fine and continued to put the last of the dishes away.

"Come on, Connie, that can wait until later. I want to talk to you," Victor said.

"Okay, I'll be out in a minute," she replied lightly.

"I want to talk to you now," Victor said more firmly, the tone in his voice causing Connie to turn from her task and look at him. Marsh, who was standing behind Victor at the sink, also stopped and turned.

"Sure," she said quietly, "I'll just put—" Victor grabbed her by the arm and started to pull her away from the counter. Connie yelped in pain as he had grabbed her injured arm. Marsh stepped immediately between the two, appearing to tower over Victor.

"Let her go," he said quietly, with clear intent to beat Victor to a pulp if necessary.

"This isn't your business, Galahad," Victor said, pumping up his chest and holding fast to Connie's arm. She cringed in pain as he squeezed harder.

"I said, let her go," Marsh repeated with deadly quiet, stepping closer to Victor. "You want to discuss this further with me—that's fine. But let her go now." Victor released her arm and gave her a slight shove toward the counter. Marsh reached out to steady her, and then turned to follow Victor. Connie grabbed his arm to stop him.

"No, Marsh, don't. Please just let him go," Connie pleaded.

"I've had enough of him, Connie. He will not treat you like that in my presence," he said angrily. Connie went out to the back deck to deal with Victor. Marsh slammed his fist on the counter and stood there a few moments longer. No one had noticed Deandra standing in the open dining-room doorway. She'd watched the entire exchange. She stepped back into the living room and closed the door quietly. Sitting back down at the table with Tina and Emmett, she seethed in silence.

14

The contents of the envelope lay strewn about the kitchen table. The private detective she'd hired had dropped off the package earlier in the day. Her hand shook as she picked up a picture from the pile. Gingerly she laid it back down. In her distracted state she pressed both palms over the face in the picture and patted it lightly. Viola rose slowly from the table and poured another shot of whiskey into her highball glass. The information she'd received was disturbing, very disturbing. She wandered over to the window and looked out across the lake that bordered her rear yard. The reflection of the moon shimmered on the lake. The cool, gentle breeze coming from the open window, which usually calmed her, was ineffective tonight. Her nerves were too on edge. For once in her life she wasn't sure of her next move. The report revealed that Deandra was all she'd suspected and more. However, there was more at stake now than just ejecting Deandra from Marshall's life. More than she could ever have anticipated.

She needed to speak with Tina. Hopefully, Tina would be able to shed some light on this situation or at least point her in the right direction. She called Tina's home and one of the children advised her that his parents were currently vacationing up at the lake. It would be best to reach Tina on her cellular phone. The son willingly provided the number and Viola thanked him before hanging up. She'd call her friend with a clear head the following day.

Tensions in the cabin were running high by the third day. Victor and Connie were barely speaking. Deandra had been drinking far too much and flirting outrageously with Victor and Emmett. Tina and Marshall were none too happy with the turn of events.

After dinner Connie had feigned a headache, and retired to her bedroom to read, while Victor, Tina, Emmett, Marshall, and Deandra were sitting in the backyard talking.

"Anybody want to join me in the Jacuzzi?" Victor asked.

"That's a good idea," Emmett chimed in. "Honey, how about it?" He turned to his wife.

"Sure, I'll join you." She smiled and leaned over and planted a brief kiss on his lips.

"Marsh?" Emmett inquired.

"No, I think I'll sit this one out. I'm fine right here," Marshall replied, leaning back in his lounge chair and closing his eyes.

"Well, I'm going in," Deandra said determinedly.

"Sure, that's fine, babe. Enjoy yourself," Marshall responded with a smile.

They retired to their bedrooms to change into swimsuits. Emmett and Tina were the first to return. Tina was wearing a black one-piece bathing suit and Emmett had on a pair of knee-length trunks. Emmett tested the waters first to make sure the temperature wasn't too hot and then climbed in. Once inside, he turned to assist his wife. Tina stepped gingerly into the water. Finding the warmth of it very relaxing, she leaned back against the side, next to Emmett. His arm was draped casually along the top ridge of the Jacuzzi and she rested her head against his shoulder.

Meanwhile, Victor had been busy opening and closing drawers in a futile effort to find his swimsuit. Disturbed by the noise and cursing, Connie looked up from her book to see what he was doing.

"What are you looking for, Victor?" she asked.

"Where's my frigging bathing suit?" he asked, annoyed.

She wanted him to find it and leave her alone in peace, so she got up from her chair and pulled his suitcase out of the bottom of the closet. She opened it and handed him the bag with his swimsuits in it. He grabbed it without even thanking her. "Why is this still in the suitcase and not in the drawer, where it's supposed to be?" he demanded.

"I didn't unpack your bag, Vic. You did. I just assumed if it wasn't in the drawer, it had to still be in the suitcase," she replied casually, trying to avoid the argument she could feel was coming. She returned to her chair in the corner, picked up her book again, and curled her legs up under her.

Victor stripped off his clothes. In the dim light across the room, she watched surreptitiously as he pulled off his shirt, jeans, and briefs. She could see the smooth skin of his chest, his soft stomach, and the thick patch of hair surrounding his limp manhood. His thighs were slim and slightly muscular, just like the rest of him. She wondered why she had ever thought him attractive. She felt no stirrings of sexual excitement gazing at him. It wasn't because she was angry with him. She just found she no longer cared about him. She knew at the end of this trip she would be calling it quits with Victor. She had had enough. Victor grabbed a towel from the bathroom and headed back out to the Jacuzzi.

* * *

Emmett and Tina were still relaxing in the tub when Victor returned. He put his towel on a nearby chair and climbed into the tub with them. It was a rather large Jacuzzi, with the capacity to seat eight. Victor settled in on the opposite side and leaned his head back, letting the warmth of the bubbling water soothe his jagged nerves.

"Where's Marsh?" he asked, noticing Marshall was no longer seated on the patio.

"He said something about taking a drive," Emmett replied.

"Did Deandra go with him?" Vic asked.

"No, I believe he went alone," Emmett answered. Just then he let out a low whistle under his breath as he saw Deandra coming through the doors back out to the patio. Vic turned quickly in his seat to see what Emmett was looking at. She was wearing a red string bikini. Her voluptuous breasts were barely contained by the small triangles of material. A slightly larger triangle covered her pubic area. Tiny red strings rose high over her hips, holding the material in place, exposing the full length of her firm thighs and legs. Victor made a grimace, then expelled a breath of air. "Damn girl, you look hot!"

Deandra grinned in acknowledgment. "I was hoping you would think so," she said coyly. She turned her back on them, and walked deliberately over to the picnic table, giving the men a clear view of her naked ass, with another tiny red triangle of material fading into a red string that disappeared between taut, round butt cheeks. She tossed her sandy hair over her shoulder as she looked deliberately back at them and asked, "Can I get anyone a drink?" She was pleased by the open admiration she saw in Emmett's eyes and the clear, unbridled lust displayed in Vic's. She turned back to the table, away from them, and secretly smiled to herself. Marshall was going to be sorry he had been ignoring her. She poured herself another glass of white wine and returned to the Jacuzzi. Vic jumped up from his seat to assist her into the hot tub.

Tina sat rigidly next to her husband. *How dare this brazen hussy come out here dressed like that.* She glanced at her husband and saw Emmett was barely able to stop licking his lips as he looked at Deandra, and Vic looked like he could pounce on her at any moment. She had never felt so disrespected and angry. She wished Connie or Marshall were here to see this, to stop this. But she was determined she was not going to leave her husband alone out there with Deandra.

Tina sat there silently, while the three of them joked and laughed through several rounds of drinks. Deandra was obviously tipsy, and the fourth glass of wine, along with the heated water, began to cloud her already poor judgment. She tried to stand in the middle of the tub and Victor had to reach out and steady her on her feet. Tina looked desperately around, hoping Marshall would walk back in and see his spectacle of a girlfriend and do something.

Connie, curious about the noise coming from the backyard, was standing at her bedroom window watching. She could tell Deandra was drunk. Connie felt sorry for Tina as Deandra started dancing unsteadily in the middle of the tub. It was embarrassing. Horrified, she watched as Deandra raised her arms above her head and began tugging at the string around her neck. "Oh no," Connie said aloud, involuntarily reaching out and touching the glass of the window, as though she could stop what was about to happen.

Tina was equally horrified by the impromptu striptease taking place in front of her. She jumped up from her seat and tried to stop Deandra from removing her top. But Deandra was much taller than Tina, and she pushed her away easily. Emmett and Vic sat rooted to their seats. Deandra succeeded in undoing the knot on her top and the red triangles fell easily away, exposing her full breasts and salmon nipples for all to see. She continued to sway and dance in the moonlight. Tina climbed out of the tub and stormed into the house. Reacting to his wife's rage,

Emmett grabbed a nearby towel and tried to cover up Deandra's nakedness. Deep in the throes of her dance, Deandra struggled to pull off her bottom as well. Victor sat there, enjoying the show, and made no attempt to assist Emmett.

A car door slammed, and Emmett called out loudly, "Marsh! Marsh!"

Marshall came quickly around the side of the house. Taking in the scene, he immediately made his way toward the hot tub.

"Deandra!" He called her name loudly.

She looked up from her drunken haze. "What do you want?" she slurred, wobbling unsteadily on her feet. Standing at the side of the tub, Marshall reached in to pull her out. With Emmett's assistance he was able to get her onto the deck. Wrapping the towel firmly around her, he scooped her up in his arms. She continued to protest and punch at his chest as he carried her into the cabin. Annoyed, he strode through the living area to their bedroom, where he deposited her on their bed, none too gently.

"Bastard!" she spat at him from her position on the bed. "I was just trying to have a little fun. You're no fun anymore."

"You're disgusting. What were you hoping to achieve, and what happened to Tina? She was out there when I left," he asked.

"You mean the little woman? She couldn't handle it. Her husband probably hasn't seen a real woman in years. She got upset and ran in the house. Where the hell were you, by the way?" she demanded. "Out there pissing around with Connie again? Every time I turn around, you're up in her face. Did you think I didn't notice? Maybe I wanted someone to pay attention to me for a change," she said, and started to cry.

Marshall knew it was the alcohol talking. This wasn't the first time she had done her exhibitionist act, and he was sure it wasn't going to be the last. But he was certain this was the last time she was going to embarrass him this way. He looked at

Deandra whimpering with her face in a pillow. He knew she would be asleep before long. Exasperated, he sat down on the end of the bed and put his head in his hands.

Connie had witnessed the whole scene from her bedroom window. She saw the glee on her boyfriend's face as Deandra gyrated in front of him. She knew the only reason he didn't assist Emmett was because it would have exposed his erection, had he stood up. After Emmett passed Deandra over to Marshall, Emmett quickly disappeared in the house in search of his wife. Connie watched in disgust as Victor rose from the Jacuzzi, his erection bulging against his swim trunks as he retrieved a beer from the cooler. With one hand lifting a beer to his lips, he slipped his free hand inside his trunks, and walked off into the woods.

She turned off the light in her room and climbed into bed, hoping she would be asleep before he came back.

15

The following morning Tina and Connie were sitting in the swing on the front porch, both nestling mugs of hot cocoa that Tina had made for them. The rest of the cabin was quiet, so they assumed they were the first to arise.

"I don't understand why Marshall puts up with her," Tina mused as she looked out over the front of her property. "He could do so much better."

"That's what you said about me." Connie laughed.

"True, but I think you've decided to do something about your situation. Am I right?" Tina asked.

"Yes, you are. I'm over Vic. As soon as we get back, I'm telling him to move out. I know you hoped being here would bring us closer together, but it's really just shown me what a loser he really is," Connie said, sipping her cocoa.

"I've had people get drunk at my home before, and most times I can handle it. Last night when she started shaking her body and rubbing up against the men in that disgusting manner, it was all I could do to maintain my temper. I wasn't really surprised it turned into a striptease, because that's the kind of hussy she is. There she was, shaking her boobs in my husband's face. I have never been so disrespected in my life," Tina said, starting to get upset again. Connie reached over and patted her on the hand.

"I know it was upsetting and I'm sorry you had to witness such an ugly display. But don't let her get to you. She's not worth it," Connie said, trying to console her.

"If it weren't for Marsh, I swear, I'd throw her right out on her ear," Tina said angrily.

"I know you would and I'd help you. But we do have to think about Marsh. Can you imagine how embarrassed he's going to be facing everyone today?" Connie said.

"Don't worry about me," Marshall advised after hearing the latter part of their conversation.

Startled, both women nearly lost their cocoa mugs. Tina was the first to respond. "Marsh!" said Tina. "What are you doing up so early?"

"I've been up for several hours," Marshall said as he came up the front steps to the porch and sat on the railing next to them. "I didn't really get a good night's sleep, so I took a canoe out on the lake for a while. I'm really sorry about Deandra's behavior last night, Tina. I didn't get all the details, but I can tell from what I just overheard, she must have upset you, and I wouldn't want that to happen for anything in the world. You know that. If you want, we can leave today," he said seriously.

"No, Marsh. I don't want you to go. It wasn't your fault. I know that. Those things happen when people drink too much. I'm not so fragile that I won't get over it." Tina smiled at him. Marsh was such a good guy. He didn't belong with a hoochie like Deandra.

"Good, I'd hate to abandon Emmett. We're supposed to go fishing today. I'm going to the shed to check out our equipment, so you can find me there if you need me." He stood up and leaned over to plant a kiss on Tina's cheek. Then he looked at Connie and kissed her on the cheek as well. When she looked at him quizzically, he said, "Just because." He bounded back down the steps and disappeared back around the side of the cabin.

"His mother must be throwing fits about this fling he's having. I can't imagine Viola sitting idly by accepting this relationship," Tina stated with surety. A thoughtful expression crossed her face and she added softly, "That's who you should be with."

Connie stared into her mug. She'd spent a lot of time this week thinking about Marsh and what went wrong, but she couldn't admit it to anyone. "Why do you say that?" Connie whispered back.

"You know why, because you're perfect together. Do you think I haven't noticed the chemistry between you two all these years? Why you let other people get in the way is beyond me. You're just mucking up the waters with these other dead-end relationships," Tina said emphatically.

"It just never seemed to be the right time for Marsh and me," Connie said, and looked away wistfully. "Now with Deandra in the picture . . . ," she continued, and then shrugged her shoulders.

"Humph!" said Tina, dismissing Deandra. "It's never too late. What's the real story between Deandra and you? I thought she was just jealous at first, but there seems to be more to it than that. She really doesn't like you. Do you know why?" Tina asked.

"The root of her problem, only her psychologist knows for sure," Connie said, and smiled at Tina. "I honestly don't know, but the more time I've spent around her, the more familiar she seems to me. I can't put my finger on where I know her from, though." Connie paused and looked out over the lake. Her mind drifted back sixteen years to her first slumber party and the disastrous results.

"Nah, it couldn't be," she mused aloud as the faces of the girls at the party flashed through her mind.

"Couldn't be what?" Tina asked. Her curiosity was suddenly piqued.

"I don't think it's possible," Connie said, and shook her head to clear her mind. She heard her mother's voice in her ear as she hissed at Andie, *"You're nothing but a common whore, just like your mother."* "No!" she cried aloud as Andie's face appeared in her mind. The sadness in her eyes so compelling. Agitated, Connie got up from the bench and walked to the edge of the porch. Could Deandra really be Andie from high school? If she was, it would certainly explain the animosity toward her.

Tina was growing concerned with Connie's agitation and mumbling. "Connie, what's going on? What do you remember?"

"I'm sorry, Tina. I can't talk about it yet, because I could be wrong. I need to find out more before I say anything, and it was such a long time ago, it shouldn't matter anyway," she said with more ease than she felt.

"Well, you let me know when you're ready to talk about it. I'm very curious," Tina said as she rose from the swing and turned to Connie. "Come on, let's go start breakfast. I imagine the rest of the house will be up soon. Marsh and Emmett will probably need a packed lunch if they're going out on the boat."

Tina's cell phone suddenly began to play a little tune indicating she had a call. She excused herself and walked into the cabin while she answered it. When Connie entered the cabin a few moments later, she could hear Tina's half of the phone conversation. She was puzzled by Tina's agitated tone.

"I'm not sure, Vi. I mean, I can ask, of course." There was a pause in the conversation as she listened to the caller's response. Then she continued, "I'll do it now and get back to you. Huh, yes, she's here. Actually, we have a full house this week. Marshall and Deandra, as well as Connie and her boyfriend, are visiting." She paused momentarily. "It certainly has. Hey, let me check into that for you and I'll call you back later. I may even have the information upstairs in my address book. Yes, yes, I promise I'll call you back today. Okay, bye."

"I don't mean to be nosey, but was that Mrs. James you were speaking with?" Connie inquired.

"Yes," Tina said as she headed toward the stairs. She looked back at Connie standing in the kitchen doorway with a concerned look on her face. "Not to worry, dear. I need to get some information for Viola and then we can start on that packed lunch for the men, okay? I'll be right back," she said, and disappeared up the stairway to the loft.

Connie shrugged off the conversation and began to take the meat and condiments from the refrigerator to make lunch for Marshall and Emmett. Whatever it was did not concern her and she decided to stay out of it.

The house was quiet when Deandra finally rolled out of bed that morning. Tina and Connie decided to go into the small village to do some shopping, and Marshall and Emmett were already out on the water. Deandra entered the living room to find Victor reading the newspaper and sipping a cup of coffee. With his feet resting on the coffee table, Victor looked up lazily over the top of the newspaper and took in Deandra's loosely tied robe and wildly tousled hair and puffy eyelids.

"Guess who finally decided to crawl out of bed or from under the bed. Looks like you had a wicked night," he remarked, and laid the paper down in his lap.

Deandra made an ugly face at him and continued to the kitchen. He quickly laid the paper on the couch next to him and jumped up to follow her. He pushed his way into the kitchen to find her pouring a cup of mudlike coffee from the drip coffeemaker.

"I guess I really screwed up last night," she said and took a sip of the lukewarm coffee and clicked her tongue against the roof of her mouth in distaste. "Ugh," she said.

"What did you expect, princess? That coffee has been sitting there for two hours," Victor said as he leaned against the door frame, admiring the lean curves of her body. "It's never a good idea to offend your hostess," he added.

"My mouth tastes like the bottom of a birdcage. Where is everybody?" she asked thickly, shrugging off his criticism of her behavior. She'd already admitted her lack of self-control. Being around Connie was beginning to take its toll on her nerves. Her robe hung open down to her waist, revealing a generous portion of breasts. The belt was loosely tied at the crotch and he could see she still wore the string bikini bottom from the night before.

"The ladies, I believe, are on a shopping spree in town, and Emmett and Marsh are out fishing," he replied.

"So why aren't you out fishing too?" she replied, and then stretched her frame from head to toe like a kitten just waking from a long nap, her hands outstretched toward the ceiling. Her robe opened completely as she stretched, revealing her voluptuous breasts.

Victor felt an excitement growing in his loins and he moved from his position by the door and approached her. "Do I look like Huck Finn to you?" he asked. "I like my fish fried, grilled, or blackened on a plate with some potatoes and greens. I can't be bothered with all that other crap."

He aggressively cupped one of her bare breasts in his hand and began to nibble softly on her neck. Deandra giggled and playfully tried to push him away. "I thought that was what real men do. You know, communing with nature, fishing, chopping wood, and bringing home the bacon," she teased.

"Look, all a real man needs to know is how to commune with a woman's nature. I can bring you all the bacon you need, extremely thick bacon if you get my drift," he remarked as he slid his hand up her thigh and nestled his palm in the moist warmth between her legs.

She exhaled a sharp intake of breath and eased away from his probing fingers. Turning her back on him, she tried to ignore the tingling sensation the heat of his hand created. She retied her robe and picked up her coffee cup to take a sip.

"Scared?" he asked.

She looked at him over the rim of her cup and replied, "Never that, darling, never that. Maybe it was time I learned to practice a little discretion, like your girlfriend, Connie."

"Connie? Connie who? You and I have unfinished business," he reminded her, slowly running his hand along the outline of his stiffened rod.

"Later, Victor, later," she said, and walked out of the kitchen. The last thing she needed right now was to be caught in a compromising position with Victor. She sensed Marshall was probably still pissed with her over last night, because he never bothered to wake her this morning. She wasn't ready to switch camps yet. Not until she was sure the next bed was going to be much softer than the one she was in. Victor was tempting for certain, but flirting with him was ultimately more delicious because he was Connie's man.

Victor watched her leave as he finished his coffee. He wanted Deandra now, not later. He glanced at the clock and calculated they would be alone for at least another hour. He thoughtfully placed his cup on the counter and rubbed his hand across his goatee. Then he headed toward Deandra's bedroom.

He knocked on the door and barely waited for her to respond before he entered the room. She was standing at the mirror, studying her face, and looked only mildly surprised to see him in her room. She turned from the mirror and allowed her bathrobe to slide off her shoulders onto the floor. Victor whistled softly under his breath as she stood there naked, except for the bottom of her bikini bathing suit. Her voluptuous breasts were gorgeous, and her slim waist graduated into curvy hips and long, endless legs. He crossed the room in a few quick strides. He grasped her chin in his hand and kissed her along the length of her neck.

"You got something for me, kitten," he whispered huskily in her ear.

"I don't want to get caught with you, Victor," she replied as she exhaled deeply in response to his lips on her skin.

"They won't be back for a long time, sweetheart," he replied, and cupped her breast in his palm. He leaned forward and captured her rosebud nipple with his mouth. Sucking gently, he swirled his tongue teasingly around its rigid peak.

It had been a while since Marsh had touched her, and her body was responding to Victor's closeness. She would show Victor what he was missing with that insipid good girl, Connie.

"Are you sure?" she gasped, and began to unbuckle the belt on his pants. Her movements were rushed and eager as she pushed aside his pants and slipped her hand inside his briefs, caressing the stiffening rod inside.

"Oh, baby," he replied, and placed his hand on her shoulders to guide her down to her knees.

Deandra obliged willingly and took his pulsing rod eagerly into her mouth. She grabbed his ass cheeks with her nails and sucked his dick with an expertise he'd never known. Alternating between firm, aggressive sucking and gentle tongue-lapping, she brought Victor to the edge of release several times.

He entwined his fingers in her silken hair and held tight to her head. When she wet her finger and shoved it into his anus, Victor couldn't hold it any longer and pulled out of her mouth abruptly and shot his hot, sticky cum all over her breasts.

"Damn girl! Shit!" he cried as he sat down on the edge of the bed. He took a minute to gather himself and then smiled at her sitting on her haunches in the middle of the floor. "Damn, you're good," he said, and laughed. He reached over and pulled her toward him. He smeared his cum across her nipples and around her breasts with his hands, and his manhood began to stiffen once again. He tried to pull her onto the bed and she resisted.

"Not on the bed, Victor," she said, afraid to muss the sheets and leave telltale signs. She stood up and faced the dresser and spread her ass cheeks invitingly. The triangle patch of the red string of the bikini was like an arrow pointing the way through her ass cheeks to the treasure inside.

Victor retrieved a condom quickly from his pants and donned it. He ran his hands along her firm, round ass before parting her cheeks and slipping into the warm, wet depths of her heat, right alongside the string of her bikini.

Deandra gasped as she was filled with his engorged staff. She leaned on the dresser for support as Victor began pumping and grinding deep inside her body. In her desire to orgasm quickly, she slipped one hand inside her thong and began aggressively fingering her clit. Her body bucked and arched in response to the double stimuli.

Victor stood upright and cupped both breasts with hands pulling her up against his chest. With deep upward thrusts he pushed his manhood repeatedly up inside her body as far as he could.

Deandra leaned back weakly against his chest and continued to stroke herself until heat flushed her body and her essences spilled over his dick.

He quickly recognized her orgasmic peak and pushed her forward onto the dresser again. He grabbed her hips and pulled her ass tight against his groin as he pumped a second hot juice stream into her depths.

She liked fucking for the sake of fucking as much as he did. He had only touched the tip of the iceberg, and he was determined to get down and dirty with her again. He started toward her and said, "It's been a long—"

"You'd better get out of here," she interrupted quickly, and started pushing him toward the bedroom door.

Conversely, Deandra's mind was on getting him out of this room before someone came home. She'd enjoyed herself, but reality was quickly setting in—and she wasn't ready just yet to give up Marshall or all he had.

"Come on, girl. Slow down. Ain't nobody here, but you and me," he replied as he buckled the belt on his pants.

"Out, out, Victor," she said, and waved him off. She turned toward the bathroom. "I've got to take a shower before they get back here. I think you may want to do the same."

He looked puzzled for a moment and then asked, "How will I explain my change of clothes?"

Exasperated, Deandra replied, "Chances are, she will be too engrossed in whatever my boyfriend is doing to even notice you." She entered the bathroom and closed the door.

Victor stood there a moment longer, digesting her last remark. She was probably right. Connie had been spending a lot of time around Marsh since they got there and she certainly had been turning a cold shoulder to him. It might pay to keep an eye on those two. After all, he was still living in Connie's house and didn't have solid plans to leave yet. He left the room and headed for the bedroom down the hall to shower and change.

Marshall and Emmett returned by late afternoon with a huge catch of fish. While Tina and Connie began preparations for dinner, the men cleaned and packed the fish in the freezer for storage. Emmett gave Tina one large bass for the evening's dinner. She seasoned the fish and then covered it with sliced onions, red peppers, green peppers, and garlic. She wrapped it in heavy-duty foil and put it aside for grilling on the barbecue later.

Deandra opted to stay out of everyone's way until dinner was served and was relaxing in the backyard on a hammock. Victor, in a benevolent mood after his afternoon tryst, had offered to get the grill ready for dinner.

The group had a quiet, reflective dinner a few hours later.

While Tina tried to lighten the mood with tales of the day's shopping trip, her stories were met with mild interest and polite laughter. Marshall pitched in once or twice with an anecdote about their fishing experience today. It garnered no better result. It seemed everyone was more interested in how much longer they would be on the island. After dinner Deandra surprised everyone by assisting Tina with the dishes and cleanup. She told Connie it was her turn and that she was free to relax. Truthfully, she was hoping to score a few brownie points with Marshall, who'd been rather reserved in his treatment of her since he'd returned from his outing.

Freed from evening chores, Connie decided to take a walk down to the lake. This time she avoided the dock, where she could be seen. She needed some private time. Thoughts of Andie Moore had been flitting in and out of her head all day. Andie had been tall and lean. Deandra was tall and stacked. Andie could easily have filled out and lost that gangly look. Her hair had been darker, but Deandra's hair could easily have been colored blond. Connie was growing more certain than ever that's who Deandra Morgan used to be.

She leaned against a tree and gazed out across the water. The light from the moon reflected on the still lake. Every now and then she would see circles appear as ripples in the lake where a fish or lake creature crested the surface of the water. In the near distance little forest creatures could be heard rustling through the bushes. This cabin and setting had always been so peaceful and tranquil. The past few days, in contrast, had been so disruptive and uncomfortable for all of them. Deandra's performance last night was the icing on this cake from hell. It was those very antics that troubled Connie so much.

She closed her eyes and tried to recall that night so many years ago. Her parents had gotten into a very heated argument when her father came back after dropping Andie off at home. Connie couldn't remember ever having heard her mother so distressed. Arlene Jefferson had always been the epitome of a gracious hostess. She was always cordial, even in the face of distasteful people or circumstances. Connie grew up emulating her mother's sense of style and grace.

Connie breathed deeply of the night air and cleared her mind. Suddenly she heard her mother's voice, angry and indignant.

"Did you know about this? How did that—that child get into my house?"

"Arlene, please calm down. The other girls might hear you," her father said as he tried vainly to stop the tirade from escalating.

Arlene was not to be placated. "I don't give a flying fuck who can hear me. That bitch should never have sent that child over here in the first place!" she screamed in protest.

"Arlene, maybe Julia didn't know she came here. I'm sure she would have prevented her child from suffering this kind of embarrassment," he said as he tried to reason with his wife.

"How dare you try to defend that bitch or her bastard child! Do you know what that little whore was doing—she was masturbating and performing oral sex in my house. In my house! In front of our child! And you dare to excuse her and her filthy whore of a mother!" she exclaimed in total disbelief.

"Arlene, what the child did was wrong. I agree with you, but continuing this tirade is only going to upset Connie that much more. Did you stop to think about that? She's already had quite a shock this evening. We need to make sure she's okay with what's happened."

"Connie, yes, my baby is very upset. This is your fault, Carlton Jefferson. This is your fault!"

Connie remembered the silence that had followed. Her mother had gone into her sitting room and slammed the door.

A short time later her father had come into her bedroom to check on her. Petra, Debbie, and Emily were trying to console her when her father knocked on the door. She remembered how she'd rushed into his arms and held on to his waist for dear life. She didn't understand then what caused her parents to fight about Andie or her mother. Rehashing it now only served to bring back bad memories. What happened was Andie's fault, and she still could not understand why her mother blamed her father. Why she'd said it was his fault. As she reflected back on that night, she had an uneasy feeling that it had something to do with her father and Andie's mother. She just wasn't sure how the two were connected.

She sighed deeply and headed back through the woods toward the cabin. These new revelations were more disturbing than she anticipated, but she was positive that Deandra was Andie. It could be the reason for Deandra's unexplained animosity toward her.

Upon her return to the cabin, Connie retrieved a book from her bedroom and settled in the living room to read. She snuggled into one of the large chairs and opened her book. Shortly thereafter she was joined by Tina, who'd brought along an afghan she'd been crocheting on her visits to the cabin. Tina smiled at Connie, and they relaxed into a comfortable silence. Victor had taken the car into town again and Connie was relieved to see him go. Emmett was tired from his fishing trip and had retired to his bedroom. Marshall and Deandra were sitting in separate lounge chairs on the back patio.

"Marshall, I'm sorry about last night. I don't know what got into me."

"I'm not sure what got into you either, Dee. I've come to the realization that whatever demons are haunting you, I can't help you with," he replied.

"I'm so afraid of losing you that it makes me crazy sometimes," she said.

"Dee, perhaps I'm the one who hasn't been fair to you. At first, being with you was fun and exciting. You did things that embarrassed me, but I honestly didn't have any long-term plans for us, so I kind of ignored your behavior," he said, and rose from his seat. With his hands in his pockets he looked down at her and continued speaking. "When you began to make it clear that you wanted more out of the relationship than I did, I should have stopped seeing you."

"No, Marshall, please don't say that," she pleaded, and rushed from her seat to wrap her arms around his waist. "Marsh, please," she whispered with desperate urgency.

"I was selfish," he continued, but did not return her embrace. "You're a beautiful, extremely sexy woman and I enjoyed being with you, but I never intended to make this a permanent arrangement." He gently pushed her away.

"How could you do this to me?" she cried. "I love you, Marshall!"

He shook his head sadly. "I'm sorry, Dee. I never meant to hurt you."

Her pride would not allow her to beg anymore. She didn't want the others to know she'd been dumped. At least he owed her that much. "Don't tell the others," she said, and brushed the tears from her cheeks. "I don't want their pity. At least let me leave this place with what little dignity I have left."

"It's nobody else's business, Dee. Nobody has to know right now," he agreed.

"Thank you," she said, and turned away and entered the cabin through the kitchen door.

She walked past Connie and Tina in the living room on her way to her bedroom. She was tempted to ignore them, but realized that wasn't a good idea. It might make them suspicious. She forced a smile and bade them good night instead.

A few hours later the house was silent when Marshall ventured upstairs to his bedroom. His hope of Deandra being asleep was quickly dashed when he saw her sitting in a chair near the window. She was wearing a long sheer nightgown and her hair was combed down around her shoulders. She was a vision of beauty, but he knew there were serious cracks underneath the surface of the vision. He began to undress for bed and slipped into a pair of long pajama bottoms before getting into bed.

Deandra waited a bit before she slipped in bed beside him. She sidled up close to him and pressed her breasts against his back. She wrapped her arm around his waist and slipped her hand inside the waistband of his pajamas. With easy familiarity she grasped his member in her hand and began to squeeze it gently.

Marshall sighed deeply. This was wrong, it was wrong to make love to her again when he'd already broken up with her. This is why he'd kept her around longer than he should have. He covered her hand with his and gently removed it from his penis.

"Please make love to me one last time, Marsh," she whispered, and slipped her hand between his ass cheeks. She pressed her middle finger against his anus and got the reaction she'd hoped for when he moaned aloud and his manhood stiffened in response.

He turned on his side and faced her. "Dee, please. This is not a good idea. I don't want to . . ." He stopped in midsentence as her lips closed around his rigid dick. The heat from her mouth sent shock waves to his brain.

Deandra sucked his dick with all the desperation and expertise she could muster. She'd agreed outside on the patio that the relationship was over, but when she'd walked past CJ in the living room, she realized there was no way she was giving up so easily.

Marshall gave up fighting a whole lot quicker than he knew was best for the situation. He rolled onto his back and allowed her to suck his dick to her heart's content. He hadn't changed his mind about ending their relationship; he simply wasn't beyond one last fuck with a beautiful woman. Especially, a woman he'd enjoyed fucking. When he'd had enough of her titillating him, he climbed between her legs and eased the gown up around her hips. He remembered to sheath his dick before sliding inside her throbbing heat. Her walls closed tightly around him, sucking him deep into her depths.

Her mouth was wet and eager as she kissed him passionately. She raked her nails along his ass and up his back. He belonged to her and she wanted to be sure CJ knew it. His dark skin wouldn't show bruising so easily and a well-placed hickey would be useless. It was unlikely that anyone would see scratches on his back. She began to moan loudly. She followed that with soft whimpering and began increasing the tempo.

At first, Marshall was too engrossed in fucking her to realize how loud she was getting. When she screamed his name aloud, he suddenly stopped his intense stroking and looked at her.

"Dee, what are you doing? Be quiet," he urged.

She giggled in response. "I'm sorry, it was just so damn good when I came, I couldn't help it. I promise, I'll be quiet," she said, thoroughly pleased with herself. She was certain CJ had heard her in the room down the hall.

Marshall's mood suddenly changed. He knew exactly what she'd done and why. He cursed himself for allowing her one last hurrah—one last chance to make a spectacle of them both. He pulled away from her and got out of bed. He retreated to the bathroom and flushed the condom down the toilet. He returned to the bedroom and put his pajama bottoms back on, while she watched in silence. This time he added his pajama shirt and then headed toward the door.

"Where are you going?" she hissed.

"I'm going to get a drink," he replied.

"You wouldn't need a drink if you'd finished the job you

started," she said, nastily referencing the fact that he had not climaxed.

"I shouldn't have started it in the first place. Don't worry, it won't happen again. That I promise you," he replied angrily. He was angrier with himself than he was with her. He knew what she was about and he'd allowed his dick to think for him.

Alone in the bedroom down the hall, Connie had indeed heard Deandra's impassioned cries. She cringed with anger and jealousy. She remembered what it was like to make love with Marshall, vividly remembered. The thought that after all Deandra had done, Marshall was still involved with her, baffled Connie. If he couldn't see past her sexuality to the real woman Deandra was, then perhaps he wasn't the man Connie thought he was after all.

She turned over in bed and clutched her pillow to her chest. Tears stung the corners of her eyes. The part of her heart that loved Marshall James was breaking all over again.

16

Viola drove up to the small villa on the beach and parked in the sandy driveway. Tina's directions had to be wrong. She couldn't imagine she lived in such a small home. She collected her purse and a folder of papers off the seat and exited the car. In her high heels she walked up the wooden steps to the front door. There was no bell, so she opened the screen and knocked. A voice from inside bade her to wait just a minute.

She looked around while she waited. Exotic flowers grew in wild bunches around the landscape. The villa was painted a pale yellow with white trim. The door opened suddenly, and she found herself staring at an earthy bohemian-looking woman with wild flowing black hair and sparkling brown eyes. The woman was dressed in a paint-splattered apron over loose-fitting shorts and a tank top. Flat sandals and an ankle bracelet of seashells adorned her feet.

"My God, as I live and breathe, Viola James!" the woman exclaimed, and pulled a stunned, speechless Viola into her home and gave her a sincere, welcoming embrace.

Viola nearly stumbled as the woman released her and tried

to regain her composure. This was not the polished, austere socialite she remembered. Her voice cracked as she accepted the truth. "Arlene?"

"Well, who did you come here looking for?" Arlene Jefferson replied with a hearty laugh.

"Oh, my word! What has happened to you?" Viola questioned.

"I learned to live life," Arlene replied as if that explained it all.

"You look positively uncivilized," Viola said with a giggle as she began to feel relaxed with her old friend.

"Come on in and have a seat," Arlene said, and directed Viola into her small kitchenette. "Would you care for a glass of my infamous 'Key Limeade?' "

"I'd love some," Viola replied as she glanced around the small villa. She noticed dozens of paintings, matte canvases, and an easel, along with an array of painting utensils, in the corner of what would normally have been the dining room.

Arlene dropped some ice cubes into a tall glass and poured a generous amount of limeade in before she handed it to Viola. She wondered what would bring Viola two hundred miles to see her. She hadn't seen her in many years and was curious how she'd found her.

"What brought you all the way down here, Vi? I haven't seen you in at least ten years," Arlene asked as she took a sip from her own glass.

"It's a very delicate matter. So delicate I hesitate to bring it up, but it involves my son—"

"Marshall? Is he okay?" Arlene asked with concern. She remembered him being a very handsome young man.

"He's fine. It's just that he's fallen into the clutches of a rather unsavory young woman and I'm not in the least bit happy about it," she replied. She was almost afraid that going any further would get her tossed out on her ear, but she was doing this for her son, and Connie.

"I had the young woman he's currently dating investigated, and there were some issues that were uncovered in their investigation that I needed to speak with you about," she said cautiously.

"Speak with me about? How could I be involved?" Arlene asked. Her posture became tense and she prepared herself to hear Viola's news.

"Your connection is rather indirect. What I discovered has a greater impact for Connie. Did you know that your daughter and my son are friends? I recently found out the two of them have met socially," Viola said.

"No, I didn't. Connie never mentioned it. So how is she involved in this situation?"

"I think the woman Marshall is dating may have an ax to grind with Connie, and Connie is not aware of it. The woman has changed her name and appearance. I also believe this other woman may be dangerous, and I'd hate to see Connie get hurt," Viola explained as she laid the folder on the table. She pulled out several photos and spread them on the table. There was a mug shot of a much younger Deandra amongst the pile. The placard she was holding in the picture identified her as Andrea Moore.

Arlene rose abruptly from the table and walked to the sliding glass door leading to the beach. Her body went rigid as old angers surfaced. "How did this happen?" she hissed through clenched teeth.

"I'm sorry, Arlene. Really I am, but if what I suspect is true, we have to tell Marshall and Connie so she can protect herself. Is this woman who I think she is?" Viola asked as she rose from her seat and approached Arlene. She took her lack of response as confirmation and placed a comforting hand on Arlene's shoulder. "I'm so sorry for opening old wounds, my friend, but you needed to know. Now we have to tell Connie. They're all at Tina's lake house together."

Arlene flashed a panicked look at Viola. The panic faded as quickly as it had arisen. If they were all at the lake house together, then Connie was not alone with Andrea. It would keep until they returned and she could figure out the best way to explain the situation. "I don't think Connie is in any danger, but she should know what she is facing. I would prefer to tell her myself. When are they supposed to return?"

"In a few days, I believe. I will wait until then to tell Marshall about this Andrea person and all she has been up to. Please don't wait too long to tell Connie," Viola urged.

Arlene turned from the window, her demeanor weary and tired. She slowly said, "It's so funny how things always manage to come full circle. How that woman managed to get back into my daughter's life after all this time is pure insanity."

Viola gathered her papers and photos, and then shoved them back inside their folder. She hated to leave her friend in such a dispirited mood, especially since she was the cause of it. She felt compelled to offer what comfort she could, but wasn't sure of what to say. "Carlton was a wonderful surgeon, Arlene. He was well respected by everyone who knew him," Viola said.

"Yes, Carlton was a brilliant surgeon. But being the wife of the surgical chief of staff was no picnic," Arlene said, and sighed deeply. She took a deep breath before she continued to talk. "That's why I live every minute of my life now doing exactly what I want, like painting and living here at the beach. I don't have to answer to anyone anymore about what I do, nor do I have to worry about what anyone else is doing. My Connie is a strong, self-reliant woman. I raised her to be stronger than I was."

"I've met Connie and you did a fine job, Arlene. Your daughter is an extraordinary young woman. I wish my Marshall would realize that," Viola said with a careless wave of her hand, as if she could so easily dismiss the news that brought her there. She continued, "Anyway, I've had enough of this wistful talk. Would you like to join me for dinner for old times' sake? I'm staying at the Ocean Key overnight. We could dine there and you can stay the night with me, and we can catch up on the last several years. I'll drop you off tomorrow on my way back to Jupiter," Viola suggested.

"You would be seen with me in my uncivilized state?" Arlene chuckled as she considered the idea of dinner with her old friend.

"Yes, I would. As a matter of fact, I want to know the secret to your happiness. You were positively bubbling when I first got here," Viola reminded her. She started toward the front door to put the folder back in the car, out of sight.

Suddenly a handsome young man entered from a door on the far side of the kitchen. His exuberance preceded him into the room as he called out a greeting to Arlene. His body was still partially wet from a dip in the ocean and his tight swim trunks left very little to the imagination. He swept into the kitchen like an ocean wave and pulled Arlene into his arms for a passionate kiss.

She giggled girlishly as she pushed him away to inform him they had company. She pointed to Viola, who was standing at the front door with her mouth agape.

"Oh, my bad. I'm sorry. I beg your pardon, ma'am," he replied, and walked briskly across the room to extend his hand in greeting. His long, lean, but muscular, body glistened with droplets of seawater. A towel was slung casually over his shoulder.

As Arlene made introductions, Viola tried valiantly not to stare at the gifts with which this perfect, nearly naked boy toy was endowed.

"Vi, I would like you to meet my friend Joshua. Joshua, this is a very old friend of mine, Viola James," Arlene said as she nearly keeled over with laughter from the expression on Viola's face.

Viola shook hands with the young man and he quickly excused himself to the bedroom. Once the bedroom door closed, Viola stared at her friend in horror. In a burst of air, she expelled the breath she had been unconsciously holding. "How old is he? Twelve?"

"Don't be silly. He's legal," Arlene said, and guffawed. "You just ought to get one. Bet it will put a smile on that sour puss of yours."

They both burst out laughing as Viola fanned herself and pondered the possibilities.

Deandra woke, once again, alone in the bed. She had no idea if Marshall ever returned to their room the night before. She'd taken two sleeping pills and was awake for at least an hour after his abrupt departure, but he had not come back to bed. In the morning he was gone again—his pajamas in the chair indicated he'd already showered and gone downstairs.

She rolled over and checked the clock on the bureau: nine o'clock. She decided she'd spent enough lazy time around this cabin and needed to get some exercise. She got up, showered, and donned her running suit and sneakers. A short time later she left the cabin through the front door and headed for the road.

Victor watched her departure from the landing upstairs. He wasn't in the mood this morning for a jog or he would have joined her. He had a bit of a hangover from the party he found last night. He decided he would wait for her return. There were things they needed to talk about. He made his way back to his bedroom and returned to bed.

Connie had gotten up early as usual and assisted Tina with breakfast. Her demeanor that morning had been rather restrained and quiet. When Tina asked what was wrong, she had replied she wasn't feeling good.

"Is there something I can pick up for you in town?" Marshall asked. He was concerned that her reserved behavior had something to do with him.

"No, thank you. I'm fine," she replied a little more sharply than she intended. When all eyes turned to her, she quickly apologized. "I'm sorry, Marshall. I didn't mean that the way it sounded," she said, and put the dish towel down on the counter. "I'm going out to get some fresh air. Excuse me," she said, and exited through the back door.

"Did something happen, Marshall?" Tina asked. It was obvious to her that Connie was somehow upset with him.

"Not that I'm aware of, but I think this little vacation has given us all more angst than we intended," he replied. He was certain Connie had heard Deandra's loud sexual cries the night before and was troubled by them. It had been a mistake, and unfortunately, one he wouldn't be able to erase anytime soon.

Marshall and Emmett wanted to get some work done on the cabin and headed toward the shed in the backyard. Marshall noticed that Connie was headed toward the dock for some solitude. Tina retired to the loft upstairs to begin putting things away for the trip home. It would probably be several months before they returned to the cabin again.

When Deandra returned from her jog an hour later, it seemed as if the cabin had been abandoned. It was eerily quiet. She retrieved a bottle of water from the refrigerator and jumped nervously when she turned around to find Victor standing in the doorway staring at her.

"Why are you always sneaking around, Victor?" she demanded angrily.

"What's wrong with you, fly crawl up your ass?" he retorted.

"Yes, as a matter of fact, and its name is Connie," she replied, and took a long drink from the bottle.

"What did she do to you now?" he asked, and walked into the kitchen and faced Deandra.

"It's her damn goody-two-shoes act. They all treat her like she's a fragile princess who can do no wrong. Well, they're wrong about her. She's not good at all," she cried emotionally.

"Hey, babe," Victor said, and brushed a tear from her cheek. He caressed her face with his palm. "She's not half the woman you are. I've told you that before," he whispered against her face, and gave her a light kiss.

"She's ruining everything for me, Victor. I was finally going to get everything I always wanted and she interfered again."

Victor slipped his hand under the elastic of her running bra and cupped her breast. At the same time he planted soft kisses along her chin and down the side of her neck.

Deandra sighed contentedly. "Why didn't you stop her, Victor? You were supposed to stop her from going after Marshall."

"I tried, honey, I tried," Victor replied. He pulled the bra over her head and latched onto her rosebud nipple, sucking deeply.

The ache between her legs was growing unbearable. She rubbed her hand along the rigid length of his dick, then slipped her hand inside his briefs. Gently she cupped his balls in her palm and rubbed the tiny pods. She eased her hand between his thighs and tickled his sensitive scrotum with her nails. "Why can't we ever get what we really want, Chuy?" she asked breathlessly.

"We're the same, Andie. You and I have always understood each other better than anyone else can. We're the same kind of people. We go after what we want, no matter what it takes." He grabbed her hand and pulled her out of the kitchen down the back hallway to the laundry room. The urgency to fulfill his desire was reflected in the forcefulness of his movements. He shoved his pants down and unleashed the beast waiting to return to its familiar, comfortable lair. As he lifted her atop a shelf in the corner, he confessed his need for her. "I've missed fucking you, baby. There's never been anybody like you, Andie."

Deandra wiggled out of her shorts and eagerly wrapped her legs around his waist, pulling his engorged dick deep within her cavernous depths. "I missed you too, Chuy," she cried as his thickness filled her.

He lifted her off the table, and with her ass securely held in his muscular arms, he fucked her like he hadn't in a very long time. She responded wildly without any pretense of inhibitions and gave him as good as she got. When he eased her down to the floor and continued his assault on her body, she matched his rhythmic stroking with wild, aggressive bucking.

They called out each other's true names as they climaxed simultaneously with mind-numbing explosiveness.

"You know we belong together, Andie," he said as he straightened up and pulled her to her feet. He started to say something more when he noticed a look of horror on her face. He turned quickly to see Tina standing in the open doorway, her arms loaded with linen and her mouth ajar in shock. He quickly shut the door and addressed Deandra. "It's okay. She won't tell Connie. She wouldn't want to hurt her. Don't worry. No one else will find out."

Deandra didn't respond as she slowly fixed her clothes and put her bra back on. It was really over now. Any chance she might have had of salvaging her relationship with Marshall, now or later, was gone. Chuy didn't understand.

"You don't understand, Chuy. It's not about hurting Connie. She'll tell because she doesn't think I'm good enough for

Marshall. None of them do, and now she has the proof she needs," she mumbled. "You let me down, Chuy. We should never have been at this stupid cabin together. You were supposed to keep that bitch away from my man. That's all I asked you to do and you couldn't even do that!" she yelled viciously.

"Where's the money, Andie? You promised to pay me. You said you would give me twenty thousand dollars to screw that whiny bitch for a few months. Well, it's been almost a year and I haven't seen a dime," he argued back.

"I was going to get it for you as soon as I could get access to his money. I told you to be patient. Now we're both going to end up with nothing!"

"Look, calm down. We can find another mark. There's a sucker born every minute. Remember how we used to say that. We'll find someone else, Andie," he said coaxingly in an effort to calm her down.

"I thought he was the one. I really did. I wanted it so bad this time," she moaned, and leaned on his shoulder.

"I'm the one, Andie. I'm the one who loves you. You belong with me, you always have. One day you will see that. Now we'd better get out of here before she comes back," he said, and opened the door. He allowed Deandra to leave first and waited until he heard her bedroom door shut before he exited the laundry room.

Tina had retired to her bedroom in the loft on trembling legs. She could not believe what she had just witnessed. Even more troubling was she did not know what to do about it. If she told Connie, who already seemed disheartened this morning, it may have a negative effect on her confidence. That child had the worst luck when it came to men. If she said nothing, that whore, Deandra, was going to get away with it. That idea did not sit well with her either. She decided to stay in the loft and avoid contact with anyone until she could talk to Emmett alone.

Dinner was a very quiet affair. Everyone seemed lost in their own thoughts. Connie retired early to bed and one by one the others followed suit.

17

The next day Viola dropped Arlene off with the promise they would get together again soon. She had reminded Arlene to call Connie soon and tell her the truth. Viola had called Marshall as soon as she began the long drive up State Highway 1, leaving Key West and heading toward Palm Beach. She wanted to check in on how everything was going at the cabin. He didn't answer his phone, and as the morning dragged on, he hadn't returned her call. She'd called again around two, but still the call went to voice mail. It was now late afternoon and Marshall had not called her back. She was getting worried. It was not like him to ignore her calls.

Victor and Connie were sitting in lounge chairs near the barbecue while Marshall and Emmett were gathering the yard tools and storing them in the shed for the next visit.

"I'll be moving my things out when we get back, but I guess that comes as no surprise to you," Victor stated without looking in her direction.

Relieved, yet saddened by still another failed relationship, Connie wistfully asked, "What happened to us, Victor?"

Victor scoffed and took a swig of his beer before answering her. "No man wants to be a substitute forever," he replied.

Taken aback by his response, Connie looked sharply in his direction and responded defensively. "What are you talking about? You've never been a substitute. Substitute for what?"

"Not what, Connie. Who," he said, and tipped his beer in the direction of Marshall, who was standing near the shed. "The Boy Scout over there. I've seen the way you look at him. You'd think the motherfucker walked on water the way you idolize him. Well, I've never been a Boy Scout and never will be," he finished bitterly.

"That's not true, Victor. I've never compared you to Marsh," she protested, but what he said made her wonder. Had she subconsciously compared the two? No, she was sure she hadn't.

"Sure you have," he said, rising from his seat. "But you know what, that's okay, you'll never have him, because you can't compete with that." He pointed to Deandra standing next to Marshall, laughing with him and Emmett. Her hair twisted in a knot at the back of her neck, she was wearing a short midriff top and low-hung shorts exposing a fair amount of tanned, olive skin. She was beautiful in a seductive, flirtatious way. "That's the kind of fire a man wants in his bed—even the Boy Scout. . . ." He paused to let his point hit home and then walked away toward the lake.

Connie sat there quietly as tears stung the corners of her eyes. It wasn't fair that the Deandras of the world always got the good guys and girls like her ended up with the users, like Victor, or all alone. She brusquely wiped the tears from her cheeks and decided this wasn't her fault. It was true that in her eyes Victor could not wash Marshall's drawers, but their relationship was over long before this trip, and she wasn't going to shoulder all the blame so easily.

She entered the cabin in search of Tina and found her upstairs in the master suite putting away linens. She walked across the room and stood near the dresser, contemplating how to ask her question without raising an alarm.

"Is there any way I could leave the island tonight?" she queried less casually than she felt.

Tina stopped folding the towel in her hands and looked at Connie. She wondered if she had somehow found out about Deandra and Victor. "Has something happened?" Tina asked, and sat down on the bed. She patted the spot next to her for Connie to sit down as well.

Connie did not want to be drawn into a conversation. If she did enter one, she was afraid she would reveal too much. She stayed rooted to her position by the dresser and replied, "No, nothing's happened. There is an urgent matter I need to take care of at home."

"So you and Victor are leaving now?"

"No, just me. I have to go," she insisted, and willed the tears not to betray her.

Tina rose from the bed and crossed the room. She took Connie's trembling hands in hers, holding them tightly as she spoke. "I can take you into town and you can catch the last ferry, but how are you going to get home from there? It's a three-hour drive. You can't take a cab that far."

"I didn't think of that part. I'll hitch a ride or something," she replied uneasily. She hadn't contemplated any further than getting off the island and away from Victor.

"No matter what has happened, waiting until tomorrow and leaving with the rest of us is best. It's only one more night," Tina stated coaxingly.

"One night too many," Connie mumbled stubbornly, refusing to give up her escape plan.

Realizing whatever was on Connie's mind was troubling her deeply, Tina tried to get her to open up. "Talk to me," she implored.

"I want him out. I want him out of my house and out of my life," she replied vehemently.

"Oh—Victor, you know then . . . ," Tina commented as she incorrectly assumed Victor had confessed. She shook her head in disgust.

"I know what?" Connie looked at her quizzically. "That he's a weasel, a liar, and a user. Yes, I know that. What do you know?"

"Uh, nothing," Tina said rather unconvincingly. Emmett had warned her to keep her mouth shut, but Connie was her friend and she was entitled to know.

"You're a very bad liar, Tina. Is there something else I should know about Victor?" she pressed.

"Well, Emmett told me not to say anything and to mind my own business, but I really wanted to tell you. Then I realized you two were probably breaking up anyway, so it didn't matter. I just didn't want to see you hurt anymore."

"What happened?" Connie asked, not at all liking the direction this was taking. She was getting nervous inside.

"Victor and Deandra," Tina spat angrily.

Connie felt a tightening in her chest as a foreboding sense of not knowing what was coming, but needing to hear the words anyway, crept up her spine.

"I walked in on Victor and Deandra yesterday afternoon," Tina continued.

"Doing what?"

Tina looked at her friend, her eyes imploring her not to make her continue. She derived no pleasure from being the one to tell her. She didn't like reliving the scene in her mind either— a clear vision of Victor's naked ass pumping frantically between Deandra's spread thighs flashed before her eyes. She shook her head and shuddered with revulsion. "They were both in the laundry room in the back of the house and I opened the door and saw them."

"Doing what? Kissing? What?" Connie nearly screamed in her anxiety.

"They were having sex," Tina answered quickly.

Connie could feel the blood leaving her face. The coldness started at her forehead and moved slowly down her body until her fingertips felt numb. Even though she somehow knew this is what Tina was going to tell her, it was different once the words were spoken. Bile tried to force its way from her stomach, up through her throat, and into her mouth.

Swallowing hard, she gasped, "Are you sure?"

"I may be old, but I ain't that damn old I don't recognize it when I see it. Yes, they were having sex on the floor in my damn laundry room of all places." Tina responded indignantly to the doubt in Connie's voice.

The events of the evening were beginning to fall in place for Connie. "He knew you would tell me. That's why he suggested he would move out," she laughed bitterly. "How fucking noble of him. Oh, I hate that man!" she screamed aloud.

"I'm sorry. I thought that was why you were in a hurry to leave."

Connie flopped down on the side of the bed. "No, he said some rather nasty things about me earlier and I just wanted to go home and put all his shit in the street before he got home. I didn't want to endure watching him pack and listen to his mouth the whole time he did. Now I just want to burn it all."

"Well, honey, this ain't the movies, so there will be none of that. Do you want Emmett and me to come home with you?"

"No, I've got until tomorrow to think of something." She grimaced. Marshall's face flashed across her mind and she suddenly realized he also needed to know. "Oh, my God, did anyone tell Marshall?" she asked.

"Tell Marshall what?" Marshall asked from the stairwell.

Startled, Tina and Connie looked quickly at one another and instantaneously came up with the same response. "Nothing," they gushed in unison.

"It didn't sound like nothing to me," he replied, and looked from one to the other for an answer.

"Well, then, you shouldn't make a habit of sneaking up on other people's conversations," Tina joked, and quickly changed the subject. "What brings you up here?"

"Emmett wanted to ask you about some things in the garage—if you want to keep them or not. So I came to find you." He accurately guessed their conversation had something to do with Deandra, but he decided to let it rest for now.

"Okay, you can tell him I'll be down in a few minutes," Tina replied.

Marshall took one last look at Connie. She was clearly disturbed by something. He wouldn't pry now, but he wanted to let her know he was done with Deandra. He wanted to admit he'd made a mistake, and then see if she planned to stay with Victor. Although, from what he'd observed, he was almost certain her relationship with Victor was over. He turned without a word and went back down the stairs.

"Whew!" Tina said as she breathed a sigh of relief. "I know he has to find out sooner or later, but I'd rather Emmett told him than me."

"I agree with you. I'm going down to my room for a while if you should need me," Connie offered, and then took the stairs to the first level and headed for her bedroom.

In her bedroom Connie sat down in the chair next to the window. She reflected on the recent events. This week had turned into a total disaster. Instead of reconnecting with Victor, their time together showed they were not meant to be together. However, she'd known that since shortly after they started dating. She allowed him to show blatant disregard for her feelings, whenever he felt like flirting with other women. Why had she put up with his behavior and prolonged the inevitable? It wasn't the sex, although sex with Victor had been exciting and fun in the beginning. However, something happened a few months ago that had turned him angry and bitter. Whatever it was, he took those feelings out on her. She should have ended the relationship a long time ago, and then she could have avoided this latest humiliation. Deandra once again couldn't keep her legs closed to any man within arm's reach. She may have changed her name, but not her tactics. No man was off-limits. She could only hope Marshall would wake up and realize with what kind of woman he was in love.

Restless, she made her way downstairs. The living room was empty, so she was able to go out the front door unnoticed. The porch swing looked inviting and she eased back into its wooden frame to relax in the late-afternoon breeze.

Connie wasn't sure how long she'd been out there when she heard a rustling nearby. She opened her eyes as Marshall climbed the steps to the porch and sat on the railing opposite the swing.

"You look tired, Connie," he said.

"I guess I am. This week has worn me out in more ways than one," she replied, and gave him a weak smile.

"Is it anything that I can help you with?" Marshall inquired. He knew it had been as trying a week for her as it had been for him.

Sure, you can dump that guttersnipe and take me away from here, she thought. "No, but thanks for asking. I told you before I didn't think my relationship with Victor would last. Well, it's over, finished, kaput," she replied.

"It probably comes as no surprise to you, but my relationship with Deandra is also over. As a matter of fact, I told her last night."

Last night? Before or after you humped her brains out? Connie wondered bitterly as she recalled Deandra's passionate cries. She looked away from Marshall, and quietly replied, "I wouldn't have guessed after her . . ." She stopped when she realized she was going too far. "I'm sorry. It's none of my business," she finished abruptly.

"I've made mistakes, Connie. I think we can agree that we both have," he answered simply. He stopped the swing and pulled her to her feet.

She didn't resist when he pulled her close to his chest and embraced her. A tear trickled down her cheek. Why couldn't Marshall have realized three years ago how much she loved him and needed him? Why did he make love to her and then leave her to be with women like Deandra? Leave her to be preyed upon by the Victors and the leeches. She wanted to push him away, but she could hear his heart beating steadily beneath her ear. His body was warm and solid.

He tilted her chin up with his palm and planted a soft kiss on her lips. When he tasted the saltiness of her tears, he stepped back. "I'm so sorry, Connie," he whispered before claiming her mouth with his.

She melted in his arms as his tongue slipped between her lips and she hungrily welcomed the sweetness therein. He held her tightly as he caressed her back with one hand and cupped her jaw with the other. Her body began to tingle in ways she hadn't experienced in a long time. When he slipped his hand under her shirt and touched her bare waist, she pulled away. She'd never wanted him more than she did right now and her body was moist and ready to reconnect with him. Yet, if she gave in to that, she would be no better than Deandra. She'd already made love to Marshall when he was attached to another woman. She would not do it again.

"I can't do this, Marshall, not again, not like this," she cried, and turned away.

"You're right. I owe you more than this. You deserve better than this heat-of-the-moment passion," he said as he reached out for her hand. "I promise you, Connie. This time I will make it right." He kissed her cheek and squeezed her hand before he entered the cabin and left her alone with her thoughts.

* * *

Deandra stood deathly still with her back pressed against the side of the cabin. She'd been about to go around the front when she heard voices. When she peeked around the corner of the cabin, she'd seen the two of them locked in a passionate kiss. First shock, then horror, and finally rage filled her being. She'd known CJ was after Marshall all along. That witch had been waiting for Deandra to make a mistake, and she'd made a mistake or two. Damn that Chuy! He always did know where to find her hot button. If she hadn't gotten caught fucking him, she wouldn't be in this mess. Now CJ was going to end up with everything she'd ever wanted. *You will not get away with this CJ, not this time. Marshall James belongs to me and I will see you dead first,* she silently vowed as she clenched her fists. No one had told Marshall about the incident yet. If she could prevent him from finding out, maybe she could salvage the relationship.

She took a deep breath and walked around to the front porch. Connie was still standing at the rail, deep in thought. Deandra smiled up at her.

"Hey, Connie, it's a beautiful afternoon and I was thinking of taking a walk. I just saw you there and wondered if you'd like to come along? I'd hate to get lost, and you're more familiar with the area," Deandra asked with forced cheerfulness.

"Thanks, but I'm okay right here," Connie replied, suddenly suspicious of Deandra's friendly demeanor. She now knew she was dealing with Andie Moore.

"Please let bygones be bygones. I know I haven't been the greatest cabin mate this week, but we may be seeing a lot of each other in the future. So we can at least be cordial, right?" Deandra said as she continued to coax her into joining her.

Connie remembered that Marshall had already told Deandra the relationship was over. She obviously wasn't accepting "no" for an answer. Connie decided to go on the walk to see what

Deandra had up her sleeve. Maybe she would be able to warn Marshall. She walked down the steps and followed Deandra toward the path leading into the woods.

When Arlene had decided to join Viola for dinner, she'd packed a small overnight case to stay over at the resort hotel with Viola. The two women freely imbibed several bottles of champagne during the evening, since neither had to drive anywhere. By the time they retired to Viola's room, any qualms they might have had were dissolved as they rekindled their friendship. Their trust of one another allowed them to openly and honestly discuss the past. They swore each other to secrecy with a toast before the discussion got serious.

Viola was the first to divulge her secret. Thirty-five years ago she'd had an affair with a man she'd met while her husband was on a business trip. It started out as simple flirtation with a man she'd met at the market. She was enormously flattered by the attention. The memories of the special romance flooded back into her mind.

She was twenty-five years old. She and Edward had been married for three years. He'd been her first and only love since high school. However, in an effort to establish his business, he was away from home frequently and spent many late nights at the office.

She'd gone to the local market one day for groceries. Her cart was filled with all manner of food items when she stopped at the flower stand to admire the beautiful arrangements displayed.

She reached out for a particularly colorful bouquet of orange lilies, pink tulips, yellow orchids, purple freesia, and baby's breath. A man brushed past her and quickly swooped in and grabbed the arrangement before she could say anything. She was stunned at how rude he was as he briskly walked away with her flowers. It had been obvious she was going to at least take a closer look at them. She looked around at the other arrangements and was disappointed to see that had been the only one of its type. Disappointed, she pushed her cart toward the checkout line. After she'd paid for her groceries, she left the store and headed for her car. She loaded all her purchases into the trunk and was about to close it when she turned around to find the same rude man approaching her. She slammed the trunk of the car and pushed the cart to the front of the parking space so she could exit. When she returned to the driver's-side door, he was standing behind the car. What did he want now? It never occurred to her that he could be dangerous—only that he was getting on her nerves.

"Unless you are planning on getting run over this morning, I suggest you move," she said, and opened the car door.

"I wanted to apologize," he said, and began to walk closer to her.

"Apologize for what?" she demanded angrily as she tossed her purse on the seat next to her.

"For being in such a rush to get those flowers, I may have seemed a bit rude," he replied, and moved closer still.

"A bit rude?" Viola said, and laughed nervously as she took note of how attractive he was as he came closer. He was rather tall, with a warm brown complexion, and clean shaven, no facial hair. His eyes were light brown with tiny flecks of gold and his mouth was curving into a smile as he submitted to her inspection. "You know I was looking at those flowers first."

"Yes, I did know," he replied. His voice was deep and belied a hint of an accent.

"Then why did you take them?" she asked, thoroughly curious and growing a bit warm under his unwavering gaze.

"Because a woman as beautiful as you are should never have to buy flowers for herself," he said, and brought the bouquet from behind his back and handed it to her.

"Oh!" She gasped at the romantic gesture and accepted the bouquet she'd coveted only minutes earlier. "You bought these for me?"

"Yes, because you are the most beautiful woman I've seen today. I was irresistibly compelled to give those to you myself," he said, and smiled warmly. "Am I forgiven for my earlier uncharacteristically rude behavior?" he asked.

She pressed the bouquet to her face and breathed deeply of its aromatic sweetness. She was flattered, and the attention of this handsome stranger made her feel giddy in a way she'd never experienced before.

"Yes, and please accept my apology for being rather sharp with you. This is a wonderfully nice gesture on your part. Thank you," she replied.

"It was my pleasure," he replied as he tipped an imaginary hat and walked away.

Viola wanted to stop him to ask his name or something, but she soon acknowledged there was nothing she could do anyway. After all, she was a married woman. She pressed the bouquet close to her heart and sighed as she got into her car to go home.

She didn't see him again for about a month—although she'd look for him every time she'd enter the market. One day she saw him exiting the market as she was driving in. She honked her horn to get his attention and was rewarded with the gorgeous smile she'd seen the first time. He waited for her to park the car and then approached.

"Good afternoon, beautiful lady. It is nice to see you again," he said as he opened her car door to assist her out.

"It's nice to see you again as well," she replied, stepping out of the car. "My name is Viola," she said, and extended her hand in greeting. She half-expected him to raise it to his lips for a kiss, but he clasped it gently in his.

"My name is Grant Carlisle," he replied. "Viola is a lovely

name. I don't wish to be overly forward, but I must admit to stopping at this market almost daily, hoping for a glimpse of you. Now that you have crossed my path again, I'm reluctant to walk away without knowing when I will see you again."

"Grant, I don't know if it is proper for us . . . ," she started. The idea of not seeing him again was troubling her as well. She was intrigued by his gentlemanly mannerisms. His proper and clipped speech pattern was enormously arousing. She wondered where he was from.

"I'm not suggesting anything untoward, I promise you. Just the opportunity to see you now and again would be enough," he replied as he pulled a business card from his wallet. "I am not blind and I can see you are married, so I only ask that you take my business card. If you ever feel the need, or perhaps an occasional desire, to speak with me, call."

She accepted the card from him. It would be nice to be able to talk to him on occasion. There was nothing wrong with that, she convinced herself. She took the card and slipped it inside her purse. "Thank you, Grant. I can't promise to use it, but I do thank you for the offer," she said with an engaging smile.

Once again he tipped his imaginary hat and walked away. Viola watched as he strolled through the parking lot. The loose-fitting jeans he wore did not disguise his well-formed buttocks. His short-sleeved shirt was tucked into the waistband of his pants and showed his trim waistline. Muscular arms bulged under the sleeves. He wore casual but expensive loafers. As she watched the fluid movements of his confident stride, Viola couldn't help but wonder what he would be like in bed.

She was not overwhelmingly surprised to see him stop next to a late-model midnight blue Lexus sedan. The shiny silver rims accented the dark blue of the sleek and clean auto. She continued to watch as he pulled out of the spot and exited the parking lot. Sighing deeply, she started to get back into her car when she realized she had yet to buy the groceries she had come for.

Viola took his business card out of her wallet several times the following week, but always returned it without making a call. Temptation was a powerful force to be reckoned with, and Viola, an often-neglected wife, found herself losing the battle. By the end of the second week, she could resist no longer. She retrieved the business card from her purse and called the number listed. A secretary answered and informed her that Mr. Carlisle was in a meeting—would she care to leave a message?

"No, no message. Thank you," she said, and placed the receiver back on its base. She was disappointed, enormously so.

Two days later she ran into him at the market. She'd seen him as she approached the checkout line. He was standing near the flower display and was smiling at her. Her heart fluttered like it had grown wings and a thousand tiny butterflies danced in her stomach. She smiled in return as she steered her cart in his direction.

"You do realize that I have been rooted to this spot for the last two days waiting for you to come by," he said, and fell in step beside her. "I'm sorry I missed your call the other day."

"I could ask how you knew it was me, but I'm not good at being coy," she replied as she gazed up at him. He was more handsome than she remembered.

"That's a good thing. Coy women or those who spend more time on pretense than on real emotions bore me," he said as he pointed to the floral displays and asked, "What suits your fancy today, madam?"

Viola perused the assortment of colorful flowers and selected one with an array of tropical flowers in deep oranges, reds, and yellows. "I like this one," she said, and ignored the voice in her mind that cautioned her about how comfortable she'd become with him so fast.

They paid for their respective items at the checkout and

Grant assisted her loading her items in the trunk. She watched the muscles flexing in his arms as he arranged the bags. Her body involuntarily flexed a few of its own muscles in a very secret place. They hadn't spoken since they'd left the store, but it wasn't an uncomfortable silence.

He stood up slowly, as though he were pondering something very troubling. A frown briefly puckered his brow. Then he smiled, almost whimsically.

She stood by the car and watched the play of emotions on his face as she waited for him to say something, anything. She didn't budge when he leaned down and pressed his cheek to hers. The texture of his skin was smooth and warm as it rested momentarily next to hers. She held her breath as he turned his head ever so slightly and pressed his lips to her jaw, just below her earlobe.

"Call me," he whispered, and then he was gone.

Viola stood stock-still, rooted to that spot and to that moment in time. There was an aching desire in her body created by the simplest of kisses. She stayed there for a few seconds more, unable to shake the feelings overtaking her. She was wading into a dangerous arena, drawn by an irresistible lure. A cool breeze blew through the area, startling her out of her reverie. She slowly got in the car and headed home.

She called Grant the next day. It started out as a call every few days, but soon they progressed to speaking almost daily. He was funny and worldly, unlike anyone she'd ever met. The only time she couldn't speak with him was if he was out of town. On occasion they would bump into one another at the market, but Viola refused to see him in any other venue. He was a friend, and as much as she was physically attracted to him, she was determined to be a good wife to Edward. Grant never pressed for more than the time they spent on the phone. He respected her wishes.

* * *

Viola sighed and got up from the bed to look out the window. She smiled at Arlene. "He was the most romantic man I'd ever met," she said wistfully, and sighed.

"So what happened?" Arlene asked as she stretched on top of the bed and reached for her glass of champagne.

Viola came back to the bed and sat down on the corner to continue her story. "One day a package addressed to me arrived at the house. It was a diamond necklace in the shape of a heart. The inscription on the card said, *I will forever celebrate the day you were born—Happy birthday to the love of my life.* It was signed by my husband, Edward, a man who didn't have a romantic bone in his body," Viola said, and took a sip of champagne.

"Wow! But that was so romantic," Arlene exclaimed.

"It wasn't my birthday," Viola said dryly. "Apparently, his secretary or the jeweler or some damn body got the addresses mixed up. Or maybe they just wanted me to know what good ole Edward was up to."

"Oh my, Viola," Arlene said, and sighed with empathy.

"Well, I immediately called Grant, crying hysterically. Here I was keeping the faith and my legs closed to all but my husband and the joke was on me. Edward was screwing around and spending our money on some other woman. I told Grant I was leaving Edward."

"What did he say?"

"He said that I was understandably upset, but I should not react in haste. I should give Edward a chance to explain."

"I screamed at him and told him I wasn't about to sit through any more of Edward's lies. I hung up with him and immediately packed a few bags and drove out to the airport. Girl, I didn't have any clue where I was going. I just had cash and credit cards and I was getting out of town."

* * *

Viola closed her eyes as she remembered that day vividly. She was sitting at the airport terminal crying. She had no idea where to go or what to do when she got there. They hadn't traveled much and Edward always handled everything. Desperate, she'd called Grant again. In less than an hour he was at the airport, suitcase in hand. She rushed into his arms the moment he came through the terminal door. His solid chest provided the comfort she was seeking and she pressed close to his body.

He kissed her tearstained cheeks and instructed her to go freshen up while he purchased their tickets. They boarded a flight bound for San Francisco. The first leg of the trip would take them through New Jersey for a quick stopover and then on to California. Seated comfortably in first class, Viola relaxed and was finally able to tell Grant coherently what had occurred. He empathized with her distressed state and his comfortable shoulder soon became a pillow as exhaustion caught up with her and she drifted off to sleep.

She slept soundly through the first leg and halfway through the second leg of the trip. Luckily, the plane from Florida was the same aircraft that would take them to California and they did not have to deplane in Newark.

She resumed her story for Arlene. "When we finally arrived at the hotel in San Francisco, the first thing I wanted to do was make love with him. He refused. He said he did not want to be the receptacle for my revenge. I needed time to clear my head and make an informed choice to be with him. He was so damned smart, it made me angry. I was already mad at Edward and I didn't want to be mad at Grant too. I hated it, because I knew he was right.

"We spent a week in San Francisco doing all those touristy things. We walked across the Golden Gate Bridge, and we went wine tasting in the Napa Valley. We even hiked through Muir

Woods. That was truly amazing. Then we left there and drove down to LA. We stayed at the Ritz-Carlton in Marina del Rey. That's where we made love for the first time."

Viola closed her eyes and was back in the Ritz for one magical moment. They'd arrived around midday and checked in. The bellman assisted them up to their room. She was standing at the window, staring out at the marina, when Grant walked up behind her. He placed his hands on her shoulders.

"Are you okay, my love?" he asked. He'd begun using the term of endearment a few days earlier. They'd had a wonderful adventure up to this point. He knew that reality would soon invade this fantasy. She was, after all, still married, and he didn't think her husband, regardless of his infidelity, was planning on giving up his wife.

"I'm fine," she replied, and patted his hand gently before walking away from the window.

"Something is on your mind?" he queried as he took in her restless posture.

"We've been together for a week and you've yet to make love to me. Is there something wrong?" she asked. They'd been sleeping in separate beds, and the more time she spent with him, the more she'd come to care for him. She wanted to share the intimacy of lovemaking with him.

"There's nothing wrong at all," he said with a laugh. "Don't think it's been easy for me to sleep in the same room with you and not breach the space between these beds, but I need to be sure this is what you want. I am not the one who is legally bound to someone else. Once I make love to you, you will not be able to pretend it never happened," he added wisely.

"That legal commitment is only a matter of time. I am through with him. I want you. I want you in every way that I can have you," she boldly admitted, and began to unbutton her blouse.

"No, do not undress yet," he said, and put up his hand to stop her.

She looked perplexed, but complied with his request. She waited patiently to see what he would do.

Grant closed the curtains and crossed the room to her side. He gently pulled her toward the bed and sat down on the edge of the mattress. There he began to slowly and methodically unbutton her blouse.

She watched his long, slim fingers as he undid each button. When her blouse was completely undone, he'd put his hands around her bare waist and pulled her closer. He slipped the blouse off her shoulders and tossed it into a nearby chair. Then he placed his cheek against hers; slowly turning his lips to her earlobe, he pulled the soft flesh into his mouth.

She shuddered in anticipation as his lips blazed a trail from her neck to the valley between her breasts. He blew lightly on the moist trail left behind, and her inner muscles contracted.

"Have I told you today that you are the most beautiful woman I know?" he whispered as his hand cupped her breast and she cried aloud. He slipped his tongue inside the lacy rim of her bra and swirled it around her nipple. She buckled slightly as her legs turned to jelly.

She didn't even feel him unsnap the hook on her bra and barely noticed as he eased the straps off her shoulder, leaving her breasts exposed. He cupped his hand under her breast and brought the smooth brown tit to his mouth. Covering it completely, he sucked gently.

His free hand was on the small of her back and he easily slipped it inside her waistband and it eased down the narrow crack of her ass. He pressed his finger firmly against her anus and she felt a rush of fluid between her thighs. He stopped holding her breast long enough to unzip her pants and slide them down over her hips. With ease he lifted her up and laid her in the middle of the bed. Clothed only in satin bikini panties, she anxiously awaited his disrobing.

Grant appreciated the slow unveiling of Viola's gifts and he was determined to give her the same pleasure as he took his time undressing. The rippled abdominals were no surprise, but for her they were a joy to behold. His manhood was already firm and erect when he slipped out of his boxers. His chest was broad, his hips narrow, his thighs strong, and his dick thick and long.

Viola audibly expressed her pleasure under her breath and he joined her on the bed. He started at her breasts once more, teasing them into an aroused state. Then he continued his path down her midsection to the top of her satin panties. With his teeth he pulled her panties down her hips and then buried his face in the curly patch of exposed hair. He used his hands to slide her panties all the way off, and then spread her legs to slip his tongue inside her sweetness.

Tears crested at the corners of her eyes as he tasted every crevice and valley of her body. He teased the tiny pink throbbing bulb with his tongue and then gently nibbled on it with his lips. When he slipped his finger inside her passion at the same time, she came violently. She thrashed wildly about the bed and screamed aloud.

He eased his way up her body again and kissed her passionately. He did not miss the tears. "Have I hurt you?" he asked. When she shook her head, he asked another question. "Have you ever had an orgasm before?"

Viola shook her head. She did not know what had just happened. It hadn't happened before, and at the moment the only thing on her mind was the painful, unfulfilled ache between her legs. "Grant, please," she whispered urgently.

When he eased between her legs and inside her body, he could feel the tension flow from her body as she accepted him. She raised her hips to meet his as he pushed his full length into her sweet depths. Together they found a rhythm that worked best for them and, with a slowly increasing tempo, pushed themselves to an incredible simultaneous climax.

Viola shuddered as she recalled that first sexual experience with Grant. She learned so much during the time she'd spent with him.

"He was an amazing lover. Not like my old stick-in-the-mud, Edward."

"But you and Edward stayed together," Arlene said.

"Yes, you see there was an image to be maintained. While Edward thought it was entirely appropriate for him to have a mistress, the idea of me seeking a lover drove him over the edge. He hunted me down and waited until I was alone. Grant was in the hotel taking care of some business. I stepped out of the hotel and Edward basically abducted me right off the street. He literally dragged me back home. Once we got back to the house, he beat me pretty badly and locked me in our bedroom. He told everyone I was in Rio on vacation when I was actually in the house recuperating for weeks. Two weeks later I discovered I was pregnant. I prayed that it was Grant's, because I knew Edward's pride wouldn't allow him to accept the child if it wasn't his. I would be free then. He avoided me the whole pregnancy. When Marshall was born, and turned out to be the spitting image of Edward, it was a turning point in our relationship. He couldn't do enough to reward me for giving him a son. He never hit me or strayed again, and neither did I, but it was never the same for me. Something in me had died the day that necklace arrived," Viola said.

"Damn, Vi. Seems everyone has some kind of skeleton in their closet. What happened to the necklace?"

"I still have it. It's locked away in a safety-deposit box. One day I may just give it to Goodwill," she replied.

"And Grant, what happened to him?" Arlene asked.

"Grant never wanted to be responsible for breaking up a family. When he found out I was pregnant, he let me know he'd be there for me if the child was his. He was as disappointed as I was when it wasn't. I didn't hear from him again until after Edward died. We see each other occasionally now," Viola said with a smile.

"Is it the same?" Arlene asked.

"Oh yes," Viola said, and smiled. "It's still the same."

"Well, you already know part of my secret, but I'll tell you the biggest humiliation of it all. It was covered up so well, it was like it never even happened," Arlene said as she rose from the bed and placed her glass on the desk. She leaned against the desk and began to recount her own dirty secret.

"I loved Carlton, like no other man in the world. He was handsome, charming, and, as you've stated, a brilliant surgeon with a bright future. It was a shame that he died so young. I mean, he was only forty-two at the time of his death. He died of a heart attack at forty-two years old. He was a doctor, for crying out loud!" she exclaimed, and then took a deep breath to calm her nerves.

"Carlton told me he was working late at the hospital. Connie was just about to graduate from high school and she'd already had that disastrous slumber party. I got a call at home from a woman whose voice I did not recognize. It was hard to understand her at first, because of all the sniveling and crying she was doing. She told me to come to a hotel in Royal Palm and that my husband was seriously ill. I asked what he was doing there and she just kept crying and telling me to come fast."

Viola sat on the bed, shaking her head. She could almost guess where this story was going. Still, like someone watching an approaching train wreck, she couldn't turn away.

"I called our attorney and went straight to the hotel. When I got there, I found that whore and my husband, my obviously deceased husband. He was lying naked and ass up in the middle of the bed, and she was wrapped in a sheet in the corner, crying. That sniveling little bitch didn't even have the decency to put his fucking clothes back on. She didn't even have the sense to put her own damn clothes on. My husband of twenty years died of a heart attack while screwing that filthy piece of trash. I had no idea until that moment that he was still involved with her. After all those years when I stood by him, he was still sneaking around fucking her. I lost my mind temporarily. I couldn't kill Carlton, so I did my best to beat the living shit out of her. The only thing that stopped me from killing her was my attorney, who arrived just in time and grabbed my arm as I was about to put her lights out with the damn clock radio."

"Arlene, I had no idea," Viola said as she now understood the trauma her friend had been through.

"My attorney took care of everything. It pays to have money, lots of money. Prominent heart surgeon dies of heart attack while . . . ," Arlene started.

". . . while trying to assist domestic violence victim. The name of the victim was never released and her attacker was never caught," Viola finished for her as she recalled the gist of the story when Carlton died. "Remind me never to mess with you," she added to lighten the mood.

"After that, I buried my husband as was befitting a man of his stature and lived in that mansion for two more years. I nearly drank myself into oblivion. I have Connie to thank for getting me together. She came by one day, gathered me up, and took me to Key West for two weeks. I've never looked back. This is where I needed to be, to regain control of my life."

"You didn't sell the house, did you?" Viola inquired.

"No, that's Connie's house, whenever she is ready for it. She says it's too big right now."

The women had talked some more, then finally settled in for the night.

*   *   *

Deandra was quiet as they followed the path into the woods. Even though sounds of nature were all around them, Deandra couldn't hear anything but the hollowness of her thoughts. She surmised Tina had probably told Connie about catching her with Victor. The reality of the loss of Marshall and the lush lifestyle she had been living as his girlfriend was finally setting in. She pictured the house, the cars, and the endless flow of money she would have had as his wife. Her head began to throb intensely as she refused to believe she'd lost it all. She didn't want to go back to her old life—back to lying on her back to put food on the table and keep a roof over her head. The only person standing in her way was walking beside her now. She watched as Connie strolled through the woods, checking out the scenery like they were on a nature hike or something. She slowed her steps to fall in line behind her old enemy.

Connie was quite aware of everything that was going on around her. She knew exactly when Deandra's steps slowed down. She knew how deep they'd gone into the woods and how to get back to the cabin. When Deandra's footfalls stopped behind her, Connie immediately turned around, prepared for a confrontation. Deandra stared at her menacingly.

"I never thought I would be the type of woman who would rather see her boyfriend dead than with another woman. I know you have been getting cozier and cozier with Marshall and you won't have him, Constance Jefferson. I swear you won't get everything I've been working for."

"Andie, I am not trying to take Marshall away from you. If things are going wrong between you, you have no one to blame but yourself. You were screwing my boyfriend while we were all sleeping under the same roof. You haven't changed a bit since high school. You still can't resist climbing on the nearest available dick, no matter what it costs you. Well, you've screwed one too many this time. I wasn't going to tell Marshall, but this little game of yours is up."

"Andie? My name is Deandra! You never could be trusted, CJ. You ruined my life once. You don't get to do it again."

"*I* ruined your life? Everything that has happened to you has been your own fault, Andie. Yes, I remember exactly who you are and what you are. Marshall deserves better than you and he didn't need me to point that out. You've done a great job of it yourself!"

Connie decided their conversation was over and started back toward the cabin. She passed a little too close to Deandra on the path. Deandra grabbed her arm and swung her around and slapped her hard across the cheek.

"Stop lying, you little bitch!" Deandra screamed.

Shocked by the force of the blow, Connie stumbled. She scrambled quickly to her feet as Deandra charged at her. Connie deftly ducked to the side and landed a solid punch in Deandra's midsection, momentarily stunning her. Connie took advantage of the moment and began to run back through the woods toward the cabin. She could hear Deandra coughing as she regained her strength.

Deandra's long legs and form as a runner allowed her to close the gap between the two of them quickly. Soon she was close enough to grab a handful of Connie's hair. She yanked her back off her feet. Connie came up swinging with all her might and the two women threw wild blows at each other. Deandra, the bigger and stronger of the two, momentarily seemed to have the upper hand, but Connie was faster and more nimble than Deandra had anticipated. Connie managed to hook her foot behind Deandra's legs and dropped her on her back before she scampered away. Unfortunately, she didn't realize she'd gotten turned around during the fight and ran off in the opposite direction of the cabin. Deandra, propelled by adrenaline, recovered quickly, tackling Connie as she reached the top of the hill. They fought to their feet again, but by then they had reached the summit of the hill and the ground was starting to crumble away under their feet. Panicked, they stopped fighting long enough to realize the predicament they were in. Deandra suddenly looked frightened.

Alarm registered on Connie's face. She was closest to the edge. Deandra reacted unexpectedly as Connie lost her footing first and began to fall backward over the cliff. Deandra instinctively reached out and grabbed her arm. She held Connie's wrist with all her strength and tried to pull her away from the edge. Seconds later the soft, crumbling earth gave way beneath their feet and they both disappeared over the edge.

Marshall returned to the living room in search of his cell phone and wondered where everyone had gone. Victor strolled in from the kitchen, heading for the bedroom upstairs.

"Have you seen Deandra?" Marshall inquired.

"Yeah, I saw her and Connie going out toward the woods about half an hour ago. That's an unlikely pair." Victor tossed the comment over his shoulder on the way up the stairs.

An unlikely pair, to put it mildly, thought Marshall. He found his cell phone tucked in the couch next to the seat cushion. He'd slept on the couch the other night after the incident with Deandra and only realized the phone was missing in the last hour. He noticed he had two missed calls from his mother. He hoped everything was okay as he pressed her speed dial code.

Viola was reading in bed when the phone finally rang. She prayed it would be Marshall as she quickly reached across the bed to answer it. She picked it up on the second ring and said hello.

"Mom, is everything okay?" Marshall asked.

"Yes, I'm fine. I was checking on you. Why didn't you answer your phone? I called you several times," she replied, and wondered how to get the conversation around to Deandra and Connie.

"I honestly misplaced it. Sorry, I didn't mean to worry

you," he apologized, although he couldn't understand why she would be worried about him. He could hear the strain in her voice and wondered if something was wrong with her.

"Is everything going well, son? Are you all right?"

"Of course, Mom, I'm fine. I'll be home tomorrow. Is there something you needed?" he asked, still not certain the call was as casual as she was trying to make it.

"How's everyone there?" she persisted.

"Well, Tina and Emmett are preparing dinner," he responded, but said no more.

"Where's Deandra?" she asked with feigned interest.

"Mom, what's going on? You could care less where Dee is and I know it. So what's the real reason for your call?"

"Well, I'd really prefer not to discuss it on the phone, but just make sure you don't leave her alone with Connie. Okay?" she replied quickly.

"Don't leave her alone with Connie? What is that about?" he demanded as his heart started to race in his chest. *That's an unlikely pair,* he remembered thinking just moments before.

"I don't want to go into it over the phone, son. It's a long story, just keep them separated until you come home tomorrow," she said urgently.

"Mom, Deandra and Connie are not here. They've taken a walk in the woods out back. You have to tell me what you know," he said with increasing concern.

"There's no time, Marshall, there's no time. You have to find them. Connie's in danger. Deandra's not who she says she is. Go, go now and find them, please!" she cried. Her worst fears were suddenly coming true. Why had she not insisted Arlene call the other night and speak with Connie? They could have averted this impending disaster.

He wanted more answers, but the fear in his mother's voice propelled him from the cabin toward the woods at breakneck speed. He knew his mother was not beyond snooping into people's backgrounds. Something unsavory had come up about Dee, and although he desperately needed to believe she was not dangerous, this whole walk in the woods with Connie was not in character for her.

He followed the path until he could hear raised voices in the distance. As he tuned into the sound, he noticed the voices stopped and the cracking of brush, along with grunts and groans, indicated a tussle of sorts was taking place. He picked up speed as he identified the direction of the noise. He burst into the clearing just as Deandra and Connie disappeared over the edge.

"No!" he screamed as he raced as close to the edge of the hill as he deemed safe. When he peered over the precipice, he was relieved to see the drop was not more than fifteen feet or so. However, Connie's motionless body lay crumpled at the bottom of the incline, while Deandra tried unsteadily to gain her footing, but was unable to stand on a badly sprained ankle. Blood trickled from a gash on her arm as she crawled toward Connie. Marshall watched in horror as Deandra leaned over Connie and peered closely at her face. Her hand came to rest on a large rock near Connie's head.

"Dee!" he yelled to gain her attention, but she did not acknowledge him. Unable to get a signal on his cell phone, Marshall frantically searched for a way down the incline. Deandra leaned on the rock and with her free hand tugged her shirt free of her pants. She then pushed herself up to a seated position and ripped off a corner of her shirt. Rolling it into a ball, she pressed it to the side of Connie's head to stem the flow of blood from a deep cut on the side of her face.

"Dee!" Marshall called again from above to get her attention; she did not respond and he watched in amazement as she tried to cover Connie's wound in an attempt to assist her. His mother had to have been wrong about her. For an instant he'd thought she was going to smash Connie's head with the rock, and the next moment she was helping her. He did not understand what was going on, but he had to get help now and figure it out later. "Dee, I'm going for help. Can you hear me?"

Deandra looked up weakly and nodded. She hadn't intended to kill Connie. Not really. She wanted to scare her and make her go away. Now she'd possibly killed her, and both of their lives would be over. Tears trickled down her cheeks as she brushed bloodied, matted hair away from Connie's pulsing wound. "Why couldn't you just stay out of my life, CJ? Why did you have to make me hurt you?" she wailed as she rocked back and forth anxiously. She hoped Marshall would hurry up.

Marshall burst into the cabin a short time later. He shouted for Emmett and Victor. Tina rushed from the kitchen and he immediately instructed her to call 911. Emmett followed closely on her heels. Tina rushed to the phone and placed the emergency call. When she finished, she turned anxiously to Marshall.

"Is Connie all right?" Tina asked, and couldn't stop wringing her hands nervously with the dish towel. How was she going to explain this to Arlene? If only she hadn't insisted on this whole vacation idea. It had just been one disaster after another.

"I don't know, Tina. She's unconscious and she appears to have a head wound," he said, and when Tina gasped, he quickly added, "It may not be as serious as it looks, but I can't tell from the top of the hill. Deandra is tending to her, but we have to hurry."

Marshall gave Emmett a brief description of the accident from what he'd seen and they raced out to the shed to see if there was anything they could construct as a stretcher or use to hoist the women up from the ditch.

Victor stood on the landing just inside his bedroom door. He'd known something bad was going to happen when those two wandered off. If Andie was tending to Connie, as Marshall stated, then it meant Deandra was the least injured of the two.

It also meant she was okay. He breathed a sigh of relief—Andie was a survivor. His minutes here would be numbered once they rescued the women. He went back into the bedroom to pack his things. He intended to make haste as soon as discreetly possible. Andie would have to fix this mess on her own.

18

Connie remained unconscious as the rescue team prepared her for helicopter transport to the nearest trauma center in Gainesville. Deandra was taken by water ambulance to a local hospital to have her less serious injuries checked out. Tina and Emmett closed up the cabin, while Marshall prepared the boat for the trip across the lake to the mainland. With bags in hand, Victor waited on the dock to leave with the rest of them.

In less than an hour they were headed across the lake and back to their cars on the mainland. Tina and Emmett were going to Gainesville to check on Connie. Marshall had to stop at the local hospital to check on Deandra. Victor did not say much of anything, and they were all surprised when he got into his car and headed south. It was a clear indication he was headed back to south Florida and did not care about what happened to Connie.

Marshall was deeply worried about Connie, but he knew his first responsibility was to Deandra, since he'd brought her to the island. The other important fact was that she was the only one who really knew what had happened out in the woods, and he wanted details. He hadn't thought to call his mother back, because he'd been too focused on the rescue efforts. He couldn't get his mind off Connie and the fear that she could die as a result of her injury. The fact that she had not regained consciousness at all was not a good sign. He debated whether or not to call his mother and decided it would be better to wait until he had more information to tell her.

He arrived at the hospital about fifteen minutes later and went straight to the emergency desk to inquire about Deandra. He found her behind a small curtain in the treatment area. He was glad to see she did not look too bad for her experience.

She looked up woefully when he entered the room. The relief she initially felt when he appeared quickly vanished as she remembered he would have a lot of questions regarding what had happened to Connie.

"Is Connie okay?" she asked, nervously rubbing her hands along her dirt-stained jeans.

"I really don't know. We'll have to go and see as soon as they release you. Have you been seen yet?" he replied.

"Yes, I'm waiting for them to put an Aircast on my ankle and give me some painkillers before I can go. The rest is just a few cuts and bruises. Nothing a little makeup won't hide," she said, trying to lighten the heavily weighted atmosphere.

Marshall was too worried about Connie to respond, and his mind quickly shifted to the road trip ahead of him. He could call a car to take Dee home and make the trip to Gainesville on his own, but questions needed to be asked and answered. He wasn't letting her out of his sight until he was clear about the nature of the accident. They'd been fighting—of that he was certain. His phone buzzed again and he looked down to see his mother's number. It was her third call in the last hour. He couldn't avoid her anymore.

"Hello," he answered, and excused himself from the treatment area. He walked toward the exit door for privacy.

"Marshall, I've been frantic with worry. What is going on out there?" Viola demanded.

"There was an accident, Mom," he started to say, but stopped at her sharp intake of breath on the other end of the line. He waited a moment, but she did not say anything. "Connie has been hurt and I'm going up to Gainesville to check on her within the hour."

"Going . . . within the hour. . . . Why are you not with her now?" Viola demanded.

"I'm at the hospital with Deandra. She was hurt as well," Marshall replied as calmly as possible. He did not want to alarm his mother and he couldn't provide her any details. Suddenly he remembered it was her warning that alerted him to the trouble. He wanted to know what she knew. "Mom, what do you know about this situation? Why did you think Connie was in danger?" he asked.

"I'm sorry, Marshall, but something about that woman you are seeing did not sit well with me. You know this. So I hired a private investigator to do just a little checking around," she said almost apologetically.

"I know, Mom. That's another story. What did you find out?" he asked.

"Deandra Morgan is not her real name. Her real name is Andrea Moore and she's a bit of a con artist, amongst a few other things. She has a police record, mostly misdemeanor issues, but still a police record! It's probably best that we discuss the details in person. What hospital has Connie been taken to?" she asked.

His head began to swim with all the information his mother had already provided. He didn't need any more drama at the moment. He slowly digested the news and started back into the hospital. He needed to get on the road. Deandra was not her name and she had a criminal record. *Why am I only mildly surprised to hear this?*

"She was taken to the trauma center at Shands."

"Fine, I will meet you there in a few hours," Viola said.

"Mom, that's not necessary. Whatever else you have can wait until I get home," he replied, and stopped walking just as he reached the curtain where he'd left Deandra. He paused outside the privacy barrier to finish his conversation.

"No, Marshall. I'm sorry, but this can't wait. I'll see you at Shands," she said, and hung up, leaving him no opportunity to debate the issue.

Marshall shoved his cell phone into the clip on his belt and stepped through the curtain. Deandra was testing her weight on an Aircast on her ankle. The nurse handed her a pair of crutches and some packets of painkillers.

"All my paperwork has been taken care of," Deandra said as she propelled herself forward on the crutches. "I'm ready to leave."

"Okay, fine," he replied, and opened the curtain for her to precede him down the hall toward the exit. When they reached the exit, he instructed her to wait there for him to bring the car around.

Marshall had been attentive to her since the accident, but she detected a distinct reserve in his manner since he'd arrived. She knew his mind was on Connie and her more serious injuries, so she decided it was best not to agitate him. She saw his car as it approached and he got out and assisted her into it. He placed her crutches on the backseat and got back into the car without uttering a word.

The drive to Shands was a long, silent one as both occupants of the car were deep in thought. Deandra wondered what had happened to Victor. She also wondered what would become of her if and when Connie regained consciousness.

Marshall was stewing in the newfound information his mother had provided. Who was this woman seated next to him? He'd always found her secretive and evasive about her past, but a criminal record and an alias were beyond anything he would have imagined. "What's your real name?" he asked without looking at her.

Startled by the unexpected question, Deandra hesitated to answer him. "What are you talking about?"

"Do you think it is appropriate to continue this masquerade?" he asked, and looked across at her pointedly.

She turned away quickly as tears stung the back of her eyes. He knew. How could he know already? She remained stubbornly silent. Connie hadn't had an opportunity, and surely, Victor would never have betrayed her.

"Who is Andrea Moore?" he asked, and refused to be ignored. Deandra remained silent, so he continued. "I heard she is a con artist and petty thief. That could explain some of the things that have gone missing around my home."

Deandra bristled at the insinuation that she had stolen from him. She hadn't needed to steal from him. He'd given her more than she could have dreamed. "I never stole so much as a dime from you, Marshall James, and you know it," she hissed angrily.

"Why all the lies, Deandra?" he asked as his anger at this whole fiasco reached a constant simmer. All of the "if only" scenarios jockeyed for prominence in his brain. If only he hadn't brought her to the island. If only he'd listened to his mother that night at the gallery, instead of his dick. If only he'd stopped seeing Dee when she paraded around naked on his boat and embarrassed him the very first time. If only he'd hooked up with Connie three years ago, instead of blowing off that afternoon in the shed and letting her get away from him. "If only" was not going to erase what happened this afternoon. It was not going to make Connie suddenly and miraculously well. This was his fault and he was going to have to live with the consequences.

"Would you have looked twice at a woman with my past? I

can answer that for you. The answer is no. You would not have given me the time of day. Yet, you met me under circumstances you felt comfortable in. So you believed what you wanted to believe. I simply went along with your game plan."

"My game plan? Who do you think you are kidding? I've gone along with your little charade simply because you amused me. You're a beautiful woman and no one can take that away from you. But the real truth of the matter is I enjoyed fucking you. That's it in a nutshell. Well, maybe a little bit of it was the fun of ticking my mother off, but you were never in consideration for a long-term commitment. Sure, I toyed with the idea that you would one day confide in me. Perhaps let me help you, but you didn't want that. You became a major embarrassment to me with your unexplainable behavior. You wanted my money and you thought I was going to be gullible enough to give it to you. Marriage was never on the table."

"You have no idea what you're talking about, Marshall. You have no clue about me or my life." She wanted to strike out at him for being so callous and unfeeling toward her. Her fists were coiled tightly in her lap.

"Do you want to hit me, Dee? Is that what you did to Connie? Lashed out at her and pushed her over the cliff? Were you planning on adding murderer to your long list of talents?" he demanded.

She turned away from him. She would not continue this discussion. Hurting Connie had been an accident. It was not the end result she'd been looking for. Yes, she had momentarily wondered what it would be like without Connie around. Still, she had only intended to rough her up a little bit and make her stay away from Marshall. Connie turned out to be tougher than she had anticipated. She hadn't expected her to fight back so aggressively. That's how the accident happened. Connie wasn't supposed to fight back. Deandra brushed the tears from her cheeks. She needed Connie to survive for her own sake.

The rest of the drive was silent. Marshall had hoped to learn some info from Deandra on the trek over. It didn't happen. So when they arrived at the trauma center, Marshall called a car to take Deandra back to South Florida. She refused, however, to go without finding out how Connie was doing first.

They walked to the intensive care unit where Connie was being treated. Tina was in the room seated next to Connie's bedside, and Emmett had gone out for coffee. Tina greeted Marshall with a hug and explained that Connie had not regained consciousness and the doctors indicated it would be a wait-and-see prognosis. She had suffered a severe head trauma, but her other vital signs were good. They would be unable to determine the extent of the damage, if any, until she woke up.

Deandra settled into a chair in the hallway outside the unit, and Marshall took a seat on the opposite side of the bed from Tina. As he watched Connie, she appeared to be sleeping peacefully. One side of her face was swollen and bruised. The cut near her temple had been closed with twenty finely sewn stitches. Her mother, Arlene, who was listed as emergency contact on her daughter's driver's license, had been contacted and was on her way. She'd demanded no stitching of any kind was to be done on anything, anywhere, on her daughter until she made a few contacts. A few phone calls later, the finest plastic surgeon in Alachua County was on his way to Connie's bedside.

Early the following morning Viola arrived at the hospital. By the time she'd arrived, Tina and Emmett had departed for home. Tina had to get back to the spa and Emmett had to return to work. They would stay in constant touch with Marshall via phone. Viola strode past a sleeping Deandra and cast a disparaging eye her way. She peered into Connie's room and saw her alone in there. Quietly she walked up to the bed. A rush of unexpected emotion caused tears to brim in her eyes. She hadn't gotten to know Connie as she hoped she would. She closed her eyes and said a silent prayer for the daughter of her old friend.

Marshall entered the room, carrying a cup of coffee. He hadn't slept at all since they'd arrived and was hoping for any sign of awakening from Connie. Thus far, there had been none. He hugged his mother and offered her the lone seat in the room.

"Why is that woman still here?" Viola whispered as she indicated Deandra sleeping in the hallway.

"She didn't want to leave until Connie regained consciousness," he replied.

"What happened?" Viola asked.

"I'm not sure. I heard them arguing and then I heard what sounded like a fight. By the time I got close enough to see them, they both were falling over the edge. I don't know who caused it or if it was an accident," he replied.

"What is her explanation?" Viola asked.

"She isn't saying," he said, and leaned his head against the wall. "We argued on the way here and I said some pretty vile things. I was worried about Connie and I was none too careful about what I said."

"I brought the information with me. When you have a moment, we can go over it," Viola suggested.

"I don't think things are going to change here anytime soon. Would you like to get a cup of coffee or something to eat?" he asked.

"Coffee is a good idea," Viola agreed, and rose from her seat. She hefted her large purse higher up on her shoulder and walked out.

Marshall took one last look at Connie and followed his mother to the elevator.

19

Deandra stirred restlessly in her chair. She opened her eyes to see Arlene Jefferson as she exited the elevator and headed toward Connie's room. Deandra subconsciously looked away, unwilling to face a confrontation with Arlene.

As she rushed toward her daughter's hospital room, Arlene paid little attention to the young woman seated in the hallway. Standing at the entrance, she took a deep breath before proceeding into Connie's room. Her daughter looked so helpless, and Arlene noticed a pallid tone to her skin. She took the seat near the bed and picked up her daughter's hand and pressed it to her cheek. Silent tears trickled down her face as she prayed.

Marshall and Viola were seated in the cafeteria when Viola pulled a folder from her purse. She placed it on the table between them and began to explain its contents to Marshall.

Deandra's mother, a white medical technician at a local hospital, was having an affair with one of the surgeons on staff. Both of them were married at the time. When she ended up pregnant, she wasn't sure whose baby it was, until the little girl was born. When she arrived with such a dark complexion, there was no mistaking who her father was, because the surgeon was black and her husband was not. The father of the baby refused to break up his family. His wife, coincidentally, had just given birth to their first child a few months earlier, also a girl. The medical technician and her husband moved to the other side of town, and with glowing references, she was able to get a new job at a different hospital. After a while the whispers and rumors died down at Sisters of Mercy Hospital, where the surgeon was on staff, but not before his wife heard them. The staff members at the technician's new hospital were a bit curious about the baby girl with the olive complexion and brown curly hair, but they were polite enough not to question her parentage. The surgeon went on eventually to become chief of staff, and his wife never mentioned his affair or illegitimate child.

Unbeknownst to his wife, the surgeon remained a benefactor to the child until his death. She attended the best schools up through high school. When he passed away from a heart attack, his wife discovered how much he'd been supporting this child, and all funds were cut off. Coincidentally, Andrea's father disappeared around this time and her mother had begun drinking heavily. Without the support of the surgeon or Andrea's father's income, it was not long before she and her mother were destitute. Her mother couldn't keep a job because of her constant drinking, so the responsibility fell to Andrea, who was only seventeen at the time, to find the money to keep a roof over their heads. She learned early on men were willing to pay dearly to have sex with her.

The investigation detailed reports from neighbors who suspected how the child was getting money to pay the rent, but the landlord did not care where the money came from, as long as it was on time. Andrea had been arrested on a few occasions when several customers had been duped out of more than their agreed compensation. However, no charges had ever been filed because the men did not want their own misdeeds to become public knowledge. There was a mug shot of Andrea Moore in the folder, as well as a mug shot of Jesus Victor Cruz.

Marshall was shocked when he saw the picture of Victor. He leaned back in his chair and anger bubbled up inside. The two of them must have been conspiring to dupe him and Connie. *What a fool I've been all along.*

"Marshall," Viola called from across the table to regain his attention. She could tell he was upset, but there was more he needed to know. "Marshall," she called again before he finally looked up at her.

"Yeah?" he replied.

"There's more," she said gently.

"Fantastic," he said sourly.

"Deandra's biological father was Carlton Jefferson."

"What!" he said, and sat forward quickly. "You've got to be kidding me!"

"No, she and Connie are half sisters," she replied.

"Oh, my God!" he said, and stood up. His abrupt action caused his chair to shoot backward across the floor. "Does Dee know? Does Connie know?" His agitation expressed itself in restless pacing in the small area surrounding the table.

"I don't think either of them have any idea. Connie was never told of her father's affair. I tend to believe if Deandra had known who her father was, she would not have been spending so much time on her back," Viola stated, unable to stop herself from taking one more dig at Deandra. Her instincts about that woman had been right all along. She was nothing but trouble.

"They will have to be told," he said.

"Arlene is on her way and she can break the news to Connie if . . . I mean, when she wakes up. In the meantime you will have to tell Deandra she almost killed her own sister," Viola said as she saw Deandra hobble into the cafeteria on her crutches. "Speak of the devil and she will appear. Well, son, there's no time like the present," she added, and collected her purse. She left the folder on the table and hastened out of the room.

Deandra saw Marshall and made her way toward the table. She sat down dejectedly and propped the crutches against the chair behind her. "Her mother is here," she said as she glanced around the room before returning her gaze to Marshall, seated across from her. "Can I have a cup of coffee? I don't have a wallet or anything."

"Sure," he replied with more compassion than he'd expressed toward her in a long time.

Her eyebrow arched in response to the inflection in his voice. Something was going on. Then she remembered his mother had departed quite quickly when she entered the cafeteria, and now there was a folder lying on the table in front of Marshall. Undoubtedly, a full dossier on her life was contained therein. She watched as he got up to get her a cup of coffee, but she never touched the folder he left behind. She didn't want to know what they knew about her—not until she absolutely had to know.

Marshall returned with a large cup of coffee for her and returned to his seat. He sat silently as she added sugar and creamer. He wasn't sure how she would react to the news and he wasn't thrilled with the prospect of telling her. "How's your ankle?" he asked.

"The same as it was two hours ago," she replied, and took a sip of coffee. She was really hungry, but not about to ask him for anything else. They had no right to go digging around in her personal life. Anger boiled just beneath the surface and she tried to keep it in check. To let it out would display weakness, and she wasn't weak. She never had been weak.

Marshall watched her intently. He could see that her knuckles were white and her fists were clenched. Her face was set and a muscle twitched along her jawline. She was very angry. He surmised she had a right to be. His mother's investigation had been invasive. She'd delved into areas that were none of her concern. He and Deandra could have gone their separate ways, with no one the wiser about her past. If not for the accident, she might never have learned the truth. She deserved the truth.

"Dee, there are some things we need to talk about."

She looked away from him toward the window before she answered. "Is it necessary to make my humiliation a public affair? Obviously, your mother has dug up something unseemly about me and you have questions. Questions I probably won't be able or willing to answer."

He acknowledged she was right. A bit more privacy was required for their discussion. "When you've finished your coffee, we'll go somewhere more discreet."

"Is it that bad?" she asked.

"Actually, yes, it is," he replied.

"Un-fucking-believable," she hissed beneath her breath. Damn Viola and her nosey, busybody self.

She finished her coffee and clumsily tried to get back on her crutches. Marshall stood up and held her arm to steady her as she slipped the crutches back into place in her armpits. Together they made their way toward the exit.

Viola returned to Connie's room to find Arlene there. The two women embraced. Tears welled up in Arlene's eyes as she spoke. "They aren't certain how long it will take for her to wake up. The doctor said the blow to her head was pretty severe. He doesn't suspect any brain damage at this point, but they will know more when she regains consciousness. There is always the possibility she may . . . may not be the same."

"Don't think the worst, Arlene. We have to have hope and faith that everything will turn out fine. She's just resting right now, gaining her strength," Viola said as she tried to comfort her friend.

"Why did this happen?" Arlene asked.

"I don't know," Viola replied sadly, and clasped Arlene's hand in hers as they stood at the bedside looking down at Connie.

Marshall asked the receptionist if there was a private area where he might have a few minutes alone with Deandra. She directed him to a private consultation room that was currently empty.

He escorted Deandra inside and closed the door behind them. He pulled out a chair for her to sit down in as she eyed him suspiciously before easing into the seat. Marshall took the seat opposite her and laid the folder on the table. He'd decided to get a few answers from her before breaking the most important news. He removed the mug shot of Victor from the folder and laid it on the table between them.

Deandra glanced at it, clicked her tongue loudly, and shook her head, but said nothing.

"How long have you known Victor?" he asked.

She stared him down, but it was useless to pretend she did not know Victor. He already had the evidence. "Since we were kids," she replied.

"What was he doing hanging around Connie? And don't tell me you had nothing to do with it. I don't believe in coincidence. Not this kind anyway."

"I asked him to keep her away from you. That's all. I was insecure and jealous of her relationship with you. I figured if she had a man of her own, she would leave mine alone," she said, the anger she felt toward CJ resurfacing in her tone.

"You two apparently have a long history of conning people out of their money," he said, indicating the closed folder.

"There's no proof of that. An allegation is not a fact. Those were unproven allegations. Therefore, I'm still not guilty in the eyes of the law," she said indignantly.

"But are you innocent, Deandra?" he asked.

"That's none of your business," she retorted. "Obviously, our relationship is over, so I don't know why you feel it necessary to try to humiliate me with this stupid file of lies."

"Why did you change your name?" He continued with the questions.

Exasperated, she sat back with her arms folded across her chest. She didn't want to think about those times. Didn't want to think about her mother and the last time she saw her. Her arms tightened around her shoulders and a lump formed in her throat. "I changed my name after my mother—" She almost said "died," but she knew it was another lie. "My mother became very ill and I had to put her in a nursing home. I couldn't care for her anymore. I wanted to escape that life and everything associated with it, so I left the neighborhood, changed my name, and moved to the better side of town."

"To find a more affluent clientele?" he queried.

She stared angrily at him, but did not answer. Yes, she had found richer clients. She found wealthy men willing to support the style of life she wanted to become accustomed to. She mixed and mingled with the movers and shakers of Palm Beach County, even if it was only under the covers. It had paid her very well. She'd left Victor behind as well, until CJ came back into her life. Then she'd made the fatal mistake of calling on his assistance one last time.

Marshall really hadn't expected her to answer the last question. It was obvious from the moment he'd met her, she was used to good things and using her body to get them. Like any number of men before him, he was willing to spoil her, if only temporarily, to slide between those silken thighs. They could blame no one but themselves and their own weakness.

"Deandra, what do you know about your father?" he asked quietly.

Her father—what did he have to do with anything? Agitated, she turned in her seat and crossed and uncrossed her arms. She did not like this inquisition and it was getting on her nerves. "He left when I was about seventeen. I'm not sure why, and my mother never shared that information with me. Why, what do you care about him?" she asked.

"I meant your biological father," he said to clarify.

"My father is Dan Moore. That's the only father I have ever known. He raised me since I was born. The man who carelessly left his seed in my mother doesn't matter to me. He never did," she said vehemently. She knew Dan Moore wasn't her biological father, but her mother never wanted to discuss the man who had fathered her. Dan took care of her and provided for her until she was sixteen. She never knew why he left.

"Were you ever curious about your real father?" he asked. He was getting to the heart of the matter, and this conversation was only going to get more difficult.

"I told you, Dan Moore was my real father!" she protested angrily. Why was he bringing this up? Did he find out that her real father was some kind of serial killer, which would explain her foray into a life of crime? There was no point to this conversation. "I don't want to talk about my father anymore. He has nothing to do with this," she said.

"*He's dead! He's fucking dead. He ruined my life and yours. Now you can finally stop moping around here, hoping he'll come and rescue you. He's gone!*" Dan Moore yelled.

Deandra placed her hands over her ears, as if they were in the room with her. She could hear them fighting again, fighting about him.

"Deandra, are you okay?" Marshall asked, concerned by the pained look on her face.

She didn't answer because she didn't hear him. She was back in her bedroom listening to her mother and father screaming: "*I've been here for the last seventeen years. I stuck by you even after you embarrassed us in front of this whole fucking town!*

You made me look like a fool and I still stayed with you anyway!"

"Why? Why did you stay?" Julie screamed, and took a deep, ragged breath through her tears. *"Did you stay to torment me? To make me pay for a mistake I couldn't help?"*

A mistake? Deandra thought. Her heart thumped loudly in her chest, and her pulse was like a drumbeat in her ears. Tears rolled silently down her cheeks. She was the mistake her mother couldn't help. She was the reason her father left. Her mother's infidelity destroyed her marriage. She surmised she'd always known their constant fighting had something to do with her, but she never accepted it, until now.

"Deandra?" Marshall called to her again. This trip into the past was going to be bad, very bad for her. He could see that already.

She looked up at him with ice in her eyes. How dare he bring up her mother's affair? How dare they invade such private moments in her life? They had no right to do this to her—none. "What—what do you want from me? Why was this necessary? What do you hope to prove?" she screamed at him, giving in to the full force of her anger.

"I'm sorry for what you've been through, Dee. Really I am," he said as he tried to comfort her.

"You have no fucking idea what I've been through," she hissed.

"Let me tell you a little about what happened back then," he said. When she did not respond, he continued. "When your mother was a medical technician, she fell in love with a prominent surgeon at the hospital. Yes, they had an affair that resulted in your birth. However, your mother and this other man were both married to other people. Dan Moore stayed with your mother to raise you, even though it was quite obvious you were not his child. The surgeon did provide financial support for you and your mother. That's how you were able to attend private schools, growing up. But when he died, his wife found out about the money and cut off all support. I guess it was also around this time that Dan Moore left and your mother began drinking."

Deandra listened quietly through her anger. Her biological father wasn't a criminal, and unfortunately, he was dead, so there was no reunion in the offing. She waited for him to continue.

"Dee, this next part of what I have to tell you is a bit of a shock. So take a minute to absorb it and then we can talk about it," he said as he prepared to drop the bomb.

She rolled her eyes at him and shook her head slowly. She was the bastard love child of some rich doctor who died and left her nothing. Fantastic, what more did she need to know?

"Carlton Jefferson was your father," Marshall said slowly, allowing the information to sink in.

Deandra did not react. Who the hell was Carlton Jefferson? Suddenly tiny lights of recognition exploded in her brain.

"*Get that half-breed trailer trash out of my house this instant. You're nothing but a common whore,*" Arlene Jefferson hissed, and paused for a moment before adding, "*Just like your mother.*" She then slammed the front door behind her.

"No, no, no!" Deandra began screaming louder and louder. She tried to rise from her chair and escape the room, but tripped over the crutches and fell to the floor. She continued screaming. When Marshall tried to assist her up, she swung at him wildly. "How dare you! How dare you do this to me!" she yelled at him as she realized CJ was her half sister. She thought about how desperately she'd wanted her dead and out of her life. She could have killed her own sister. Why had they kept this secret from her for so long?

"You needed to know, Deandra. You had a right to know who your father was," he explained.

"What am I supposed to do now? What am I supposed to say to Connie?" she asked, and then she thought for a minute. "Does she know? I mean, was she told?"

"As far as I know, she has no idea either," Marshall replied, and placed hands under her armpits to lift her off the floor. This time she accepted his help into her chair.

"I can't deal with this right now. I can't get my head around this. It's just too much," she wailed, and laid her head on the table.

Marshall left the room to get her a glass of water and returned a few moments later. He handed her the glass and made her drink some. "I'm going to take you over to the hotel down the street and get you checked in. You have some thinking to do and I know you could use a break from here. Is that all right with you?" he asked.

She nodded her head weakly. Her head was pounding and a shower would be nice. She knew he was only doing this because he felt sorry for her. It did not make her feel good to be the object of his pity, but at this juncture she had little choice, except to go along until she could figure out where to go from here. She stood up on her crutches and followed him out of the room.

20

Marshall returned to the hospital to find no change in Connie's condition. He warmly greeted his mother and Arlene, who were outside Connie's room. He explained that Deandra had taken the news very hard and he'd checked her into a hotel.

"Did she tell you what happened to Connie?" Viola asked.

"No, she did mention she'd been jealous of my friendship with Connie and felt threatened by it. I guess that's what they were arguing about when the accident happened."

"They were arguing?" Arlene queried.

"Yes, I heard their raised voices as I was trying to find them in the woods. I'm not sure how the fall happened, but I do know Dee tried to help Connie afterward. She used her shirt as a bandage and tried to stop the blood flowing from Connie's head wound. Unfortunately, I don't have any more information."

"Did anyone think to call the police?" Arlene asked. Her daughter was in there fighting for her life, and it might have been that other woman's fault. Someone needed to file a complaint so an investigation could be conducted. She wanted someone to pay for what had happened to Connie.

"It appears to have been an accident. There was no need to alert the police, and besides, they were on the scene during the rescue. They didn't see anything suspicious. If Connie's story differs from Deandra's, we can pursue it at that time," Marshall said, trying to inject a little reason to calm Arlene down.

"If Connie can tell us her side of the story," Arlene said bitterly before walking away.

"She's upset." Viola tried to explain her friend's behavior as Arlene strode down the hallway.

"She has a right to be, but if someone had told those two women years ago that they were sisters, we might not be standing here today like this."

"Their mothers undoubtedly had their reasons for keeping the secret," Viola said. She understood the need to keep secrets. She wouldn't want Marshall to know of her affair when she was younger. Sometimes secrets had to remain secret.

"Carlton Jefferson was a weasel. He should have owned up to fathering Deandra. I'm not saying he should have left his wife and child, but he should have at least acknowledged Deandra. Her life would have been so different," he said angrily.

"His wife would have left him and taken his legitimate child. His reputation would have been smeared and it would have put a halt to his fast-rising career. What kind of choice is that?" Viola asked.

"She knew anyway and didn't leave," he countered.

"She knew the rumors would die down and go away. Facing the truth publicly would have made her life a living hell. It's not something I expect you to understand. Just believe me when I tell you it wasn't that simple," Viola replied.

"But when Carlton died and the funds were cut off, it forced Deandra into a life of prostituting her body for money."

"No, that's not true. It was her mother's weakness that forced Deandra to become responsible for them both. No one forced that child into prostitution. It was an avenue she chose on her own. Yes, albeit it was the wrong choice, but if her mother hadn't been so weak-minded, life would have been different for Deandra. Her mother believed until the day he died that Carlton was going to leave Arlene and be with her one day. What kind of existence is that for anyone? She did not do right by the child of a man she supposedly loved so much," Viola said passionately.

"You're right, but where do they go from here?" he asked.

"I honestly don't know," Viola replied, and looked toward the room where Arlene was once again sitting at Connie's bedside.

Deandra showered and put on the robe provided by the hotel. She'd lain down on the bed and fallen into a fitful sleep. After an hour or so, she got up and placed a phone call to Victor.

"Hello," he said sleepily as he turned over in the bed and checked his alarm clock.

"Victor, it's me, Deandra," she said, and was warmed by the sound of a familiar, friendly voice.

"Hey, babe, how are you doing? I'm sorry I didn't come out to the hospital to see you, but things were getting entirely too hot around there," he said.

"I'm okay. I just have a bad sprain on my ankle," she replied, and hesitated before saying any more. She wanted to talk about what she'd learned, and Victor was her closest confidant.

"You don't sound like yourself. Are they giving you a hard time or something? Tell them it was an accident," he suggested.

"It was an accident, Chuy! I didn't mean for this to happen. I was only trying to scare her, and suddenly we were falling and I couldn't stop it. It wasn't my fault," she cried as tears started to pool in her eyes again.

"I know, honey. I'm sorry," he said. "When are you coming back?"

"I don't know. I just found out some very disturbing news and I'm not sure what to do about it."

"Like what?"

"Well, you know my dad really wasn't my dad. It seems that Connie and I have the same biological father. My mother had an affair with her father, so we're actually half sisters," she blurted out in a rush.

Victor was silent on the other end of the line for a few seconds as he absorbed the enormity of her news. "Get the fuck outta here!" he finally responded. They'd just struck a gold mine and Deandra didn't seem to realize it yet. "Deandra, do you know what this means?" he asked.

"What does it mean?" she asked, suddenly suspicious of the unbridled enthusiasm in his voice.

"You've just hit the 'baby daddy jackpot,' sweetie. Your father was a prominent doctor. You have to be entitled to some of the old man's money," Victor said as his excitement grew.

"I never thought of that," she said slowly. She'd caused quite a bit of trouble to that family already, intended or not. Was she up to fighting for an inheritance? Exposing her mother to the world as the adulteress she was, shaming Connie and her mother in the process. The story was dead, along with Carlton Jefferson. Did she want to revive it? If she did, would it then come out that she'd tried to kill her own sister? What a lurid crime tale that would make for the local papers. No, she couldn't do it.

" 'We're in the money. We're in the money,' " Victor began to sing happily on the phone.

"*We're* in the money, Victor? How did 'we' get in the money?" she asked as she realized how unethical and ruthless Victor was when it came to cash. This was really no surprise. Whenever they ran a scheme in the old days, it was for the benefit of both of them, not just her. He always took his cut. "I'm not going after my father's money, Victor."

"Are you crazy? What do you owe Connie? Nothing! She lived in the lap of luxury while you scrounged around the streets for something to eat. You were selling your pussy for a few measly hundred bucks a week. While she got to be the Goody Two-shoes saving her golden pussy for the real thing and living off her daddy's money." His voice dripped with derision and disdain. "What's wrong with you, Andie? You gone soft in the head or something?" he demanded angrily. She had the brass ring in her reach and she was going to let it go.

"She's my sister, Victor. She may not survive!" she cried.

"Big fucking deal! If she dies, you get everything. We got to stake our claim to that money now!" he insisted. He did not understand where she suddenly got this bleeding-heart garbage.

"No, Victor! I won't do this anymore. She's my sister and the only one I have. I have to make this right. I have to!" she screamed at him, and slammed down the phone. She sat on the edge of the bed, shaking. She'd never liked Connie, but now that they were inextricably bound to one another, she needed to find a way to mend the fence. She prayed she would get that opportunity.

A short time later, Marshall returned to the hotel room with a change of clothes for Deandra and himself. He'd gone to the store and picked up toiletries, underwear, jeans, and shirts for both of them. There was nothing fancy in the bags, just clean clothes, and Deandra was grateful for the outfit. Before he went into the bathroom for a shower, she asked him if there was any news on Connie. Deandra was disappointed to hear there was no change.

Although Viola rejoiced in being right in her assessment of Deandra, she knew Marshall had been right when he said that it was not entirely her fault. She'd been a victim of circumstance even before her birth. If she and Connie were going to be able to bond in any way, Arlene was first going to have to accept that Deandra was not responsible for her parents' actions.

"Arlene, can we talk about the girls for a minute?" she asked, and Arlene looked up wearily and nodded her head in assent. "Deandra may not be my favorite person in the world or yours right now, but she is Connie's sister. Connie won't be able to accept her if you are still harboring anger and resentment toward her."

"I'm not certain I want Connie to accept her, but I am aware it is not up to me. She is the illegitimate child of my husband. A man who lied and cheated on me from the time I married him. Logically, I know none of that is her fault or responsibility, but she is a constant reminder of the greatest humiliation of my adult life. I loved Carlton with all my heart. His affair devastated me and nearly destroyed our marriage. I guess ultimately it did destroy our marriage when he died in that hotel room with her mother. I'm sure she knows none of this, and there would be little to no value for either her or Connie to learn the circumstance of their father's death," Arlene said as she stood up and approached the bed. She brushed a strand of hair across her daughter's forehead and placed a kiss on her cheek. Then she turned and exited the room.

Viola got up and followed her out to the hallway. Arlene paused to look back at the room one more time. "Where is Deandra?" she asked.

"She's over at the hotel with Marshall. Shall I ask him to send her back over here?"

"No, tell him to have her meet me in the lobby in about half an hour. I'm going to get a room. I should be all checked in by then. Are you going to stay over, Vi?" she asked.

"Yes, I'll call Marshall on our way over to the hotel. I'd like to stay a little longer for Connie, if you don't mind the company?"

"Don't be silly. I don't know what I would do without you here."

The women left the hospital and headed for the hotel down the block.

* * *

Thirty minutes later Deandra was standing in the lobby of the hotel waiting for a woman who had instilled fear and trepidation in her young heart so many years ago. The hotel clerk called across to her and advised her that Mrs. Jefferson requested she proceed to her hotel room. He gave her the room number and she made her way to the bank of elevators. When she reached the room, she stood nervously outside for a few moments. She was afraid to knock on the door and incur the wrath of Connie's mother once again. It would have to happen sooner or later. She raised her hand and rapped lightly on the door. In a matter of moments, Arlene opened the door and ushered her inside. She was no longer the intimidating figure Deandra remembered. She was actually a little shorter than Deandra now and seemed old and tired.

"Please sit down, Andrea," Arlene said, and motioned to the chair in the corner.

Deandra did not dare correct her on her name and took the chair as instructed. She sat with her hands clasped in her lap and her eyes cast down.

"It seems we have a bit of a dilemma on our hands. First I want the truth from you, young lady," Arlene said sternly. "Are you responsible for what has happened to my daughter?"

Deandra quelled the immediate denial that rushed to her lips. It was time to start telling the truth. "Yes, ma'am, but it was an accident. I really didn't mean for Connie to get hurt," she admitted.

"I see," Arlene replied—she hadn't expected such candor. "What were you two fighting about?"

"I was blaming Connie for the failure of my relationship with Marshall. She was going to tell him something bad about me," she said uneasily.

"Worse than what he has learned these past few hours?" Arlene continued.

"Probably not," Deandra agreed.

"So you and my daughter got into a fight over a man. Knowing what you now know, Andrea, it hardly seems worth it, does it?"

"No, ma'am," she answered, feeling like she was sixteen all over again.

"What is it that you want, Andrea? Now that you know my dead husband was your father. Or should I say, how much do you want to go away and never contact us again?"

"Mrs. Jefferson, I honestly have not thought about money. I've been shocked enough by finding out that Connie and I are related. I haven't considered anything beyond her getting better."

"So how much will make you disappear forever?" Arlene persisted. She wanted to test the mettle of this woman, see what was really underneath the surface.

Deandra stood up to leave. She'd had enough today between Victor's scheming and Arlene's trying to buy her off. Her voice rose higher with every word she uttered as she grew angrier and angrier at the injustice of these people who tried to control her life. "I don't want your money. I am going to stay and try and get to know my sister. That's what I want. I want to know the sister you and my mother have conspired to keep from me for thirty-some years. You treated me like dirt when I came to your home for a party. You called me a whore and insulted my mother. What did I know? I was only sixteen years old!"

"You were performing oral sex in my house in front of my child, you little slut!" Arlene hurled the insult back at Deandra.

"I was wrong. I know that now, but I didn't know any better then. I just wanted the other girls to like me. But that was no reason to do what you did. You made the whole thing worse because of who I was, because I was *her* daughter. That part wasn't my fault. I never understood that until now."

Arlene took a deep breath to calm down. She was letting the

situation get the better of her once again. "You are right, Andrea. That part wasn't your fault, but seeing you in my house threw me for a loop and it brought everything back. I lost control, and I admit it. It was a very painful time for me."

"I understand that, Mrs. Jefferson. I may not be the sister you would have wanted Connie to have, but I am her sister. I only want an opportunity to tell her I'm sorry and ask her to forgive me. If she wants me to go away and disappear after that, I will, and without your money."

"Please sit back down, Andrea. I appreciate what you're saying, and I can only hope you are sincere. Time will tell. I'm going to order room service for us and you are going to tell me about your childhood and, forgive me, your misdeeds. I want to be able to understand you a little better before we have to tell Connie about you," Arlene said, and rose from the bed to call room service.

Deandra sat back down in her chair. This was going to be one long night.

21

Deandra was sitting at Connie's bedside two days later when she heard a small coughing sound. She looked up quickly and saw Connie's eyes fluttering open. She limped on her cast from the room to find Arlene, who was talking with the doctor at the nurse's station.

"She's waking up!" she cried with unabashed excitement.

Both Arlene and the doctor turned and made their way to Connie's room, with Deandra limping behind. Connie's eyes were closed again when they got to the room, but she opened them immediately when Arlene called her.

"Hi, Mom," she said weakly.

"Oh, dear Lord. Thank you," Arlene said as she leaned over and kissed her daughter on the forehead. "Sweetie, we were so worried about you." She stepped back to allow the doctor to examine Connie and exchanged hugs with Deandra.

Connie drowsily watched the exchange between her mother and Deandra and was confused. What was Deandra doing there, and why was she hugging her mother? She closed her eyes again. This was not making sense. Perhaps she was still dreaming, she thought as she drifted off to sleep again.

She awakened a few hours later to find Marshall sitting at her bedside. He smiled warmly at her and reached for her hand. He brought it gently to his lips and kissed the back of it. "Welcome back, princess," he said.

"Hi," she croaked weakly, and smiled. "Can I have some water?"

"Sure," he replied as he got up and poured a small glass. He tilted the straw to her mouth to allow her a sip.

"Thanks. Where's my mom?"

"She just stepped out for a minute. I'm sure she'll be right back."

"Funny, I could have sworn I saw Deandra here earlier, but I must have been dreaming."

"No, she's here too."

"What's she doing here?" Connie asked, confused.

"Do you remember what happened, Connie?"

"Yes, a little. We were fighting, and suddenly the ground started slipping away. I couldn't get my feet," she said. By reliving the moment in her mind, she felt the same fear she'd experienced at that moment.

"Where was Deandra?"

"She was standing in front of me and I was falling," she said, and then she remembered Deandra reaching out for her. "She tried to stop me. She grabbed my arm and then we both fell. Marshall, she tried to help me. Why? She hates me so much, she could have just let me fall."

"No, she couldn't. Maybe she's not as bad as we all thought."

"Hmm, I'm not so sure," Connie murmured. It didn't make sense that Deandra tried to save her, but she knew she had. She'd seen her with her own eyes.

"When you're better, there's a lot we have to talk about," Marshall advised. "In the meantime you need to regain some strength. So get some more sleep and I'll check back in on you later."

"Sure, see you later," she said, and closed her eyes again.

The next time she awoke, she was hungry. She called the nurse and they immediately sent for a tray of food. She was munching happily when her mother returned to visit.

"Well, my goodness, young lady. You look like you haven't eaten in three days." Her mother smiled, pleased to see Connie looking more like her old self.

"Has it been that long, Mom? Wow, I had no idea."

"How do you feel?"

"My head hurts and these stitches on the side of my face itch, but other than that, I'm okay."

"The doctor said the stitches should be nearly invisible when they heal. Your head may hurt for a while. That was quite a blow you took."

"Yes, I suppose I am lucky to be alive. Did I see you hugging Deandra the other day? That was kind of weird."

"I imagine it would seem so to you, but you'll understand in time. I've made peace with her."

"You've made peace. I don't understand. Why would you have to make peace with her? What did you do to her, or did she do to you?"

"It's a long story, Connie."

Connie made an exaggerated glance around the hospital room. "Am I going somewhere anytime soon?"

"Well, yes. Hopefully, you will be released to go home to-morrow. They just want to observe you one more day."

"Stop evading the subject. What's going on with Deandra?" Connie insisted.

"I really don't know where to start, honey. It happened so long ago," Arlene protested. She knew she had to tell Connie, but her daughter had only fond memories of her father. This was going to shatter that image forever. "Before you were born, your father had an affair with a medical technician at the hospital. It was a devastating blow to our marriage, but even more so, because he had a child with the other woman."

"No, I don't believe you. My dad wouldn't do that. He loved you, Mom. I know he did. He was always taking us on trips and buying us presents," Connie said, dismissing the possibility.

"Yes, dear. I do believe he was trying to make up for his infidelity all those years afterward. But this other woman had a child by him and he helped her put that child in school with you. I didn't know it at the time. Not until that party."

"What! No, no, Mom. You're not trying to tell me . . . ," she started, and heard her mother's voice in the distance.

Her mother was very upset. *"I don't give a flying fuck who can hear me. That bitch should never have sent that child over here in the first place,"* she screamed in protest.

"Arlene, maybe her mother didn't know she came here. I'm sure she would have prevented her child from suffering this kind of embarrassment," Carlton said as he tried to reason with his wife.

"How dare you try to defend that bitch or her bastard child!"

The pain in Connie's head started pounding incessantly. Andrea Moore was her father's bastard love child. What irony! She pushed the food tray away. "I need to rest, Mom. I don't want to think anymore," she said.

"I'm sorry to disappoint you, honey. Your father was a good man, but he was only human."

"That's no excuse, Mom, and you know it. He cheated on you and had a child with another woman. I will never forgive him for that," she said flatly. Another child—her father had another child, and that child was Andrea Moore.

"You have a sister, Connie," her mother said softly.

"No, I don't. My father had another child. I didn't have anything to do with that," she said, and turned to face the wall. "I don't want to talk anymore tonight, Mom, please."

"Okay, sweetie, I understand." Arlene patted her on the

shoulder gently and walked out of the room. She would try again in the morning. Connie idolized her father. She had taken this news much harder than Arlene had anticipated.

It was dark when Marshall returned to the room to find Connie staring vacantly in the darkness. He'd already spoken with Arlene and knew she was aware of her newfound relationship to Deandra. He also knew she wasn't taking the news very well.

"Hey, Connie," he said as he moved close to the bed. He leaned over and kissed her cheek.

She did not immediately respond. It was his fault. If he hadn't brought Deandra to the cabin, none of this would have had to come out. She could have kept the image of her father safe and secure in her heart and not had to deal with all the drama happening now.

"I'm sorry, Connie," he said.

"And well you should be," she responded bitterly.

"You had a right to know."

"Why? Why did I have to know? That was my parents' secret. Now it's exposed and I have to deal with it. What am I supposed to do?" she cried angrily.

"Take it one day at a time, Connie. Your mother has had thirty years to deal with this. You just found out. No one can expect you to get over this quickly."

"But they do. My mother referred to Deandra as my sister. How dare she! She is not my sister, and she never will be."

"It's going to take time, Connie. Whether you form a new relationship with Deandra is entirely up to you, not anyone else. The old one still has a lot of unhealed wounds."

"Thanks, Marsh. I'm glad someone understands," she said, and reached for his hand. She squeezed it gently and closed her eyes. "Can you sit with me for a while longer?"

"As long as you like," he replied, and squeezed her hand in return.

* * *

Connie was getting dressed to leave the following morning when Deandra appeared in her doorway. She looked at her only briefly before attempting to put on her shoes. Her head throbbed as she bent over to slip them on. She leaned back on the bed dizzy from the effort.

"I'll help you with those," Deandra said as she hobbled from the doorway to assist.

Connie wanted to refuse her help, but knew she could not do it on her own. Reluctantly she allowed Deandra to slip the loafers on her feet. "Thank you," she said begrudgingly. "My mother should be here soon. You don't have to stay."

"Connie, we need to talk."

"I don't really think we have much to say to one another, Deandra. Or should I call you *Andrea*?"

"My name is not important. I wanted to tell you I'm sorry."

"Sorry? Sorry for what?"

"I'm sorry for causing your accident."

"Let's get this part straight. It may have been an accident that we fell off the cliff, but it was not an accident that you took me out there to kill me. Yes, sure you changed your mind at the last second. Big damn deal. It doesn't take away from the fact that you wanted to do me bodily harm. Well, you succeeded, so be happy."

"I'm sorry you feel that way. I really hoped to ask for your forgiveness."

"Well, it seems that there's a lot of that floating around lately. I hope you get some, but don't look for it from me. I have no forgiveness for you or my father."

"Connie, we're—"

"No, Andrea, we're not, now or ever. If being able to claim my father gives you some sense of identity, then good for you. I always knew who my father was—I just didn't know what he was, a liar and a cheat. That's nothing for me to be proud of," she said vehemently, and walked out of the room in search of her mother.

It was a long ride to Juno Beach in the limousine her mother had hired to take them home. Connie sat quietly in one corner, while her mother read a magazine in the other. Arlene decided it was best to leave the topic of Deandra alone for a while. Connie was very bitter, and until she was fully recuperated, there was no point in creating more tension and aggravation for her.

Marshall told her he would stop by later in the day to check on her after he dropped his mother at her house. Connie was careful not to put too much hope into having a future with Marshall. The memories of their time at the cabin were still too fresh. The fact that he continued in his relationship with Deandra, even after her outrageous behavior, and slept with her when he claimed they were through, was something she could not easily dismiss.

Now that she and Deandra were purportedly related, it made the situation even stickier. How could she possibly have a relationship with him now? She realized suddenly Marshall had no idea Deandra had slept with Victor at the cabin. There was no point in telling him now.

Her mother was going to stay for a couple of days to make sure she was okay and then she was heading home to Key West. Marshall had hired a limousine to take Deandra home. He did not want to have her and Viola in the same car for a four-hour ride. Even though it seemed his mother was taking an easier tone with her lately, he did not want to push his luck. His relationship with Deandra was over, and she'd finally accepted that fact. Therefore, he did not want her to mistake his current kindness for interest.

A week would pass before Connie and Marshall sat down in her living room to discuss Deandra again. Getting back into his work routine, Marshall had been stopping by regularly for short visits. They had not touched on the topic of Deandra. That night Marshall arrived with a folder in hand.

Connie brought two glasses of wine to the living room and handed one to Marshall. "Can I offer you some cheese and crackers or anything to snack on?" she asked before taking a seat next to him on the couch.

"No, I'm fine. Thank you."

"What is the folder for?"

"My mother, in her infinite wisdom and nosiness, did a little snooping into Deandra's background while we were out at the cabin. Unfortunately, she was the one who uncovered the secrets."

"Oh," Connie said, and backed away instinctively as if afraid of hearing more bad news.

"What I want to explain to you about this file doesn't really impact you, but I think if you had a better understanding of Deandra, you might feel different toward her," he said.

"You're here on her behalf," she said, and bristled at the idea he would come to her to defend Deandra.

"No, I'm not. I'm here for you. You have a lot of pain and disappointment to deal with, but I want you to have a better understanding to make your decision."

"What decision?"

"Whether or not to have a relationship with Deandra."

"I thought I had already decided that. I don't want a relationship with her."

"That's fine. But at least understand all the facts before you dismiss her completely."

Connie sat back and folded her arms across her chest defensively. She would hear what he had to say. However, her mind was made up.

"Shortly after your father passed away, Deandra's father abandoned the family. Her mother was so distraught over your father's death and the loss of her husband, she began drinking.

Soon there was no money to pay the rent and they were about to be evicted. Deandra began running scams with a neighborhood boy to rip off older men. She would entertain the men, while her friend would break into their homes or apartments and steal jewelry and cash. It was the only way she could get enough money to keep a roof over her mother's head."

"She entertained the men how?"

"I'm sure you can use your imagination, Connie. She entertained them sexually."

"So she started this prostitution thing as a teenager and never stopped. She just found bigger fish as time went on."

"Yes, I suppose you could say that. Connie, how far would you go to take care of your mother? Is there anything you would not do?"

"Don't put me in the same league as her, Marshall. I would never sell my body for money."

"Maybe that's because you had a sense of self while growing up. She didn't. She wasn't rich like the rest of the class. She tried to fit in the wrong way. The kids at your school laughed at her and made fun of her behind her back."

Connie looked down at her hands. She remembered how upset she was when Andie showed up at her party. Nobody liked her, including CJ. Then after the party things just got worse; there were more whispers. Andie's behavior at school got wilder and wilder. The rumors were rampant that she'd slept with every willing boy in school—and some of the girls. It probably wasn't all true, but they said it anyway. After a while Andie just stopped coming to school altogether.

"Can't you find it in your heart to see what she's been through and maybe extend an olive branch of friendship?" he asked.

"What's in this for you, Marshall?"

"Helping you to find some peace. As long as you keep her at arm's length, you'll never have closure."

"She's called here a couple of times since I got home. I haven't spoken with her."

"Maybe the next time she calls, you will?" he asked.

"Maybe," she replied noncommittally.

Marshall gathered the folder and began to put the papers back inside, when Connie stopped him.

"Can I keep this for a while?" she asked.

Marshall had already removed the mug shot of Victor and any reference to him by name in the file. He didn't think she needed to know Victor was only using her to help Deandra. It wouldn't help the situation.

"Can I take you out for a bite to eat?" he asked as he downed the last of his wine.

"Yes, that would be nice," she replied, and got up to retrieve her sweater before they headed out into the chilly evening air.

Deandra was seated at her kitchen counter with an empty coffee mug in front of her. She was disappointed she'd been unable to connect with Connie. She understood the shock of finding out about her father's affair must have been a hard blow to deal with. She always knew the man who raised her was not her father, and discovering her biological dad was an important doctor of renowned status was a boost to her self-worth, even if she was his illegitimate child. He cared enough about her to provide for her until his death.

She spent most of her life resentful of Connie and the advantages her heritage afforded her. The fact that they were related was a great irony. Connie had not returned any of her messages. Victor had tried to contact her several times, but Victor was part of an old life she wanted to leave behind. She had enough money left in her bank account to cover her for a few months. It was time to decide what she was going to do with her life. She and Marshall had gone their separate ways. There was no bitterness between them. Deandra had finally accepted the relationship was not destined to last. As far as a career was concerned, she had no real clue what she wanted to do, and she was not trained for anything viable.

With thoughts of Connie fresh on her mind, she impulsively decided to try one more time to reach her. She was very surprised when Connie answered the call on the second ring.

"Hi, Connie, it's Deandra. How are you doing?" she asked anxiously, afraid that Connie would disconnect when she realized who it was.

"Hello, Deandra. I'm fine, thank you," she said a little stiffly.

"I was hoping we could get together and talk, if you're ready to talk about our parents."

"I don't imagine it's going to get any easier by avoiding the issue. So, I guess, we could talk about it sometime."

"Can we meet tomorrow? Are you feeling up to it?" Deandra asked.

"I'm much better. How are you getting around on that ankle?"

"I'm walking on the Aircast and don't need the crutches anymore. Would you like to meet at—" Deandra started, but Connie interrupted.

"Why don't you come here. I'd prefer not to discuss our personal business in a public place."

"Okay, that's fine," she replied, and wrote down Connie's address and directions. "I'll see you tomorrow at one," she said, and took a deep breath as she replaced the receiver.

Connie replaced the handset on her end and stared at the phone for a minute before sighing deeply. She returned to her garden, where she'd been planting flowers when the phone rang.

Deandra arrived promptly the following day for their meeting. She was surprised to find Connie living so modestly in a small two-bedroom villa. She did not have to wait long for

Connie to come to the door and usher her inside. A quick glance around the room took in the simple and handmade appointments. A colorful crocheted afghan was draped across the arm of a wing-back chair in one corner of the room. Several rough sculptures were on the mantel alongside scented candles of varying sizes.

"Your home is beautiful," Deandra said as she took a seat on the sofa.

"Thank you, I like it," Connie replied. "Can I offer you a cup of tea or a glass of wine?"

"Tea would be fine. If it's not too much trouble," Deandra replied. Wine would bolster her spirits, but she suspected Connie was more a tea-in-the-afternoon kind of girl.

"It's no trouble. I already have a pot boiling on the stove," Connie replied, and disappeared into the kitchen.

Deandra silently congratulated herself on guessing the appropriate afternoon libation. She watched Connie as she returned with a tray containing shortbread biscuits and two cups of tea. They prepared their tea before settling back into their seats to talk. Connie opened the conversation.

"What is it that you want from me, Deandra?" she asked.

"I don't want anything. I'm not after your money or anything like that," she said, and took a sip of tea before she continued. "Most of my life I have spent pursuing the almighty dollar in one way or another. Yes, on many occasions it wasn't always legally correct. But I'm an adult and the people I dealt with were adults. I'm not prone to pretense, so they knew as well as I did what we were about."

"And Marshall?" Connie asked. She hated the fact that Deandra had been with him for as long as she had. It was something that still rankled her when she pictured the two of them together. It was the main reason she was keeping Marshall at arm's length.

"I admit I went after Marshall for his money initially, but as

I got to know him, I really began to care for him," Deandra confessed.

"Then why would you behave the way you did? Why would you risk losing it all over someone like Victor?" Connie asked. She'd never understood why anyone would pick Victor over Marshall.

"Victor is a long story. It's like a bad habit you can't break. He's got that bad-boy thing going on. I was drawn to his fire, his familiarity. It was wrong, but I was so unhappy and afraid I was losing Marshall that I couldn't help myself. I wanted to feel better, if only for a moment, and he always knew how to make me feel better."

Connie's cup rattled back onto the saucer and Deandra's words began to sink in. Her hands were shaking as her thoughts came together. *Victor knew Deandra long before he knew me, and he'd never said a word.*

"How long have you known Victor?" Connie asked, her voice barely a whisper.

"That's something else I'm not so proud of, Connie. What I did to you regarding Victor. All I knew about you was that I blamed you for the greatest humiliation of my life. For fifteen years everything that happened to me was your fault. Your mother threw me out of your house. The kids at school started calling me names behind my back. Within a year after that my dad left us. The next thing I know I had to leave school and my mom never said why. All the bad things started happening to me after your party, so I blamed you. Then suddenly I find this Prince Charming named Marshall James, and lo and behold, who happens to be a good friend of his? You. I just wanted to eliminate the competition, that's all."

Connie listened only to half of what she was saying. She still had not told her about Victor and how long she'd known him. Deandra was blaming everything that had gone wrong in her life on a slumber party she hadn't even been invited to.

"How long have you known Victor?" Connie repeated.

Deandra realized Marshall had not told her everything. He'd obviously left Victor out of the story. She wanted the air to be cleared, so she confessed.

"I've known Victor since we were very young. We were probably ten or eleven when we met. We lived in the same apartment building."

Connie rose from her seat and walked toward the window. She didn't say anything, but her mind was a whirl. She waited for Deandra to continue.

"I only asked Victor to distract you for a while, until I could be sure I was on solid ground with Marshall. I know a lot of the things I did that ruined my relationship had nothing to do with you. I see that, now that I've had some alone time to think about it."

"Did you pay Victor to pretend he was in love with me?" Connie asked, although she already knew the answer. She'd thought she'd managed to find another loser, and all along it was someone who was only seeing her to appease someone else.

"No, Connie. I didn't pay him anything. You're a very beautiful woman and he was quite happy to be your boyfriend. I think he was happy with you until he saw how you reacted to Marshall, and then his jealousy got the best of him. He started acting out."

Connie never turned back to the room to address Deandra and her barely audible words were directed to the window. "But he approached me, because you asked him to. Is that correct?"

"Initially, yes, Connie, I asked him to seek you out," Deandra said, and hung her head.

As Connie turned back into the room, her eyes swept past the poker standing next to the fireplace. She envisioned herself picking it up and taking a few swipes at Deandra's head. She was angry. To think Deandra had concocted this diabolical plan to keep her away from Marshall. A man she'd known almost all her life. A man with whom she'd shared a mutual respect. A man she loved deeply, even if it was secretly. How was she supposed to have a relationship with this woman? Her mother wanted her to make amends, to leave the past in the past.

"You know, Deandra, I think that I could get past blaming you for my father's actions. I'm adult enough to realize none of what happened back then was your fault or mine. I can even understand where your circumstances as a young girl could have led you down an unsavory path in life. All that I can understand, and I could even have compassion for you."

"I hear a 'but' coming," Deandra interjected.

"You're right. There is a 'but,' and it's a big one. After my father died, I had to grow up rather quickly. I had to take care of my mom, because for a long time she was in a very bad way after his death. I never once blamed anybody else for what happened to my father, or to my mother and me as a result of his death. I didn't harbor this grudge into my adulthood and set out to destroy someone else's life because I was unhappy."

"I can't change what I've done, Connie. I can only acknowledge that it was wrong. I can apologize and ask forgiveness. I can try to atone for my sins, but I can't make you do anything you don't want, or are not ready, to do."

"I'm still very angry about a lot of things. After you left high school, I honestly never gave you another thought until you showed up at Tina's, and even then I had no idea who you were. So, until we went to the cabin and I discovered who you were, you didn't factor into my life at all. All the bad memories I have of you are not old, they are very recent and very fresh."

Deandra rose from her seat and picked up her purse to leave. "I'm sorry for the pain I've caused you, Connie."

"Wait, there is a problem and a reason I asked you to come here today. I know in my heart my father would want me to reach out to you. He may not have spent time with you, and he may not have publicly acknowledged his paternity, but he did provide for you for a long time. That means you were important to him." She paused as tears caught in her throat. She knew she must do this for him. "For my father I will try to put these things behind me and see where we can go from here. I make no promises, but for our father I will try," Connie said as she reached out and shook Deandra's hand.

Deandra resisted the urge to embrace her newfound sister. She would take the olive branch Connie offered and do her best to be worthy of the chance to prove herself.

22

Connie smiled as she read the postcard from Deandra. She'd enrolled in some travel courses at the local college and had gotten a job as a travel agent. She was currently traveling through Europe with a group of agents touring hotels and resorts. She sent postcards from every stop along the way.

She and Connie had come a long way in developing their relationship over the past year. They would probably never be bosom buddy friends, but they had achieved a satisfactory coexistence.

Connie and Arlene had decided together to give Deandra a large sum of money as an inheritance from her father. Deandra declined the gift and asked them to hold on to it for her. She'd said she wanted to make it on her own first, legally. If she did that, she could then feel worthy of an inheritance from her father. She was doing a good job of it already and they were planning to pass on the gift to her once she returned from Europe.

Connie and Marshall had been seeing each other steadily since the accident. They'd been taking it very slowly. It had taken Connie a long time to let go of the images of Marshall and Deandra together. Once she made peace with Deandra, she was able to move forward into a relationship with him.

Although they were affectionate with one another, they'd stopped short of becoming intimate. Building up trust had been the most important bridge between them. Marshall had disappointed Connie, unintentionally on more than one occasion, and he was determined not to be the one to hurt her again.

Marshall often stopped by Connie's for dinner. Sometimes she would cook and sometimes he would. They'd developed an easy comfort with one another and saw each other several times a week. On this particular night, as Marshall drove to her house for dinner, he'd contemplated the events of the last few years. Four years ago he'd made love to Connie during an afternoon storm. It had been a memorable moment in both their lives, and it could have been a pivotal moment, but he didn't act on it. He let the opportunity to create something with Connie slip by. He'd felt guilty about taking advantage of her vulnerability, but maybe he, also, wasn't ready to commit to anyone at that time. When they met again after that, each was involved with someone else, and the moment was gone. When the near tragedy occurred at the Millers' cabin over a year ago, it brought to light how much time they'd wasted. The accident had shown them how fleetingly it could be over. Tonight he'd decided he was going to show her he had no intention of letting her slip away again. He noticed the front door was open when he walked up the steps to the porch.

"Connie," he called as he opened the screen door and poked his head inside. She came quickly from the kitchen as she wiped her hands on a dish towel. He beckoned her outside to the porch.

"What's the matter?" she asked as she stepped out onto the porch with him. He reached out for her hand and pulled her close to the railing. Positioning himself behind her, he pointed up at the stars.

"Make a wish," he said. He placed his chin against the side of her head and breathed in the clean scent of her freshly washed and still damp hair.

Connie relaxed against his chest. *A wish*, she thought, *I've been wishing all afternoon.* She smiled as she closed her eyes and made her wish.

"What did you wish for?" he asked. He wrapped his arms around her waist and bent his head to nibble on her neck. He made a mental note: she didn't move away, or stiffen uncomfortably in his embrace as she sometimes would.

"I can't tell you or it won't come true," she replied softly as she leaned her head back on his shoulder. "Did you make a wish?" she asked.

"No, I didn't. I go after what I want. I can't wait for wishes to be granted," he replied as he turned her in his arms to face him. He looked down at her freshly scrubbed face and soft, slightly parted lips. He gently claimed her lips with his.

Connie sighed aloud, and responded eagerly to his kiss.

Marsh broke off the kiss and guided her back into the house. "What are we having for dinner?" he asked.

Connie was a little surprised and disappointed. *Dinner? Does this man ever think of anything other than food?*

Dinner was the last thing on his mind, but he didn't want to rush the moment and scare her off. She seemed comfortable with him, and it was important to him she keep this comfort level. He'd been biding his time for several months, waiting for the perfect opportunity to seal their relationship.

"Snapper. I picked one up at the market today. I've already seasoned it. I was going to let you do the grilling, though," she answered. She'd speared and wrapped two baking potatoes in foil and they were baking in the oven. The table was set for two, with two crystal candleholders topped with long-stemmed white candles.

"Hey, you've been busy in here," Marsh said as he surveyed

the kitchen. Connie checked the potatoes, while Marsh pulled two bottles of white wine from the pantry. "Chablis or Chardonnay?" he asked.

"Chardonnay, if you don't mind," she replied, and took two winesglasses from the cupboard. She set them down on the counter and began to check the drawers for the corkscrew. She found it under a pile of clean dish towels in the cabinet near the stove.

Marsh put the Chablis back in the pantry. As he turned and accepted the corkscrew from Connie, his hand closed over hers. He took the opportunity to gaze into her eyes again. "You're a very beautiful woman, Connie," he said sincerely.

"Without makeup and my hair undone?" she teased, smiling up at him.

He took stock of her as she stood in front of him: firm in all the right places, round, small breasts he had intimate knowledge of, and a gorgeous face, with doe-shaped light brown eyes. She was beautiful, but it wasn't her physical beauty he was referring to.

"I have always thought you were one of the most beautiful women I knew. But I really didn't get to know you on a personal level until the last year. Your spirit is beautiful, Connie. It's about more than how you look on the outside. I see a beauty inside you. It's something I think you keep hidden from a lot of people," he said seriously.

"Oh," she said, surprised. Embarrassed by his verbal introspection, she turned away. He looked a little too deeply into her soul. She didn't want him to see into her heart—didn't want him to feel compelled to state something he really didn't feel. "Are you going to fill those wineglasses or not?" she asked lightly, in an effort to change the direction of the conversation.

"Sure," he said, and filled the two glasses. He raised his glass to make a toast. "To us," he said.

She looked at him quizzically, then touched her glass to his.

She took a sip and found the Chardonnay quite smooth. It was a good vintage. Casually she picked up the bottle and studied the label.

Marsh took the fish from the plastic container where it was marinating and laid it out on a thick piece of aluminum foil. Sprinkling it with fresh lemon, he folded the ends of the foil together and placed it on the grill. He squeezed the potatoes to test for doneness. Finding them almost soft enough, he moved the potatoes to the back corner of the grill, so they wouldn't overcook in the oven.

Connie prepared a tossed salad while Marsh grilled the fish. Sipping the wine on an empty stomach was causing a slight fuzzy feeling in her head. She'd been working in her garden all day and hadn't taken time to eat. She knew she should slow down on the wine until they started to eat dinner, but tonight she was throwing caution to the wind. She wanted to feel as carefree and uninhibited as possible.

Dinner turned out delicious. The fish was light and moist, the Cajun seasoning giving it a little bite. They kept the conversation light during the meal. Connie spoke about one day getting her own cabin on the island with Tina and Emmett. Even though, she now knew, it could be dangerous, the solitude and ability to have someplace where she could escape the outside world held enormous appeal to her. Marsh told her he'd already purchased a lot on the island, but had put aside working on his floor plans, because he was in the middle of work on a new development. She was not surprised to learn he was designing the home himself.

After dinner Marsh sent her to the living room and said he would clean the kitchen by himself. He could see she was getting tired, and although she was not complaining, he knew her muscles were aching from the day's strenuous exertion.

She took her glass of wine with her and sat down on the sofa, while Marsh lit the fireplace. He returned to the kitchen and she curled up in the corner of the sofa to relax. She studied the room, taking in all the knickknacks and pictures she'd used to decorate the villa and give it a homey feel. It was a very comfy and friendly atmosphere. The room was fairly darkened with the slight flickering illumination of scented candles.

She could hear the familiar sound of dishes being washed in the kitchen. She was able to discern the *clink, clank* of silverware items as they bumped against one another in his hands. Pictures of Marsh began to flash through her mind: Marsh standing on the pier at the lake; Marshall at her bedside in the hospital; Marsh smiling as he teased her in a restaurant last week; Marsh asleep on her sofa after dozing off while watching television. Then she saw an image of him poised above her as he made passionate love to her four years ago. Connie came to a decision as she sat there. She was tired of waiting for him to make the first move.

Determinedly she rose from her seat on the couch and placed her empty wineglass on the end table. She wasn't drunk, but was clearly feeling the effects of two glasses of wine. She entered her bedroom and began to rummage through the drawers. It took her a little while to find the filmy white negligee she wanted. It was a last-minute purchase a few days ago. She wasn't quite sure why she had bought it. Now there was a perfect purpose. Her body ached from the work in the yard earlier in the day, but there was a distinctly different ache she was feeling in her loins, which had nothing to do with the gardening and everything to do with the man in the kitchen. Removing her clothes, she slipped into the negligee. The layers of filmy white chiffon concealed little of her naked body underneath. She added a dash of perfume on her neck, stomach, and in between her breasts, and went back into the darkened living room. She retrieved a few blankets from the closet and spread them on the floor in front of the fireplace. She turned off a few lights. The only illumination remaining was from two small candles and the glow of the fireplace. Seated on the blanket facing the fire, she waited for Marsh.

He entered the living room a few minutes later with the half-empty wine bottle and his glass of wine. He was shocked to see Connie had changed her clothes and was seated in front of the fireplace. He covered his surprise as he walked up to her. "Would you like some more wine, Connie?" he asked.

"Sure," she replied as she turned slightly in his direction.

In the darkened room, he did not realize her nightgown was see-through. But as she turned away from the fire, the illumination from the fire gave him a clear outline of her breasts under the nightgown. He wondered if she had drunk a little too much tonight. Why was she dressed like this? Surely, she realized he wasn't made of stone. He retrieved her glass from the end table and refilled it. He handed it to her and sat down on the blanket next to her. He could smell the faint sweet scent of the perfume she wore. He tried to search her face for clues to what she must be thinking, but she kept her face averted and stared at the fire. Unable to look away, he drank in the undeniable sensuality of the woman beside him. Her dark nipples were visible through the filmy material. This close to her in the direct glow of the fireplace, he could see she was completely naked beneath the gown. He felt the stirrings of arousal in his loins. He excused himself and went into the bathroom for a few minutes. Upon his return he took a deep gulp of his wine, sat back down next to her, and faced the fire. He waited for her to give some indication of what was on her mind.

After several minutes of silence Marsh couldn't wait any longer. She looked so delicious, sitting there in the firelight. His body was talking to him and he needed to know where she was coming from.

"Connie," he started, "what's on your mind?"

She sighed deeply and looked at him. She let her gaze travel from his handsome face to his broad shoulders, strong, muscled arms, and down his long legs. She could see he was already aroused. Connie wanted him tonight and wasn't sure how she could boldly tell him so. She thought the negligee would have been a big enough hint; however, he hadn't made any attempt to touch her. Was she being too aggressive? Maybe she was not being aggressive enough?

She swallowed, then said, "I want you to make love to me, Marshall. Isn't it obvious?" She swept her arms around and indicated the fireplace, blankets, negligee, and a condom packet.

"I'm not going to take advantage of you again, Connie. You may have drunk too much tonight and—" His words were cut off as she pressed her fingers to his lips.

"Stop thinking and talking so much, Marsh," she said sternly. She put her wineglass down on the floor and crawled in front of him. With her body positioned between his and the fireplace, she rose to her knees and began to pull the negligee over her head.

Marsh felt his manhood responding to her naked body. With the glow of the fireplace behind her, she was a vision of sensual beauty. He slipped his hand behind her back and glided her onto the blanket beneath him. The naked desire in her eyes was all the agreement he needed. Marsh easily slipped out of his clothes.

She watched the muscles ripple across his chest as he removed his shirt. Her body responded to the magnificence of his male form. She reached up to touch him as his body descended on hers. His lips claimed hers with a passionate desire, which she hadn't experienced in a very long time. His tongue engaged hers as he tasted the recesses of her mouth. Eagerly she returned his kisses with equal passion. Aching for fulfillment, she arched her back and opened her legs for his entry.

Marsh was in no hurry, though. Now with her voluntarily back in his arms again, he intended to take his time. His hand slipped between her open legs and firmly massaged the aching mound. She could feel his engorged member brushing against her thigh as he pulled his mouth away from hers. She gasped as he gently squeezed her breast with his free hand and ran his tongue around the peak of her erect nipples.

Crazed with desires and overcome by orgasmic sensations, she clawed wildly at his arms. She tried desperately to think, but her mind would not cooperate. She grabbed his arm in an attempt to make him fill the aching void.

His exploration traveled to her navel as he nuzzled his face in her belly, inhaling the warm musk of her body mixed with the sweet scent of the perfume. She grabbed his face and pulled his mouth back to hers. Hungrily she kissed him again. As he rose above her, she watched him slip the condom on his erect manhood. Enticingly she reached out and touched it. She wrapped her hand gently around it—it was rigid, yet supple in its latex skin. She guided him between her legs to her aching sweet spot. Simultaneously he let out a deep groan, while she emitted a sharp cry as he slipped into her warmth. Power exploded in his every movement as he rocked deeper and deeper into this woman, who'd stolen his heart so many years ago and was reclaiming it now.

Connie reveled in the passion of this man, whom she loved with all her heart. She refused to think beyond this moment of him inside her, their bodies joined as one. With a rising crescendo of shared passion, they unleashed the furious wanton desires of their hearts and crested the waves of orgasmic release.

Rolling onto the blanket next to her, Marsh pulled Connie into his arms. Held close, she marveled at the strength and desire of the man next to her. She'd set out to make this a night to remember, and he'd made love to her like no other man before or after him ever would again. Her love for him overwhelmed her.

He lay quietly with her nestled in the crook of his arm. He didn't plan for this to happen, but he was supremely glad it had.

He could tell from the way she had responded, she loved him. He was happier than he could remember being in a very long time. She was finally his, and he would do all he could to make her happy. In his mind the melding of their bodies was the beginning of the union of their lives. He pulled her close and kissed the top of her head.

Connie was feeling vulnerable. The last time they'd made love, he'd left her and hadn't come back. Now years had passed, and she wondered, what made this night different? *I'm being silly,* she thought, admonishing herself silently. She sat up and looked away into the fireplace. She brushed the tears off her face and tried to smile. It wasn't working. He wasn't fooled by her brave act.

"Connie, talk to me. Did I do something wrong?" he urged. He reached over and picked up his shirt, draping it around her shoulders, covering her nakedness.

She looked at him sitting opposite her, sincere concern on his face. She decided not to make the same mistake she had made four years ago, when she let him go without telling him how she felt. It was now or never. If he walked away this time, at least she would not have to wonder "what if" anymore. She took a deep breath and looked directly into his eyes.

"No, you didn't. It's just . . . I love you, Marshall," she admitted.

His jaw dropped open and he let out a burst of laughter. Relief flooded his face. Hurt flashed across hers. He laughed again and pulled her back down onto the blanket.

"Connie, you scared the heck out of me. I know you love me. I love you too. Couldn't you tell? Jeez, I thought I did something wrong," he said as he wrapped his arms around her.

"So we're going to see each other after tonight?" she asked tentatively. She heard him say he loved her, but she wanted to be certain. There had to be a future for them beyond tonight.

He turned her in his arms so her face was turned up to his.

"Connie Jefferson, you will not get away from me again. Do I make myself clear?" he said firmly.

"Yes, Marshall James, I understand," she replied, and smiled. Relief flooded through her body as she breathed a deep sigh of contentment.

"Good," he said, and retrieved a small box from his pants pocket. "I wanted to give this to you later, but you've left me no choice."

She opened the velvet box to find a sizeable princess-cut diamond engagement ring. Her breath caught in her throat as the sparkling ring picked up the flickering flames from the fireplace.

"I can be a bit foolish and reckless at times. I need someone to watch over me. Constance Jefferson, will you be responsible for me? Will you be my wife?" he asked as he slipped the ring on her finger.

"Yes, Marshall James, I would love to be responsible for you and to become your wife," she agreed happily.

"Great, now let me show you what you're going to be getting a lot of," he said as he picked her up and carried her into the bedroom.

When she heard of the impending nuptials, Deandra wanted to be happy for Connie, but deep inside where old wounds hide, she couldn't bear to see CJ get everything she'd dreamed of.

Her life was good now and with the inheritance that Arlene had given her she'd bought a flat in London. She'd gone there on a travel excursion and decided to stay. Without the support and encouragement of her sister, Connie, she may not be where she was right now.

She sent her well-wishes from afar, but wouldn't be attending the wedding.

No one was happier at the engagement announcement of Marshall James and Constance Jefferson than Viola James, who felt totally vindicated. She and her friend Arlene had already begun laying out their plans for the wedding. Connie hoped she would get a word in edgewise when it came to her own special day. She'd already overheard the two of them discussing the grandchildren they didn't have yet. Her wish had finally come true, and she was truly happy for the first time in her life. She intended to do everything she could to make it last. . . .

1

Madison St. Claire feigned sleep, listening as her fiancé, Alan, moved about their darkened hotel room. If he knew she was awake, he might want to have sex again. The thought clenched her stomach.

In hindsight, agreeing to marry Alan Hunsinger was not one of her brighter ideas. Their lackluster love life proved it. She planned to discuss their hasty engagement with him as soon as they returned to Detroit. When he'd encouraged her to leave her engagement ring at home while they traveled to set up a new business in the little po-dunk town of Slippery Rock, Texas, she had hoped Alan was having the same misgivings.

Unfortunately, they had been stuck in *Hooterville* for almost three weeks now and, quite frankly, she smelled a rat.

And she was increasingly concerned she may be engaged to it.

The door clicked shut and she breathed a sigh of relief, snuggling down farther under the blankets. Thanks to the sleeping aid she'd taken, her mind drifted. Who knew when they would be able to go home? She'd discuss everything with Alan when he returned.

* * *

Loud knocking on the door of her room awoke her. Before she'd done much more than open her eyes, blinding light filled the room through the open doorway.

The silhouette of a woman stood framed against the sunlight. "Sorry!" The woman's twangy accent set Madison's teeth on edge. "I said housekeepin' before usin' the pass key. I thought the room was empty."

Madison struggled through the sleep-induced fog, silently cursing Alan for convincing her to take the sleep aid the night before. "Well, obviously that's not the case."

The maid visibly cringed and Madison immediately regretted snapping at her. But before she could apologize, the maid was gone, closing the door on her way out.

Battling the sheet, Madison got to her feet and walked to throw the privacy bolt to ensure her shower would not be interrupted.

As she turned to make her way to the bathroom, something white on the floor caught her eye. She bent and picked up the paper. Walking to the bedside table, she flipped on the lamp and sank to the mattress to read the motel bill.

Evidently she and Alan had checked out: obviously a mistake. From what she'd seen of Slippery Rock business practices, mistakes happened all the time. Why would the motel be any different?

The front desk picked up on the first ring.

"Hello, this is Madison St. Claire in room 302. Yes, I received the summary, but there must be a mistake. He did? Well, why didn't you just put it on the card we used when we checked in? Oh. That's not possible. I—" She listened for a few moments, jaw clenched, then said, "I understand. What do you mean my room has been reserved? Yes, I know hunters make reservations in advance. Yes, I'll be down soon and give you another card. Sorry for the inconvenience."

What was Alan up to?

＊　＊　＊

After her shower, she packed her bags and loaded them into the car, then headed to the office to straighten out her bill. With the opening of hunting season, it might be difficult to find another motel room. Bad enough Alan had dragged her to the tiny town in deep southern Texas, but for him to have taken off and left her there was unconscionable. As soon as she paid their bill, she was going to call him and find out where he was and what he thought he was doing.

The old man at the counter looked up from his paper at the sound of the door chime.

"I'm Madison St. Claire, room 302."

"I know who you are." He took a sip from a mug emblazoned with the slogan HOT GRANDPA. His hazel gaze was hostile, at best. "Ran your card again. Denied. Again. Called the company. Card is canceled."

"That's not possible. There must be some sort of misunderstanding. My company will look into it. I—"

"Called them, too. Said you don't work for them anymore."

"What? That's ridiculous!" As soon as she paid her bill, she would call Hunsinger Properties and get everything straightened out. The old man was obviously mistaken. What a surprise. She rummaged around in her purse. "I must have left my card case in the room. I'll be right back with another card."

"Take your time. I'll be here."

With a withering glance, she stomped out of the tiny office and up the stairs to her room.

Once inside, she literally turned the place inside out, tossing bed linens, towels, and papers, moving furniture, opening drawers—all to no avail.

Her mind flashed to Alan slinking around under cover of darkness. At the time she'd thought he was being considerate. Now she knew better.

She checked her wallet.

The rat had not only abandoned her, he'd taken all of her cash as well as her credit cards.

Swiping at the wetness on her cheeks, she paced the length of the room several times, attempting to calm down and formulate some kind of a plan. What was wrong with her? She always had a plan. Why, then, couldn't she wrap her mind around a course of action for this horrible scenario? The only thought she could come up with was to go back to Detroit and strangle Alan with her bare hands. And even that would not be enough.

Sinking to the edge of the unmade king-size bed, she reached for a tissue and sniffed. What was she doing? She never cried. Never.

She'd obviously lost her touch. By getting involved with Alan the Rat Hunsinger, she'd dropped her guard, become lax.

Darkness descended while she sat there, wracking her brain for a plan. She was a woman of action. Women of action . . . acted.

She retrieved her briefcase and opened her laptop, only to cuss a few seconds later when she was denied access to the corporate Web site of Hunsinger Properties. What was going on? After trying a few more times, she logged out and back in as Alan. Just as she'd suspected, he'd neglected to change his password. She clicked on the Projects file.

"Son of a bitch!" Flopping back against the pillows, she ground her teeth, blinking back fresh tears. Damn. It was even worse than she'd expected. There was no Slippery Rock project. No construction bonds to sell.

She'd been set up. A few more clicks to various files confirmed it.

A glance at the digital clock surprised her. Boy, it was really dark for four-fifteen P.M. The clock was obviously wrong.

She shoved back the sleeve of her raw silk suit to check the gold watch strapped to her wrist. The clock was correct.

Thunder rumbled, vibrating the bed.

It was past checkout time. What was she going to do? Where

was she going to go? She flipped open her cell phone and punched the speed dial button. The phone emitted a chime. She squinted in the darkness to read the letters on the screen.

No Service.

"Stupid building probably has tons of crap insulating it, blocking my signal." Stalking to the door, she stepped onto the balcony and tried again.

Chirp. No Service.

Fat raindrops dotted the pavement of the parking lot, splattered the steps leading to her floor.

She had to get out of there. The manager would soon be looking for her, wanting his money. Money she didn't have.

Damn Alan!

Keeping a wary eye on the office window, she made her way to her Camaro, not taking a deep breath until she'd reached the safety of the leather interior.

She winced when the motor began to purr, casting a nervous glance at the office as she eased the car toward the exit.

Stopping at the end of the drive to decide which way to turn, she remembered her gas card. Rummaging through the console, she closed her fingers around the hard plastic and blinked back tears of relief.

It was the first credit card she'd ever had and had been rarely used in recent years. Alan probably didn't even know it existed. She kept it in the car for emergencies. Her current situation certainly qualified as an emergency.

Now she didn't have to worry about getting a new motel room. Assuming the card was still valid, she could use it for gas and food, sleeping in her car on the way back to Detroit. Although the idea of sleeping in her car was personally repugnant and very likely dangerous, what other choice did she have?

There may be a perfectly logical reason for Alan the Rat deserting her. She'd decide if she wanted to hear it after she strangled him.

The card worked. With her tank full and loaded down with

snacks from the gas station's convenience store, she set off down the highway toward the interstate, windshield wipers beating in time to the pouring rain.

She touched the stiff paper in her pocket and silently pledged to send a cashier's check for her motel bill as soon as she got back home.